THE MAN IN THE MOONLIGHT

HELEN MCCLOY

AGORA BOOKS

ABOUT THE AUTHOR

Helen McCloy was born in New York City in 1904 to writer Helen Worrell McCloy and managing editor William McCloy. After discovering a love for Sherlock Holmes as young girl, McCloy began writing her own mystery novels in the 1930s. In 1933, she introduced her psychiatrist-detective Dr Basil Willing in her first novel, *Dance of Death*. Dr Basil Willing features in 12 of McCloy's novels as well as several short stories; however, both are best known from McCloy's 1955 supernatural mystery *Through a Glass, Darkly* — hailed as her masterpiece and likened to John Dickson Carr.

McCloy went on in the 1950s and 1960s to co-author a review column a Connecticut newspaper. In 1950, she became the first female president of Mystery Writers of America and in 1953, she was honoured with an Edgar Award from the MWA for her critiques.

A DR BASIL WILLING MYSTERY

THE MAN IN THE MOONLIGHT

HELEN MCCLOY

To my father

Persons of Interest in this **MYSTERY**...

PATRICK FOYLE

...Assistant Chief Inspector commanding the Detective Division of the New York Police Force. Like most men of action, Foyle is a romantic.

DR FRANZ KONRADI

...Refugee biochemist whose age seems to be between thirty-five and forty. He has a few white hairs vivid against his dark head, and his grave, aquiline profile could grace a coin.

GISELA VON HOHENEMS

...Dr Konradi's secretary and an Austrian refugee. *Pretty* isn't the right word for Gisela. The subtle spirit that lives in her eyes makes pretty faces seem trite. This is not beauty, but sorcery.

RAYMOND PRICKETT

...Professor of Experimental Psychology. With his long, white face, pointed teeth and steel-rimmed spectacles, he looks like a scholarly shark.

IAN HALSEY

…A sullen young student who helps in experimental work. His mouth is small and close; his eyes hard, bright and impenetrable.

MALCOLM SOUTHERLAND

…One of the trustees of Yorkville University. He has a hard, Roman face, its bleakness emphasised by cold blue eyes and the bluish tinge of steel-grey hair.

JULIAN SALT

…Professor of Social Anthropology. He has a rather blunt profile with an air of vigilant audacity. Reddish gold hair, golden hazel eyes, sun-browned skin, and tawny tweeds make him look like a figure carved in sandstone.

AMY SALT

…Whom most men would consider seductive. She has a slender round figure, fresh pink and white skin, and her round eyes set wide apart have the perpetually startled expression of a blue-eyed kitten.

KURT DIETRICH

…A boy with a smooth, immature face and fair silky hair. He is a German exchange student at Yorkville University.

BASIL WILLING

...Vienna-trained psychiatrist attached to the district attorney's office. Dr Willing wonders why other people's love affairs seem silly and faintly disgusting.

Objects of Interest in this **MYSTERY**...

- A missing BULLET
- An amethyst FINGERING PIECE
- A bowl of STRAWBERRIES
- A blank CARTRIDGE
- A small glass PHIAL
- A bottle of WINE
- A folder of MATCHES
- A lump of METAL
- An indoor SQUASH COURT
- A NOTE
- A TYPEWRITER

1

EXPLOSION

The day Dr Konradi was murdered dawned clear and
windy — a fragrant spring day with a cool breeze.

Patrick Foyle sat on the campus of Yorkville University,
looking at a sheaf of printed bulletins the Dean had given him.
*Assistant Professor Julian Salt — primitive cultures of Mexico...
Professor Albert Feng Lo — concepts of abnormality... Professor
Raymond Prickett — conditioned response and remote association.*

Foyle's pipe was drawing evenly. The lawn at his feet
sloped down to the East River where the water reflected the
innocent blue of the sky. It was hard to realise that this was as
much a part of New York as Police Headquarters and General
Sessions. Here, if anywhere, his boy would hear no talk of
crooks or graft or murder. Then Foyle noticed the piece of
paper.

A bit of rubbish would not have drawn his attention in a
public park. But here, where not a single peanut shell or paper
bag disturbed the neatness of gravel path and privet hedge, a
stray bit of paper could not escape notice. It floated before the

wind like a kite, twisting, rising, and falling, until it came to rest on the grass. He rose, but the wind snatched the paper away. Clenching his pipe stem between his teeth he charged after it and this time the wind let it lie. He returned to his bench and smoothed the paper on his knee. It was a carbon copy of a typewritten note. It began abruptly without date, address or salutation and ended in the middle of a sentence:

I take pleasure in informing you that you have been chosen as murderer for Group No. 1. Please follow these instructions with as great exactness as possible.

You will enter Southerland Hall from the east entrance just as the library clock is striking the hour of eight (8:00) in the evening of May 4 (Saturday). You must be out of the building by eight forty-five (8:45). This, however, will give you ample time for the murder.

You must be as quiet as possible and be careful not to show a light as you might attract the attention of the night watchman. If you are not out of the building by eight forty-five (8:45) you will find yourself in a very peculiar and unpleasant situation.

Once inside Southerland Hall, you will proceed directly to the laboratory, where…

"You've found it!"

Foyle looked up. A man was standing on the path — a man without hat or overcoat. His face was the saddest Foyle had ever seen.

"I've lost some papers." He spoke with a faintly foreign intonation. "I saw you run after that paper in the wind. I thought — perhaps—"

"What sort of papers have you lost?"

"Notes on chemical experiments. I doubt if you'd understand them. They're in German and technical."

"Well, I don't understand this." Foyle grinned as he held out the paper he had found. "Do you?"

The man crossed the grass to the bench with a quick, resolute step. His age seemed between thirty-five and forty. Yet the hand that took the paper trembled slightly and Foyle noticed a few white hairs vivid against the dark head in the sunlight. His grave, aquiline profile would have graced a coin.

"Just a gag," said Foyle. "But it gave me a turn. College boys sure do have queer ideas of what's funny."

The man lifted unsmiling eyes. "How do you know it is just a — gag?"

"What else could it be? If anything like that were meant seriously, it would be in code. Besides — a real killer never uses the word *murder.* Political murderers call it *direct action* or *liquidation.* Husbands and wives call it *avenging honour* or *defending the sanctity of the home.* Even gangsters don't murder you — they rub you out or bump you off. Whether a murderer is speaking French or German or Choctaw, he steers clear of plain words like *kill* or *murder.*"

"You seem familiar with murder and murderers."

"I'm a police officer." Foyle displayed his gold badge. "Assistant Chief Inspector commanding the Detective Division. I came here to see the Dean about sending my eldest boy to Yorkville. I never had a chance to go to college myself, but I want him to go. My name's Foyle — Patrick Foyle."

"And mine is Franz Konradi."

The name meant nothing to Foyle.

"As a police officer you believe this letter could not have been written by one of your American gangsters?"

Foyle looked at him suspiciously, but there was no hint of humour in those sombre eyes. "I don't know just where you come from, but I guess you haven't been over here very long.

Gangsters don't say please. And they don't threaten people with 'very peculiar and unpleasant situations.' Neither do they make carbon copies of their correspondence."

Konradi stood twisting the letter in long fingers.

"What's it got to do with you?" asked Foyle.

"I believe my laboratory is the only one in Southerland Hall — I know I am the only chemist with rooms in that building. And this is Saturday, May 4."

"Then it looks like somebody's ribbing you."

"Ribbing?"

"Playing a joke on you."

"But my colleagues aren't given to joking, and I doubt if any student would enter my laboratory uninvited. I'm a research professor in biological chemistry. Everyone knows I'm engaged in experiments that can't be interrupted."

Foyle permitted himself another grin. "I don't know about Europe, but over here our students go for gags in a big way. And nobody's safe — not even research professors in biological chemistry. Maybe this is part of a fancy initiation into some fraternity."

"I only hope you're right." Konradi dismissed the subject with a fatalistic shrug. "I suppose I've reached that unenviable state of mind where every molehill seems a mountain and every pin dropping sounds like an explosion—" The sonorous note of a bell cut him short. He started violently. "Only the library clock. You see—" He held out a hand that was still shaking. "I've lost my nerve. Courage is a curious thing, isn't it? Sometimes I think it is only the active form of fear. There's no chemical difference between fear and rage. The only difference is in conduct—" He drew fingertips across his forehead as if brushing aside a veil. "I think I have been working too hard. I must take a rest — a long rest — soon." His eyes were on the river and he seemed to have forgotten Foyle.

"If I were you, I'd give this Southerland Hall a wide berth at eight o'clock."

Konradi's eyes came back to Foyle. "I shall. But one thing puzzles me. How do they expect to get in? The laboratory doors are always locked when I'm not there and the windows are made of unbreakable glass."

"Has anyone a key besides you?"

"The Dean and the janitor. And my secretary."

"Well, I don't suppose the Dean or the janitor are in this. What about your secretary?"

"Gisela?" Konradi frowned like a man pricked with sudden, unwelcome doubt. "It's impossible. She would never—" He left the sentence unfinished.

Foyle studied him curiously. "If this has you really worried, why don't you see the Dean? Isn't he in charge of discipline?"

"I don't believe I'll trouble Dr Lysaght about it." Konradi handed the letter back to Foyle. "One must not be what you call, in English, a spoil-sport."

He smiled for the first time and even his smile was sad. Then he said something so startling that Foyle was at a loss for a reply.

"If anything should happen this evening, I want you to remember one thing: I am just finishing important research, and nothing would induce me to commit suicide while it is still pending. Please understand that, Herr Inspector, and remember it. No matter what happens — no matter what seems to happen — I shall not commit suicide." He bowed with a hint of alien formality and turned away.

Speechless, Foyle watched the tall figure with its resolute stride decrease among the lengthening shadows. The sun was setting behind the trees. Suddenly, the wind seemed chill and unfriendly. In spite of his overcoat, the Inspector shivered as he rose and walked toward the library. Konradi had left so much unsaid. It was only natural he did not confide in a chance acquaintance. But why wouldn't he confide in the Dean?

Foyle met no one on the campus. The gravel path led him into a big, cobblestoned quadrangle bounded by the campus and three buildings. On his left stood the great, grey library parallel with the East River. Opposite him, to the South, was a chapel. To the West, facing the library, stood a three-storied brick building, windows regimented as those of a jail. The only sounds that disturbed the academic peace were the cooing of pigeons and the splashing of a fountain in the centre of the quadrangle.

The Inspector compared his watch with the library clock and saw that the clock was one minute faster. Carefully he set his watch at 5:29 to coincide exactly with the clock. He had no plan of action yet. He still believed the letter was a sophomoric hoax. But it sounded like a rather morbid hoax and he had a vague feeling that something ought to be done about it. He started to walk across the quadrangle to a path that led southwest, between the chapel and the brick building. As he drew near the building, he noticed an inscription engraved on the stone above the main entrance:

1924

SOUTHERLAND HALL

ERECTED BY MALCOLM SOUTHERLAND, AB.

Of the Class of 1915
and Trustee of Yorkville University.

Foyle studied the east entrance of Southerland Hall with interest. There was plenty of space around the building planted with trees and shrubs. To the Inspector trees and shrubs meant only one thing — cover. He saw at once that the "murderer for Group No. 1" would have all the cover he needed to approach Southerland Hall unobserved.

The Inspector frowned. And just then the academic peace was shattered by a pistol shot.

2

EXTRAVAGANZA

The sound came from Southerland Hall. Foyle ran up three steps and tried the door. It yielded and he found himself in a long corridor. The air had the moist, unnatural freshness that means air-conditioning. A cry reached him through the first door on the left. He pushed it open.

He had a fleeting impression of a lecture hall, people and machinery, including a phonograph and a moving-picture camera. But his attention centred on a small man holding a large revolver. There was an acrid smell unfamiliar to the Inspector — he knew only that it wasn't cordite. With his left arm covering his heart, he seized the cartridge cylinder in his right hand so that it could not rotate again. He thrust his thumb between hammer and breech so the hammer could not reach the next cartridge.

"Don't move!" Wresting the revolver from the other man, Foyle backed away until the whole room came within his vision. He saw a frayed, shapeless woman in an old-fashioned hat who seemed like a faded photograph of herself taken in 1928. He saw a sullen young man in a shaggy plaid jacket and disreputable, grey flannel trousers. He saw a table covered with a black mat fastened to the legs with tapes. On the mat, under hot floodlights, lay a wailing, naked baby about four months old. But none of these people appeared to be wounded and no one else was in the room.

Foyle turned back to the man who had held the revolver. A long, white face, pointed teeth and steel-rimmed spectacles made him look like a scholarly shark. He was rubbing his right wrist with his left hand.

"What's the meaning of this?" he demanded. "Who are you anyway?"

"Just what I was going to ask you! I'm Assistant Chief Inspector Foyle of the New York Police Department. I was passing this building and I heard a shot."

"I suppose a shot means only one thing to a policeman!" Thin lips split into a toothy grin. "You're barking up the wrong tree, Inspector. I'm Professor of Experimental Psychology here — Raymond Prickett is my name. The baby on the table is my son and I'm using him in a series of experiments on fear in infants. There are two ways of exciting fear in an infant. One is to drop it — on something soft, of course — and the other is make a loud noise close to its ear. I prefer the loud noise because I want to get the Moro reflex as well as the gross reaction and I find a revolver shot the best noise for the purpose."

"Got a permit for this gun?"

"Naturally."

"What if you hit somebody with a stray bullet?"

"I'm using blanks." Prickett's gaze dwelt on Foyle with sudden interest. "I'd like to test your hearing some time, Inspector. Most people who hear a shot unexpectedly, mistake it for a backfire. But you didn't."

"I'd be a swell cop if I couldn't tell a revolver shot from a backfire!" Foyle was growing uncomfortable under that probing, impersonal gaze.

"That's interesting. I could use some of my students as controls and—"

"No, thanks. It doesn't seem to be doing the kid much good."

The baby's cries had subsided to a catching of the breath but its cheeks were wet with tears.

"That's what I say!" came a plaintive cry from the faded woman. "But I'm only his mother—"

Prickett interrupted hastily. "Inspector Foyle — my wife. And this is Mr Halsey, one of my students who helps me in my experimental work."

The young man in the plaid jacket nodded curtly. His mouth was small and close; his eyes hard, bright and impenetrable. Probably working his way through college by helping Prickett, thought Foyle. That would explain the trousers and the rather tense, self-contained manner.

Mrs Prickett could not be side-tracked so easily. "Inspector, do you think these experiments are bad for baby? They won't let me comfort him when he cries because they say that encourages self-pity."

"If a man can't experiment with his own child—" began Prickett.

"Because he is your own child you shouldn't want to experiment with him!" wailed Mrs Prickett.

"I thought emotional shocks gave kids complexes and things," ventured Foyle.

"My dear Inspector, please spare me the vulgar superstitions of the Freudian mythology!"

Halsey intervened in a taut, vibrant voice. "I'll have to go, Dr Prickett. I've an appointment at six."

Prickett glanced at his watch. "Time for one more reaction! You'll find it interesting, Inspector, if you stay."

"Oh, must you?" moaned Mrs Prickett. "Baby hasn't got over that last shot yet!"

"That's just why I want to see the effect of another shot on him now," explained Prickett with angelic patience. "I want to see if repetition of the fear stimulus will strengthen or weaken the startle pattern."

"Ian!" Mrs Prickett turned to Halsey. "Don't you honestly think all this is bad for baby?"

Halsey looked at her without sympathy. "No."

"Well, you don't have to be so blunt about it, do you?" suggested Foyle.

Halsey was focusing the moving-picture camera directly above the baby at a distance of six feet. "I believe in speaking the absolute truth in all circumstances," he announced solemnly. "What we call 'courtesy' is simply a conventional form of lying and I won't sacrifice my intellectual honesty to mere convention."

"You'd have to if you were on the Police Force." Foyle's tone was deceptively mild. "What's the movie camera for? And why the black mat?"

"The Moro reflex — as we call the startle pattern in infants under four months — is too quick for the human eye," answered Prickett, reloading his revolver. "To study it we take a moving-picture record at the unusual speed of 64 pictures to the second and then project the film in slow-motion. The subject is set against a black background so every detail of his white body will show."

He bent toward the table as he attached the revolver to an electrical apparatus. The "subject's" face puckered, and it bawled lustily.

"An interesting example of conditioning," Prickett

informed Foyle. "After I've experimented with babies for a while, they begin to scream the minute they catch sight of my face."

"Sort of inconvenient around the house when they're your own babies," ruminated Foyle.

"Not at all." Prickett answered serenely. "When the experiment is over it will be a simple matter to recondition the child by getting him to associate my face with something pleasant like food or affection. Now, Marian," Prickett turned to his wife, "do try to overcome your personal bias. When you hear the baby cry don't think of him — think of the unborn generations that will benefit by whatever slight stress we may be causing his nervous system today. The sooner we understand the origin and development of fear habits the sooner we'll be able to conquer fear by emotional education. Ready, Ian?"

"All set."

Marian Prickett closed her eyes and put her fingers in her ears. Prickett, with notebook open and fountain pen poised, sat at a desk near the door into the hall. The door was open — Foyle realised that he had left it open when he rushed into the room. Before he could call anyone's attention to the fact, Prickett pressed a switch button and the blank shot exploded. The baby jerked its arms and legs and began to yell once more. The moving-picture camera hummed in Halsey's hands.

"*Cry perceptibly louder and more persistent after fourth shot,*" muttered Prickett, scribbling furiously. "Of course we can't tell until we project the film, but I did have an impression the eyes blinked. Possibly a delayed Moro with a superficial resemblance to the Strauss startle-pattern…"

Then Marian spoiled everything. Running to the table she snatched the baby into her arms without a thought of the unborn generations' emotional education.

"There! There! Did the horrid old pistol frighten mother's precious honey-baby? But he mustn't cry…"

Prickett and Halsey looked at each other with inexpressible disgust.

"Perhaps you'd better go, Ian. It's too late to do anything more this afternoon." Prickett detached the revolver from the electrical apparatus and dropped it on the desk. "Get those films developed as soon as possible."

"Okay." Halsey was packing the roll of film in a flat tin. "We got the Moro anyway. So long, Inspector!"

He left the room, shutting the door softly. Prickett eyed his wife with sardonic resignation as she covered the baby's face with kisses. "It's only perverted sexuality on your part, Marian. If it were not, you wouldn't want to kiss him on the mouth."

"Animal mothers lick their young and nobody calls that perverted sexuality!"

"My dear Marian, you know nothing about animal psychology."

"You don't have to know anything about animal psychology to know that animals aren't perverted!"

"Indeed!" A faint pink stained Prickett's high cheekbones. "We're boring the Inspector." Prickett turned to Foyle. "I'm sorry the experiment was such a flop. If you'd like to see another—"

"No, thanks."

A tap fell on the door. "Come in!" called Prickett.

A girl appeared on the threshold. Foyle had a glimpse of dark beauty, subtle and strange. A cluster of white violets nestled on the shoulder of her black tweed jacket and she seemed to bring a breath of grace and elegance into the bare room.

"Where can I find Dr Konradi?" She spoke in a soft contralto. "Mr Southerland is asking for him."

"I'm afraid I don't know," answered Prickett. "I haven't seen Konradi all day."

"He must have gone home." She seemed to be thinking aloud. "He isn't in his office or his laboratory and yet — it isn't like him to leave so early."

"I met Dr Konradi on the campus a while ago," volunteered Foyle. "I think he was on his way home."

"Oh, thank you. I can probably reach him there by telephone. Mr Southerland is anxious to see him."

As soon as the door had shut, Marian Prickett found voice. "It's sheer impudence for that girl to call herself Konradi's secretary! Anybody can see what she really is. And no secretary's salary ever paid for those clothes."

"Perhaps she has means of her own," suggested Prickett.

"Nonsense!" Marian thrust the baby's arms into a small, pink sweater. "Everyone knows you can't take money out of Austria — especially a refugee."

"Who is she?" asked Foyle.

"Gisela von Hohenems — a daughter of Count Alois von Hohenems." Prickett was searching among the papers on his desk. "But she has sense enough not to call herself Countess now she's at work in this country. Did you notice where I put that revolver?"

"On the desk."

"That's what I thought. But it isn't there." Prickett glanced around the room. "I usually keep it locked up. Not really necessary, but it seems wiser."

"No doubt." Foyle's tone was dry. He surveyed the room. But the revolver was not there.

"Let me see." Prickett frowned. "I was talking to Ian. I took it out of the vice and put it down on the desk and I'm sure I haven't touched it since." He returned to the desk. "It must be here." But it wasn't. "I suppose I picked it up again. Funny I don't remember. Of course Marian's hysteria distracted me, so I scarcely knew what I was doing."

"The door was open," said Foyle.

Prickett appeared to give a demonstration of his own "startle pattern". "Wh-what do you mean?"

"I left the door open when I came in and it stayed open during your experiment. That desk is beside the door. We were all talking and watching Mrs Prickett and the baby after the experiment. And the baby was making a lot of noise. Anyone coming along the hall could have noticed the revolver on the desk and taken it — without our seeing or hearing a thing."

"But — why?"

"Maybe somebody wanted a revolver and didn't want to bother about a permit."

"The door's closed now."

"Halsey closed it when he went out. And Miss von Hohenems closed it again after she looked in."

"Ian! I wonder if he—"

"Would he be likely to?"

"Well, no. I've always cleaned the thing myself."

"What about the lady?"

"Gisela? What would she want with a revolver?"

"I don't know. But someone wanted it and took it."

Prickett laughed. "I suppose a police inspector can't help suspecting everybody. But this is a university — not a gangsters' hide-out. And the revolver isn't dangerous — it's loaded with blanks. I must have put it down somewhere else and forgotten about it — like the absent-minded professor in the funny papers."

"Things do seem to get lost around here," remarked Foyle.

"When I saw Konradi on the campus just now, he was looking for some papers he had lost."

"That's odd," admitted Prickett. "I can't imagine his mislaying anything of importance."

"Is he German?"

"Austrian." Prickett stuffed some papers into a briefcase. "Surely you've heard of him? He's one of the foremost authorities on chemical factors in cancer. But that didn't keep the Nazis from sending him to their concentration camp at Dachau when they took over Austria."

"Why?"

"Perhaps his grandmother was Jewish — perhaps he turned off the radio when Hitler was speaking. The surprising thing was his escape. I don't know how he managed it. He won't talk about it. But I never heard of anyone else escaping from Dachau."

"Are you ever coming, Ray?" Marian paused in the doorway, holding the baby.

"Just a minute." Prickett hurried into a light overcoat, seized a soft felt hat and stuffed the bulging briefcase under one arm. "Will you lock the door, Inspector? It locks when you shut it if you release the catch."

"Sure." Foyle closed the door — he heard the lock snap into place. "Konradi's laboratory is in this building, isn't it?"

"Next room to this." A thin smile sharpened Prickett's lips. "If you want to see something luxurious in laboratories you should get him to take you in there. Malcolm Southerland lavished money on the equipment. He's even had the building air-conditioned and special glass put in all the ground-floor windows so Konradi can absolutely control the temperature for delicate biological experiments. God only knows what it cost, yet I can't induce Southerland to buy a Darrow

Photopolygraph for the Department of Psychology, and that would be only $1000."

Marian Prickett had gone ahead. A man in dark blue shirt and trousers was pushing a mop languidly across the tiled space before the entrance. At sight of Prickett, he took a key from his hip pocket. "You're last to leave, sir. I was just gonna lock up."

"Sorry to be late, Ezra," said Prickett. "This is your night for choir practice, isn't it?"

"Yessir." Ezra was staring curiously at Foyle.

The Inspector decided that his dash into the building had not escaped notice.

"Oh, by the way." Prickett halted. "You didn't happen to pick up my Colt 45 revolver just now?"

Ezra looked hurt. "Would I be breakin' the Eighth Commandment, Dr Prickett, sir?"

"I only thought you might have seen it and carried it off to the Dean — not realising I use it for experiments."

"I'll look for it. Whereabouts you lose it, sir?"

"I didn't exactly lose it. I thought I laid it down on my desk — but now I can't find it. Not that it matters," went on Prickett cheerfully. "It'll turn up!"

3

EXCITEMENT

Daylight was ebbing fast when Prickett left Foyle on the steps of Southerland Hall. The Inspector didn't like darkness. He remembered a precinct captain who sent out his night patrol at noon during an eclipse of the sun, with the remark: "It only needs a shadow across the sun to send this district into action."

The roofs of the University made a dark, ragged margin against the wan sky. Trees and buildings looked flat and insubstantial, as if cut out of paper. Streetlamps were lighted along the paths, but there was still enough daylight to absorb their radiance. Foyle, as he walked through the dusk, had an irrational feeling that anything might happen.

The disappearance of Prickett's revolver might be Prickett's carelessness. The preposterous letter to the "murderer for Group No. 1" might be somebody's idea of a joke. But the two taken together — and the odd behaviour of Dr Konradi. That letter had alarmed him, yet he would not say why, and he would not confide in the Dean. A man who had lived through the Nazi occupation of Austria would not be easily alarmed.

Foyle played with the idea that this mysterious "Group No. 1" was a Nazi cell. That might explain the pompous style of the letter and its naïve use of the word *murder* — it had been written in English by someone who thought in German. But Nazi agents in America would scarcely plan an assassination on paper and in English without using a code.

Whoever wrote the letter was obviously familiar with Yorkville University and Southerland Hall. Therefore the Dean seemed the person to consult. He was the only member of the University Foyle had met whom he trusted. Konradi was too enigmatic and Prickett's amused superiority had alienated Foyle completely.

The Dean lived just beyond the library in a house of salmon-pink brick with a white porch, white shutters, and white ruffled curtains. The front door was a sheet of plate glass. Foyle could see the river through another glass door opposite which led to a garden on the embankment. He rang the bell, and the door was opened by an elderly maid.

"I'm sorry, sir, but the Dean is not at home. Is there any message?"

Foyle hesitated. What sort of message could he leave? Dr Lysaght would be very sensitive to any hint of scandal involving the University. And suppose the thing were a mare's nest after all?

"No message. When will Dr Lysaght be back?"

"Not until late. This is the night of the Alumni Dinner. Will you leave your name, sir?"

The waxed hardwood floor reflected the crystal chandelier like a golden mirror. The woodwork was white, the walls papered in cream colour sprigged with rosebuds. Foyle decided it was fortunate Dr Lysaght was not at home. Vague, twilit forebodings could not survive in such a bright, conventional atmosphere.

"No. I'll come again."

Night had fallen. The stars greeted Foyle with a friendly twinkle that seemed to say: "You see, it was just a false alarm. You can imagine anything at twilight."

He followed the path briskly. Once outside the University walls, he breathed more freely. He walked down 83rd Street to York avenue. The neighbourhood was strange to him. Though he knew many Germans lived nearby, he was surprised to see a shop window filled with Nazi publications in German and English. As he had expected, there were a number of small restaurants catering to the University trade. His choice fell on a clean, quiet-looking place, largely because a man he had noticed on the campus was just entering. Steins and meer-schaum pipes were ranged around the top of an oak wainscot, and the crowded room reeked with tobacco, sausage, cheese, and beer.

"Perhaps you would prefer dinner in the garden?" suggested the headwaiter. The "garden" proved to be a typical Manhattan back yard: a trellis against the board fence, but no vines. A crazy pavement replaced grass. Six little tables were lighted by a string of Japanese lanterns, but only one was occupied. Foyle recognised the man he had seen entering the restaurant. It was a rather blunt profile with an air of vigilant audacity. Reddish gold hair, golden hazel eyes, sun-browned skin, and tawny tweeds made him look like a figure carved in sandstone. *That young fellow is going to amount to something someday,* thought Foyle, *and he knows it already. ...*

A woman with him sat with her back toward Foyle. He saw only a long evening coat of sapphire blue wool, a froth of short pale curls, and a blue slipper with a tall heel and a pret-tily arched instep. Something glittered on the hand that lay along the arm of her chair — a shapely hand with long, oval nails that made Foyle wish he could see her face.

By the time the Inspector had progressed to apple strudel and coffee, he was so happily replete that he decided his feeling of uneasiness had been caused by hunger. *If ever I see Prickett again,* he reflected, *I must ask him if superstitious people aren't usually underfed.*

The man, who had been speaking in a low murmur, raised his voice suddenly. "...You know what you mean to me, Amy. Life without you is hell. I'll go to pieces. There won't be anything left."

Like most men of action, Foyle was a romantic. This fervent speech engaged his sympathy. But the man and woman were too absorbed to be aware of him.

"I can't imagine why you insisted on this last meeting." The woman's voice was clear and cold as spring water. "My mind is made up. I told you that in November. It's painful for us to see each other now and it doesn't do any good. What's finished is finished."

"Give me another chance!" Foyle didn't like to hear any man plead quite so abjectly. "Amy, darling, we could be so happy! You know we could."

This time Foyle cleared his throat. The man looked up with a quick frown. "We can't talk here."

Foyle couldn't hear the woman's answer. But it silenced the man. He looked at her with an expression hard to analyse — more bitter than simple despair. Foyle wished he could tell him that in twenty years he would laugh at the memory of this as he would laugh now at the tragedies of his childhood.

It was the woman who signalled the waiter with a nod of her elaborately curled head. The man paid the check and pushed the change toward the waiter. The woman rose, drawing her long, deep blue coat around her with a flash of pale blue skirts beneath. About her throat was a short necklace of sapphire and turquoise. Her eyes were more nearly turquoise than sapphire — round eyes set wide apart with the perpetually startled expression of a blue-eyed kitten.

Alone in the garden, Foyle took out his pipe and fumbled for his tobacco pouch. His fingers encountered the sheet of paper he had found on the campus. By the fitful light of the paper lanterns he read it again:

...You have been chosen as murderer for Group No. 1...you will enter Southerland Hall from the east entrance just as the library clock is striking the hour of eight (8:00) in the evening of May 4 (Saturday) ...

Foyle shook the ashes from his pipe and looked at his watch. Then he stuffed pipe and pouch and letter into his pocket and called for his bill. It was already 7:43. He must hurry if he wished to be at the east entrance of Southerland Hall when the library clock struck 8:00.

The moon had risen and was almost full. The Inspector felt as conspicuous as an actor on a spotlighted stage. Once inside the walls of the University, he left the path and walked in the shadow of the trees where the turf hushed every footfall. The long windows of the library blazed with light, but the chapel and Southerland Hall were dark. Foyle made a circuit of the Hall. As he rounded the southwest corner, he thought he heard the swift tapping of an expert typist. But every window was dark. When he paused to listen more carefully, he heard nothing. He decided that his nerves had played a trick on him.

He found a second entrance on the west side and tried the door. It was locked. He came back to the east side without seeing any sign of life. But the east door was ajar. He went up the steps and looked in — the corridor was dark and silent. He pondered the situation, then retreated and slipped between two syringa bushes to the left of the entrance. He had not been mistaken about the cover around Southerland Hall — the syringa hid him completely. Any of the other bushes opposite was tall enough to hide someone else from him.

Inside the shrubbery, he found himself next to the front window of the lecture hall where Prickett had conducted his experiment. Cautiously parting the branches, Foyle could see the front door. The moon bathed path and lawn. Only the blackness of the shadows betrayed the faintness of that deceptive light.

A sound startled him. It was the library clock. He counted the strokes — six...seven...eight. He drew a deep breath and waited. Something moved in the shadow under the trees. Through a lacy web of leaves, Foyle saw a man coming furtively across the turf. Not a professional criminal — a professional would realise that a furtive manner is more likely to attract suspicion than behaviour that appears normal.

The man had to pass into the moonlight when he mounted the steps. Foyle recognised Ian Halsey. His feet moved silently on rubber soles. Though he wore no hat or overcoat, his hands were encased in heavy gauntlets. He didn't seem surprised to find the door ajar.

Halsey slipped into the building. The door closed behind him noiselessly. A moment later a tiny thread of light showed at one edge of the window beside Foyle. A dark shade inside the glass made it impossible to see more, and he could not have seen that much if he had not been standing inside the shrubbery.

He stepped out of the bushes as quietly as possible and tiptoed up the steps. He turned the knob so slowly that it made no sound and pushed the door open.

The corridor was almost in darkness, but there was a faint, fan-shaped glow from the door of Prickett's lecture hall which stood half-open. Farther down the corridor, on the other side, moonlight filtered through the dusty panes of a window at the end of a passage where the janitor kept his mops and pails.

Foyle touched the hinges of the front door. A film of grease came off on his fingertips — someone had gone to great trouble to make that door noiseless tonight. He left it ajar. The tiled floor made it possible for him to move forward without fear of creaking. The stairway was opposite the door of the lecture hall. By standing in the shadow under the stairs he could look into the room without being seen. What he discovered puzzled him more than ever.

The only illumination in the room came from a candle Halsey was lighting in a green china candlestick on the table. The black mat was gone. In its place stood an array of objects that suggested a rather frugal picnic. A sherry glass and a bottle of wine labelled *California Wine Growers Association.* A tin of Chesterfields, a folder of matches and a glass ash tray. A box of Butterthin Biscuits. A glass bowl filled with strawberries. A Corona portable open and ready for use. A book with a gay paper jacket — *Victorian Murderers,* by Wilson Steele.

In the still air, the candle flame stood straight as a spear and Halsey's shadow, monstrous against the wall, moved only when he moved. He dropped his lighted match on the tiled floor where it burned itself out. He poured a glass of sherry and sipped it while he ate the strawberries one by one with gloved fingers. When he had finished, he pushed the bowl aside. Under it lay a greenback — Foyle couldn't see the denomination. Halsey folded it and put it in his breast pocket. He lit one of the Chesterfields from the tin, and dropped his second match on the floor, treading out the flame. Then he began turning the pages of the book, pausing to read every few moments.

He's a cool young devil! And I don't like those gloves — the Inspector was thinking of fingerprints.

Halsey looked at his wristwatch. Still moving slowly, he crushed his cigarette in the ash tray and lit a second one, dropping the match in the tray. The cigarette hung limply from his lower lip as he sat down at the table and began to type. He glanced at the open book from time to time as if copying something. The steady tap-tap-tap reminded Foyle of the sound he thought he had noticed when he walked around the building. Only that was before Halsey appeared.

Abruptly the boy dropped his second cigarette in the tray and pulled the paper from the typewriter. Going to the other side of the table, he sat down again and began with a pencil to correct what he had typed.

The Inspector heard a quick, resolute step. He had heard it only once before, but he would have known it anywhere. The candle flame choked, and the shadows danced as the front door was flung wide. The round face of the moon peered through the opening and the tall figure of Dr Konradi followed his own shadow down the corridor swiftly.

Foyle's eyes remained on the front door. It was moving — closing. He dashed forward — just too late. He heard a key turn. As he stood wrenching vainly at the doorknob, he heard a shot. It was followed by a scream from Prickett's lecture hall — an inhuman scream that clung to a high note, wavered, and fell a long way into silence.

Foyle ran into the lecture hall. Halsey was standing with his gloved fist against his mouth, staring toward a door to the next room. It opened upon darkness — the moon was on the other side of the building. Across the threshold sprawled the body of a man, face down. The top of his skull was smashed like an eggshell. Before Foyle knelt and turned the head gently to see what was left of the face, he knew it was Konradi. A thimbleful of powder and an inch of lead had reduced a rare and ardent mind to this ugly thing.

Foyle saw the revolver beside Konradi's hand. The explosion had gone into the head through the roof of the mouth. No other mark of violence. No smell of chloroform, no visible symptom of a narcotic drug. How often had he heard medical examiners say that these things together were clear proof of suicide, and yet — *Please understand that, Herr Inspector, and remember it. No matter what happens — no matter what seems to happen — I shall not commit suicide.* Foyle felt a hand on his shoulder and looked up.

Halsey's grey eyes were cloudy and unfocused. He stuttered, "H-How did you get in here?"

"That's beside the point now," said Foyle bitterly. "Turn on the lights, will you?"

Halsey walked to the nearest switch as if he were wading knee-deep in water. He fumbled for the button. Every movement was heavy with the conscious effort of a man fighting against drunkenness or sleep. There was a click, but no light. "The lights won't go on!" His voice cracked. "Let's get out of here!"

"The front door's locked."

"Locked?" Halsey ran to the window. He put forth all his strength trying to raise it. "It's nailed down." Gasping for breath, he beat his fists against the glass. "Let me out! You devil! Let me out! Oh, God, I forgot!" He sank to his knees with a sob. "Unbreakable glass in all the ground-floor windows."

The two looked at each other. They both heard a stealthy sound — the unmistakable sound of a door opening.

"What are we going to do?" Halsey's voice was shrill. "We're locked in with a murderer!"

4

EXASPERATION

The sound appeared to come from the next room. Foyle took out his revolver. (In New York, all policemen are required to carry arms off duty — even chief inspectors.) He walked to the table and blew out the candle.

"You — you won't leave me alone in the dark?" whimpered Halsey.

"That light was too good a target." Foyle groped his way toward the door into the next room and paused by the threshold. There was a rustling sound beyond in the darkness — like dead leaves stirring in the wind. He had to step over the body to enter the room.

With the revolver in his right hand, he felt his way along the wall with his left, moving as quietly as possible. His eyes grew accustomed to the faint light that came through unshaded windows from the open night, and he could see the glitter of glass. This was a chemical laboratory and it must be Konradi's, for he had said he was the only chemist in the building.

Foyle's groping hand encountered a wire cage and he saw

something move within. Little eyes, shiny as black pinheads, caught the faint light — mice for some experiment. They had made the rustling sound when they were roused from sleep in their straw bed.

There seemed to be no other living thing — no sound of human breathing or movement — no sound at all but the slow drip of a leaky faucet. Whoever had been in this room a moment ago had escaped into the hall.

As Foyle moved cautiously, he heard a thunderous crash of breaking glass. A bell began to ring — the shrill, nagging clamour of a burglar alarm. He forgot caution and ran into the corridor. Four closed doors faced him, but he remembered the window in the janitor's passage. He collided with a mop handle, and cool outdoor air bathed his face. A jagged hole gaped in the dusty glass — large enough to admit a man. So this was their unbreakable glass!

Beyond the shattered window the moonlight flooded a lawn that sloped upward to the campus. One of the bushes near Southerland Hall began to move. It was a human figure moving into the moonlight out of the shadow cast by a bush. As Foyle started to climb through the window, he had a blurred impression of a solitary figure running over the crest of the hill.

A heavy grip fell on Foyle's collar, twisted it viciously and dragged him through the window, while a triumphant voice shouted, "Gotcha!"

The Inspector shook off his assailant with a jerk of his shoulders. "If this is a sophomore's joke—"

The man wasn't listening. He called to a figure that came running out of the shadows. "Here he is, sir! Th' other fella got away, but I caught this one red-handed — the dirty bum! He was tryin' to escape an' broke a window. Lissen, you!" The grip descended on Foyle's collar again. "You'll have ta pay for that window!"

Again Foyle shook himself free. "If you'll listen—"

"Inspector Foyle! What are you doing here?"

Foyle turned. The man was Prickett. "I apologise," he panted. "Woodman — our watchman — is a little impulsive."

"Is this guy a cop?" The watchman retreated.

"Yes, Woodman. I'm afraid we've made a mistake. But it doesn't make much difference."

"Oh, doesn't it?" Foyle controlled his temper.

"My dear Inspector, I can clear up the whole thing. It's just an experiment in the psychology of crime. Not a wholly original experiment — I've borrowed freely from Blane and Bickford. But I've also introduced a few improvements of my own. At least, I like to think they're improvements. The burglar alarm for one thing. And the unbreakable glass for another."

"And Dr Konradi lying in there with his brains blown out!" roared Foyle. "Is that part of the original experiment? Or one of your little improvements?"

"You…you're joking!"

"I don't joke about crime. I don't experiment either."

Woodman's mind moved more slowly than Foyle's, but at last he caught the drift of Prickett's words. "Say…what's all this about an experiment, Dr Prickett?" he demanded furiously. "Why, you — you said I was to keep a special watch on Southerland Hall because you'd seen tramps hanging around. You said—"

Prickett ignored this. "Inspector, you can't really mean that Konradi is dead?"

"Didn't you hear a shot?"

"I thought it was a backfire on East End Avenue."

"How did you happen to run around here just now?"

"Why, I…" Prickett moistened thin lips.

"Just passing by, eh?"

"No. I had to lock the door and—"

"Oh! So *you* locked us in! Didn't you hear Halsey pounding on the window and yelling to let us out?"

"Of course. I thought Halsey's reaction interesting."

"You mean to say you heard him yell and you hadn't sense enough to unlock the door?"

"I don't like your tone, Inspector. I couldn't unlock the door. That would have ruined the experiment."

"Why did Konradi come back to Southerland Hall after telling me he wouldn't be here this evening? Was that part of the experiment?"

"Konradi had nothing to do with it."

"And I suppose your revolver had nothing to do with it either!"

"My revolver?"

"You said it would turn up. It did. It was used to kill Konradi. Maybe you were studying his startle pattern and forgot to use a blank instead of a bullet."

"But I lost the revolver this afternoon — I couldn't have used it this evening."

"You might have pretended to lose it. You might have slipped it into that briefcase you took home with you. Is there a telephone in Southerland Hall?"

The front door was still locked, the burglar alarm still ringing. Prickett took a key from his pocket and Foyle unlocked the door. Automatically, he felt for the switch. Again there was a click, but no light.

"I...turned, off the current by removing part of the main switch," volunteered Prickett.

"Another of your little improvements?"

"No, I got that from Blane. Darkness intensifies the emotional reaction of the subject."

"Where's this main switch?"

"In the basement. I can fix it in a minute." Prickett groped his way toward the stairs.

"And turn off that blasted burglar alarm!" Foyle turned to Woodman. "Where's the telephone?"

"They got phones in them offices." He pointed to the closed doors on the right. "I gotta passkey and…"

Woodman's voice faded as the lights blazed. He could see Konradi's body through the open door of the lecture hall on the left.

"Good Lord! I forgot all about Halsey!" Foyle crossed the lecture hall to where the boy was lying unconscious. "Help me get him into one of the offices."

Woodman unlocked the first door on the right. Between them they carried Halsey across the corridor. The office was more personal than the lecture hall. Distempered walls and tiled floor were the same, but there was a Persian rug, a mahogany desk and armchairs. Halsey sprawled in one, limp but still breathing.

Foyle reached for the telephone and paused "When you collared me so efficiently you said something about the other fellow getting away. Did you get a look?"

"Sure." Woodman locked the door of the lecture hall where the body lay and returned to the office. "He run up toward the campus an' I seen him good when he crossed the open space in the moonlight. Little runt, he was — short an' thin — an' he had a felt hat with the brim pulled down over his eyes. He run in short steps like he wasn't used to runnin'. His head was bobbin' up an' down. It took him two-three minutes to get to the top o' that hill. Geez! It burns me up to think I didn't go after him instead of you!"

The alarm bell ceased ringing like a sudden cessation of toothache. Foyle called the radio room at Police Headquarters.

Precious minutes had been lost. But how could you make haste alone in an isolated building with the lights off, the windows nailed down, and three men to watch every minute?

"A short, thin man with a felt hat." Foyle was speaking into the telephone. "Runs in short steps — unused to running. Last seen in grounds of Yorkville University going toward the East River. Probably bloodstains on hands and clothing. Not much to go on but send it out. And now give me Homicide."

Halsey moaned and struggled into an upright position. "What happened? How did I get here?"

"You passed out and we lugged you in here." Woodman took a flask from his hip pocket.

Halsey shook his head. "I never touch the stuff."

Foyle hung up the receiver and swung round. "I saw you walk into a bottle of wine a little while ago."

"Did you?" Halsey was still dazed.

"Why did you say all the ground-floor windows were made of unbreakable glass?"

Halsey hesitated like an actor uncertain of his cue. Then he said, "Well, they are."

"Not the one in the janitor's passageway."

"That's right. I must've forgotten that one."

Foyle eyed him steadily. "You're the young fellow who always tells the absolute truth, aren't you?"

Halsey flushed. "Why are you questioning me?"

"Why not?" Foyle's voice was tired. "I was at the front door when I heard a shot and a scream. By the time I got into the room you were standing beside a dead man and a revolver — Prickett's revolver. Prickett missed it this afternoon just after you left the room."

"What about the guy who broke the window an' run up the hill?" put in Woodman.

"We've no proof he was the murderer. Anyone locked in

a dark building when there was a shot and a scream might break a window if he couldn't get out any other way." Foyle's eyes searched Halsey's face. "Why the winter gloves?"

Halsey looked down as if he had forgotten the heavy gauntlets. "I-I like to keep my hands clean."

Foyle took a pencil and a pad of paper from the desk. "Where do you live when you're at home?"

"Here in New York. East 61st Street."

"Your father's name?"

"John H Halsey."

Foyle's gaze travelled from the dirty white tennis shoes to the disreputable flannel trousers. "Not the president of the Mercantile Bank and Trust Company?"

"Yes, he is. What's so funny about that?"

Foyle realised the boy was the heir to all those financial forces known vaguely as the "Halsey interests." He didn't bother to maintain a neat appearance or a pleasant manner because he didn't need to. Even in a murder case, it would be impossible for the police to subject him to severe questioning. Yet everything he said suggested he was concealing something.

Prickett appeared in the doorway.

"You've been a long time since the lights went on," complained Foyle.

"I stopped to look at the broken window. I thought there might be traces. But I couldn't find any."

Foyle realised that Prickett was the shortest and thinnest of the three men. "Ever run in a track meet?"

Prickett looked as if he thought the Inspector's mind was going. But he answered quietly, "No, never had time for sport. I worked my way through college."

Foyle's glance rested on the felt hat Prickett was carrying.

"While we're waiting for the Homicide Squad, I'd like to hear a little more about that experiment you staged this evening."

"I had no wish to involve anyone but Halsey and myself," Prickett hastened to explain. "I was horrified when I saw you climbing out that window and another man running up the hill in the moonlight."

"Could you identify that other man?"

"I'm afraid not. At the time, I thought it was Konradi."

"But Konradi was tall!"

"That was why I mistook him for Konradi. He had the same height. But now I come to think of it he was more muscular than Konradi — large as well as tall. And he was wearing a felt hat, while Konradi usually went about the campus bare-headed."

Foyle contemplated Prickett until the silence grew significant. Then he said, mildly enough, "Woodman has already described the man in the moonlight as short and thin and wearing a felt hat."

"That's right," put in Woodman. "Little runt, joggin' along at a clumsy trot like he wasn't used to runnin'."

"On the contrary, the man sprinted like an experienced track runner," said Prickett firmly. "Arms bent at the elbow, head up and legs moving in long, easy strides. I am a trained observer, Inspector, and Woodman is not. I saw the figure quite distinctly in the moonlit space beyond the shrubbery and I am prepared to swear in court that he was unusually tall."

"Short an' thin," muttered Woodman.

Foyle looked from one to the other. "We-ell," he drawled. "Somebody's lying."

They heard footfalls, up the steps that led to Southerland Hall and down the corridor.

Foyle raised his voice. "You boys took your time!"

"Maybe it's Ezra, the janitor," said Halsey. "He goes to choir practice every Saturday evening, but he should be back by this time."

The footfalls halted as soon as they reached the room where Foyle and the others were sitting. A young man in tawny tweeds stood on the threshold. The light from the desk lamp caught the gold in his reddish hair.

"Hello, Prickett. What the hell is going on?"

"Who are you?" countered Foyle. "And what are you doing in here?"

The young man stared. "Just what I was going to ask you. This happens to be my office. I am Julian Salt, Professor of Social Anthropology."

"*Assistant* professor," murmured Prickett.

Salt bowed with irony. "Thank you, Prickett. Assistant Professor of Social Anthropology is quite a mouthful, but the distinction is important. Assistant professors can be fired and professors can't." He moved into the light and Foyle recognised the bold, blunt profile of the man he had seen at dinner. Though Prickett was the full professor and Salt the assistant, Salt had the air of assurance and prosperity. "Did you break that window on the north side?" he asked Prickett.

Foyle answered, "Apparently it was broken by the murderer."

"The — what?"

"Dr Konradi has been murdered."

Salt looked at Prickett for confirmation. "Good God!"

Foyle gave Salt no time to recover. "Where were you at eight o'clock this evening?"

"Konradi—" Salt dropped into the nearest chair. "Are you sure it wasn't suicide? These refugees—"

"I asked you where you were at eight o'clock."

"Oh." Salt looked up. "I was dining with my wife at a

restaurant on York Avenue. No, that was earlier. We separated about quarter of eight and she took a taxi downtown. By eight, I must have been somewhere on the path between the chapel and this building, walking toward the library. I reached the library a little after eight and I'm sure the librarians in the Science and Technology Room will tell you I've been there ever since. But I've no alibi for eight o'clock. I didn't meet a soul."

"What brought you here just now?"

"I came out of the library and saw lights in my office across the quad. I knew Ezra was at his prayer meeting, or whatever it is, so I decided to come over here and investigate." A gold case gleamed in Salt's hand as he offered Prickett a cigarette.

"Did you hear any sound like a shot at eight o'clock or a little later?"

"I believe I did." Salt lit a cigarette for himself.

"You weren't alarmed?"

Salt's light hazel eyes twinkled. "I thought it was one of Prickett's experiments."

"Did you see anyone on the campus when you were crossing on your way to the library?"

"Good Lord! I did see someone running toward the river just after I heard that noise."

Foyle's attention quickened. "Can you describe him?"

"'Him'?" Salt smiled through the cigarette smoke. "It was a woman. I couldn't see her distinctly, but I have an impression she was in evening dress — high heels; long, pale dress; and long, trailing dark coat that streamed behind her as she ran."

5

EXILE

The long, candle-lit table was festive with a wintry glitter of crystal and silver. Red roses were piled in the centre of white damask. A butler was pouring white Burgundy. Basil Willing suppressed a yawn and racked his brains for an excuse to leave early.

He knew he had only been invited because some other man had failed his cousin Cynthia at the last moment. She was a cousin by marriage on his father's side and that made their relation intimate enough for her to conscript him but not quite intimate enough for him to refuse point-blank. He appreciated the white Burgundy because he could not afford imported wines at home. But he never quite appreciated Cynthia and her friends after a long day at his psychiatric clinic.

He could hardly believe his good fortune when he was called to the telephone. He took the call in the library.

"Sorry to interrupt you on a party," came the familiar voice of Inspector Foyle. "I called your house and they gave me this number. I'm out at Yorkville University. Say, didn't you study psychiatry and criminology in Vienna? Ever hear of Franz Konradi?"

The bookshelves seemed to fade. Basil saw Vienna of the Twenties — a city ravaged by defeat and inflation yet leading the world in medicine and slum clearance. A city where a great radiologist couldn't afford to buy his equipment and made it with his own hands. Basil saw a crowd of young men at the door of an amphitheatre, himself among them. Someone was saying, "No room inside — Konradi's lecturing today on chemical factors in nervous disease." Through the half-open door he could see the firmly modelled, thoughtful face of the lecturer.

"Yes, I've heard of him."

"Well, somebody has blown his brains out."

Basil stared at the telephone. It had taken nature and society so long to develop a brain like Konradi's.

"Right down your alley, doc!" the Inspector was saying cheerfully. "It happened during a psychological experiment — at least, that's what they say. Sounds phoney to me. That's where you come in. I want you to tell me if it's on the level. There's a guy here named Prickett and he's a three-ring circus all by himself — but wait till you see him. Can you come right away? I'm at a joint they call Southerland Hall."

Basil had no trouble finding his little Buick convertible squeezed between two big limousines. He turned east at 72nd until he came to the river. Curious he hadn't heard Konradi was in this country. He knew men who had studied with Konradi in Vienna for years. When he was first arrested, they raised money to ransom him. But the Nazis, who released Freud and Louis de Rothschild for ransom, refused to release Konradi, and the money had been returned to each contributor. None of these had ever spoken of Konradi's being in America. If they had known, they would certainly have mentioned it to Basil. Why had Konradi avoided his former students?

He came to a tall iron fence. Beyond was an open park and scattered buildings. This must be the southern boundary of the University. There was no entrance for cars at that point, but a small gate led to a footpath. He parked his car and proceeded on foot, hoping to meet someone who could direct him to Southerland Hall.

The path wound uphill in an S-shape. As he entered the first loop of the S he had a glimpse of two figures in the second loop, quite near as the crow would fly, but a long way around by the path. The girl was in the shadow of the trees. The moon fell full upon the boy's fair silky hair and immature face.

Basil hurried on hoping they could tell him if he were going in the right direction. But when he rounded the second curve, there was only the girl.

"I beg your pardon," he said conventionally. "But is this the way to Southerland Hall?"

Her response was unconventional. "You shall not go there!"

"Why not?"

She was still in shadow. Her face was only a dim oval, but her aplomb told him she was pretty. She seemed to be wearing a long, dark coat and a long pale dress. "It's closed at night." The "o" sound was round and delicately alien. "You wouldn't be able to get in."

"You didn't say I *couldn't* — you said I *shouldn't.*"

"My English is not very good. Shall, will, can, may — it's all so confusing."

"I'll have no trouble getting in," he went on. "I'm meeting someone there by appointment."

"Oh." She caught her breath. She came closer and he was

conscious of a faint fragrance of white violets. "You're too late." Her voice was low and urgent. "Don't go. Please!"

"All this is only whetting my curiosity. Nothing could keep me from going there now."

She was quite close. Her eyes were large, dark, and brilliant. "Nothing?" A soft insinuation was in her voice — an inflection so faint that it might be his imagination.

"If you're trying to vamp me, you've chosen quite the wrong moment."

"You are rude!" In anger, her "r" was as alien as her vowels.

"Sorry. But I really have an appointment and I am late." He started down the path. As he expected, there was a step behind him.

"Don't go so fast! I will show you the way."

"Oh, you've changed your mind?" He noticed she wasn't having trouble with *shall* and *will* now.

"If I don't show you, someone else will."

"And if you do, you can keep an eye on me."

"Why should I wish to keep an eye on you?"

"That's what I was wondering."

They came to a chapel. A lighted building stood on the left. "Why — there are lights!" Her voice wavered.

"Anything strange about that?"

"I don't know. I hope not. Well, there is your Southerland Hall. Good night!"

"Wait a minute. Where are you going?"

"That hardly concerns you!"

"Perhaps not. But it may concern Inspector Foyle."

"Who?"

"An inspector of police. Something rather extraordinary has happened at Southerland Hall tonight and the police are in charge. They'll want to know why you were so anxious to keep me from coming here."

Basil could feel rather than see that she was peering at him in the darkness. "What has happened?"

"They'll tell you."

"And if I refuse to come, I suppose you'll drag me!" She stepped into the light from the open door. It was a pale face shadowed by a thick cloud of dark hair. *Pretty* wasn't the right word. The subtle spirit that lived in her eyes made the pretty faces he had known seem trite. This was not beauty, but sorcery.

The corridor was crowded with men. Basil recognised Homicide Squad detectives and he assumed the others were local precinct men. But the boy lounging in the third doorway on the right didn't look as if he had ever been subjected to police discipline. His sullen face lighted as he saw the girl with Basil.

"Gisela! Have they dared to drag you into this?"

Her eyes were wide with fear. "What has happened?"

"Don't you know?"

"Ian, tell me quickly!"

The first door on the right opened and Foyle stood on the threshold. "Mr Halsey, I asked you to wait in Dr Prickett's office with the others."

The boy turned. "Who are you to order me around?"

Foyle's glance took in Basil and the girl as if Halsey didn't exist. "Miss von Hohenems? I am the officer in charge. Please come into Mr Salt's office." He stood aside to let them pass.

Gisela turned when she reached the centre of the room. "I am Dr Konradi's secretary and—" She was looking at a pile of notebooks on the desk. "What are you doing with his laboratory notes?" Her voice was suddenly breathless.

"Sit down, please." Foyle closed the door and came forward. "You must prepare for a shock."

She sank into the chair without taking her eyes from Foyle. "He is — dead?" The words were scarcely audible.

"Murdered."

"Oh, no! They couldn't!" Tears stood in her eyes. She did not seem aware of them or anything else in the room.

Under the harsh ceiling light, her face had the white lustre of a pearl. Basil had seen that lucent pallor before — in the faces of anaemic patients. She seemed about twenty-six or twenty-seven — she must have been a child of four or five months during the World War. In Vienna he had heard tales of Austrian children who developed anaemia during the food blockade.

She wore no hat. She had thrown a sport coat of purple homespun over her shoulders without waiting to slip her arms into the sleeves. Her dress was a white silk jersey that clung to breast and waist and fell in supple, swaying folds to her feet. The sort of dress a woman wears for dinner at home to relax, but scarcely would choose for a late excursion among the bypaths of an unfrequented park. The hem was green with grass stains; the high heels of her white sandals were muddy.

"'They'?" said Foyle at last.

Gisela looked as if he were speaking a language she did not understand. With an effort she brought her attention to bear on what he had said. "They have agents everywhere. Dr Konradi had no other enemies." Even now, 3000 miles from the headquarters of the *Geheime Staats Polizei,* she would only speak of "them" and "they."

"Have you any reason to believe that Konradi was being pestered by Nazi agents?"

Foyle's blunt use of the word *Nazi* disturbed her. "No. No reason whatever." She was no longer a woman grieving for the dead, but a witness in a murder case — a frightened witness answering each question warily.

"We already have proof that the murderer was not a Nazi." Foyle took a sheet of paper from the desk. "This is a list of the people who were in Southerland Hall when Dr Prickett's revolver was stolen. Ezra, the janitor, was working in the corridor all afternoon where he could see everyone who entered or left the building. His own name is not on the list because he has an alibi for the time of the murder. He sings in the choir of a Harlem church and the whole choir as well as the rector swear he was there at eight o'clock. I've also eliminated myself." Foyle smiled. "And Prickett's son, who is only four months old. That leaves eight people. One of them stole the revolver that killed Konradi and we think it safe to assume that the thief and the murderer are the same person, for murder is generally a one-man job outside gangster cases."

Foyle read the list aloud:

- *Malcolm Southerland, trustee*
- *Raymond Prickett, Professor Experimental Psychology*
- *Marian Prickett, his wife*
- *Julian Salt, Assistant Professor of Social Anthropology*
- *Amy Salt, his wife*
- *Albert Feng Lo, Visiting Prof of Abnormal Psychology*
- *Ian Halsey, undergraduate student and assistant to Dr Prickett*
- *Gisela von Hohenems, Dr Konradi's secretary.*

"Now you see why we are so sure the murderer was not a Nazi." The Inspector's glance rested on Gisela. "No German or Austrian name is on the list — except yours."

She sat still and white save for dark hair and burning eyes. "You are not accusing me—?"

"Not at all. But I'd like some particulars. Why did you leave Austria?"

"My father supported Dr von Schuschnigg's campaign against them. My father was too old to survive a concentration camp. The day before they crossed the border, I drove him from Vienna to Slovakia. We were just in time. We went to Prague, but I couldn't find work there and we had very little money. The Dean, Dr Lysaght, was in Paris then and he wrote me suggesting I come to America. We had known him years ago in Vienna when he spent his sabbatical year there. I left my father in Prague until I could get enough money to bring him over here. I learned to type in New York. When Dr Lysaght heard that Konradi wanted a secretary who understood German he got me the job."

"Was that the first time you met Konradi?"

"Yes. Of course, I had heard of him all my life. We both lived in Vienna for years, but we never met."

"Do you know anything about Konradi's family? Or where he was born?"

"He had no close relatives living. I believe he was born in Styria. He spoke German like a Styrian."

"You are Styrian, too?"

"No, my family came from Vorarlberg."

"Your father's name?"

"Alois von Hohenems."

Foyle jotted it down. "And now" — he settled back in his chair — "when did you last see Konradi?"

"This evening a little while ago."

"Where?"

"At home. I have a small apartment at the east end of 79th Street."

"Was he there often?"

"No. He had never been there before."

"Why did he go there this evening?"

"I don't know. He came while I was at dinner — about

54

quarter of eight. I think he was worried about something. He said he had been walking and thinking ever since he had left his laboratory this afternoon. But before he could say more, the phone rang, and a man's voice asked for Dr Konradi. He seemed surprised. He said, 'I told no one I was coming here.' Then he took the phone and frowned as he listened. After a while he said, 'Very well, I'll come at once.' And then: 'Of course I understand. I won't mention your name to anyone. The whole thing must be kept quiet.' He hung up the receiver and I asked if there were anything wrong. He answered, 'No, nothing of importance.' But he was still frowning. Then he said, 'I must go to the laboratory, but I'll be back soon.' Those were the last words I heard him say."

Foyle broke the silence. "Did you recognise the voice on the telephone?"

"No. It was a lisping voice. I don't know anyone with a lisp."

"A lisp can be assumed — like a limp. Did Konradi ask who was calling?"

"No. I've told you everything he said." Her eyes dilated with horror. "You think that was the voice of the — murderer?"

"Yes," answered Foyle grimly. "And someone Konradi knew and trusted. He wouldn't have gone back to Southerland Hall alone at that hour if he hadn't recognised the voice. I saw him enter the building myself. He was in such a hurry he went straight to his laboratory without stopping to switch on the lights in the corridor. He never suspected a trap."

"If only I had known—" Her voice was more vibration than sound. They could hardly hear her. "If only I had followed him sooner—"

"You were following him when I met you?" suggested Basil.

"Yes." The word came with a sigh. "He said, 'I'll be back

soon.' And he didn't come. I watched the clock until I couldn't stand it any longer. My apartment is opposite the southern end of the University grounds. So I threw on a coat and started to walk to Southerland Hall. When you asked me the way here, I thought you must have something to do with the man who phoned. I was afraid Konradi was in some danger. That was why I tried to keep you from coming here."

"'Some danger'? As vague as that?"

"Yes."

"And yet you sounded rather — definite when you tried to keep me from coming here. Remember?"

For a moment there was colour in her cheeks. When it faded, she was paler than ever. "I had no definite reason to believe Konradi was in danger. It was only a feeling — an impression."

"Who was the boy talking to you on the path a moment before I spoke to you?"

"Boy?" She had regained control of her voice. Her eyes were wide and blank. "There was no boy. I didn't meet anyone on the path but you."

Foyle waited. But Basil had no further questions at the moment. Then Foyle asked, "Why did Southerland want to see Konradi this afternoon?"

"I don't know."

"How long was Southerland in the building?"

"About ten minutes — I don't know exactly. I was in Konradi's office when Southerland came. I left him there while I crossed the hall to see if Konradi was in his laboratory. He wasn't but he had left the door unlocked. I never knew him to do such a thing before. I went into Dr Prickett's room to ask him if he'd seen Konradi. You must remember that because it was you who told me Konradi had left the building. When I went back to tell Southerland, he wasn't in Konradi's office where I had left him — he was just coming out of Konradi's laboratory. I told him Konradi had gone and suggested telephoning him. But Southerland said he couldn't wait any longer. As soon as he'd gone, I locked the laboratory and the office and went home."

Foyle opened one of the notebooks on the desk. Basil could see the paper, white with lines of faint green instead of the usual blue. It was covered with small handwriting in black ink — equations, formulae and dates interspersed with comments in German.

"Did Konradi keep anything in these besides laboratory notes?" asked Foyle. "Anything the Nazis might have wanted, such as letters from anti-Nazis in Germany?"

Gisela, her voice low and troubled, answered, "No. He always destroyed letters from Germany as soon as he received them."

"If Konradi made a discovery of commercial or military value, who would have the patent?"

"The University. Any discovery made by a member of the faculty becomes the property of the University automatically, so they can use the royalties to finance further research in the same field. But—" a fugitive smile touched her lips "—I can't imagine Konradi concocting a new poison gas or a kiss-proof lipstick. He was a biological chemist, you know — not an industrial chemist. Cancer interested him. It's too slow a death to have military value and I don't see how a study of it could be put to commercial use."

"But if Konradi had found a cure for cancer? Surely that would have commercial value?"

"When I first came here, he told me he was trying to discover ways to avoid cancer — not ways to cure it. That sort of discovery is never commercialised."

Foyle glanced at Basil for confirmation. He nodded. "It's

only in copybooks that an ounce of prevention is worth a pound of cure. Fortunes are made through patent medicines, but I don't believe anyone has ever made a cent through preventing disease."

Foyle had laid his mine carefully. Now he exploded it. "In view of all this, how do you explain that seventy pages have been stolen from Konradi's most recent notebook?"

"Stolen?" The white silk jersey shimmered as her breast rose and fell in a quick breath. "Are you sure?"

"This book is seventy pages short as compared with the others. They're all alike except for that. I happen to know that Konradi was looking for some missing laboratory notes this afternoon a few hours before his death. Didn't he ask you about them?"

"No."

"The last entry is dated February 28. My men have searched his laboratory, his office and his apartment without finding any notes for March and April. I can only conclude they have been stolen."

"But — why?"

"We've been rather counting on you to tell us that. As Konradi's secretary you must know what subjects were discussed in the notes for March and April."

"But I don't. I-I haven't typed any recent notes."

"Surely you have some idea what work he was doing. You saw him every day. I understand you were often in the laboratory."

"I'm sorry. But I never understood anything I saw him do. I didn't even understand the notes I typed. You see, I've never studied chemistry."

Foyle received this with open scepticism. Basil wondered. Konradi could have had his pick of Yorkville graduates who knew chemistry as well as German and shorthand. Had he preferred Gisela because she was a fellow refugee — and lovely? It seemed out of character for a scientist of Konradi's standing to mix work with sentiment or pleasure.

"Who were Konradi's friends among the other chemists on the faculty?" continued Foyle.

"I can't recall seeing him with other chemists. Their laboratories are all in the School of Medicine. He rarely had occasion to go there."

"Do you mean to say he never discussed his work with other men working in the same field?"

"He didn't make friends easily."

"Where were the notes kept when not in use?"

"In a safe in the laboratory. Sometimes he took them home with him."

"Who had the combination?"

"No one but Konradi."

Basil intervened. "No doubt Dr Konradi's laboratory assistants can tell us what was in the missing notes. No need to bother Miss von Hohenems about it."

Gisela lifted stricken eyes to him. Her voice was thin and brittle. "Dr Konradi had no assistants."

"Isn't that rather unusual?" Basil's voice was casual.

"I don't know. I tell you I don't know anything about chemistry."

"Who cleaned the laboratory?"

"The janitor — under Konradi's supervision. The mice were usually kept in the animal room at the School of Medicine. The mechanics there looked after his laboratory equipment when it needed repairing."

She realised that some further explanation was needed. "Perhaps…" She seemed to grope for words. "Perhaps Konradi thought new assistants would be more hindrance than help. You see, he was repeating from memory experiments he had already made in Vienna. He was forced to leave all his records in his Viennese laboratory when he was arrested and of course he couldn't recover them when he escaped."

Basil could almost see Storm Troopers invading Konradi's, laboratory — disciplined stupidity destroying knowledge. Had there been violence? Had Konradi known what was coming and waited with resignation? Or had they taken him by surprise and burst into the room during some delicate manipulation? And could this have anything to do with Konradi's murder at an American university a year later?

Of all his questions Basil put only one to Gisela, "Was Konradi arrested for political activity?"

"No. He never took any part in politics. They arrested him because he was a Jew. There was some technical charge — lack of National Socialist spirit or some such formula that could be stretched to cover anything. But the real charge against him was his race, just as that was the real charge against Freud."

"What became of the laboratory assistants he had in Vienna?" asked Foyle.

"There were only two. Both died at Dachau. I am very tired. May I go home now?"

"Yes." Foyle spoke with more consideration than he had shown previously. "I think I'll send Sergeant Samson with you — in the circumstances."

The door closed. Foyle pushed aside Konradi's notebooks with a weary gesture. "What did he look like? The boy she wasn't talking to. A track runner?"

"More like a Fra Angelico angel. Altogether too exquisite for an adult male."

Foyle was baffled. "I certainly haven't met any angels around here!" He gave Basil a condensed account of his experiences. "Now you know about as much as I do. How are we ever going to clear away this fog of lies and get down to the facts?"

"I don't want to clear away the lies." Basil stretched his legs and leaned back in the comfortable armchair.

"But only the facts—"

"You forget that lies are facts — psychological facts. You policemen and lawyers make a great mistake when you shut up a liar and prosecute him for perjury. If you'd only listen to him long enough, you'd learn everything there is to know about him — or her. You should read Jung. 'Every myth is an important psychological truth — so is every lie.'"

"But that's screwy. How can a lie be truth?"

"A lie doesn't reproduce external facts faithfully — it is a product of the liar's own mind, and therefore a clue to the quality and content of his mind. The liar, like any other story-teller, must draw upon his remembered experiences to build his fantasy, and his choice of detail is guided by his tastes and emotions. So if you want to learn something about a man's emotions and memories listen to his lies. Wasn't it Emerson who said, 'I always listen carefully when a man boasts, for then he is unconsciously revealing his ideal'?"

Foyle rose abruptly and went to one of the north windows. He jerked a cord and the shade shot up with a clatter. "See that lawn sloping up to the campus?"

Basil rose slowly. "What about it?"

"A single figure ran up that slope tonight just after the murder and disappeared among the trees on the campus. That was all I saw. Three other men claim to have seen it. One says it was a short, thin man running awkwardly; another says it was a tall, large man moving like a track runner; and the third says it was a woman in a long, trailing dark coat and a long pale dress. At least two of them must be lying. What would you and Jung make of that?"

"Where were the three men at the time?"

"Two were standing on the lawn about six feet from this window. The third was crossing the quadrangle."

"Then all three were lying. Because you can't see any figure distinctly by moonlight at a distance over 16 meters. Even when the moon is full its light is no stronger than the light of one candle at 12 feet, and it's 24 hours short of full moon tonight."

"I suppose they might have been honestly mistaken," admitted Foyle.

Basil smiled. "Mistakes, like remorse, are always dishonest. What happens in mis-observation? A witness sees something indistinctly because the light is poor and he's excited. He remembers it vaguely. Then he's asked to describe it. Unconsciously he draws on his emotions and memories to build up details — just as if he were lying consciously. A man's mis-observations may tell you as much as his deliberate lies. Self-deception and deception are both creative efforts of the mind. That's proved by the fact that they have the same effect on blood pressure and—"

A knock fell on the door and a voice cried, "Medical examiner wants you, chief. He can't find the bullet!"

6

EXAMINATION

B asil Braced himself for an unpleasant moment. But the still, sprawling figure was as remote from life as a cast-off glove. The flat glare of flood lamps made it seem like an effigy of a man with his brains blown out. It lay on a bench. A stolid young man whom Basil recognised as Dalton, an assistant medical examiner, was bending over it.

"Hello, Willing! I'll be with you in a minute, Inspector." His hands were busy.

Basil noticed a moving-picture camera, a chronoscope, and a sphygmomanometer for taking blood pressure.

"Prickett's?"

"Yeah," responded Foyle. "This is where he experiments. He's made a great discovery. He's found that if you fire a revolver beside a baby's ear the baby will jump. This stuff on the table is what he says he was using for the experiment tonight. Everything belongs to Prickett except that Corona portable — just like my own — he borrowed that from Halsey. Does the set-up look phoney to you? Or is it really an experiment?"

Basil considered the wine and cigarettes, the book, the box of crackers and what remained of the strawberries. "It might be. Is this the revolver?"

"Uh-huh. No fingerprints but Konradi's so the murderer must have wiped it clean after Prickett used it this afternoon. Prickett swears he didn't. As I see it, the murderer wore gloves and tried to make the crime look like suicide by pressing Konradi's fingertips to the gun after firing it."

Basil broke the revolver and found two spent partridge cases inside.

"Blanks," explained Foyle. "Prickett identified them as the kind he's been using."

"Where's the cartridge case the murderer used?"

"We can't find it."

"But revolvers don't eject spent cartridges!"

"I know — but we still can't find it! The murderer must have taken it away with him."

"Why take the cartridge case and leave the revolver?"

"Would I know? He just did, that's all."

"But why?" insisted Basil. "A suicide couldn't remove a spent cartridge after it was fired, and a murderer wouldn't if he wanted the crime to look like suicide."

Dalton came toward them holding a pair of forceps, rubber-tipped so they wouldn't scratch the surface of a bullet and confuse the minute marks left by the rifling of a gun barrel. His shirt sleeves were rolled to the elbow and his jaw moved steadily masticating a cud of chewing gum. "Here's the wad." He held out a bit of blackened cotton. "Looks like old-fashioned black powder." He touched it with the tip of his tongue. "Yeah — you can taste the saltpetre."

"I don't want the wad — I want the bullet!" snapped Foyle. "We've searched both rooms and it isn't here."

"Maybe it went out a window."

"They're nailed down, and they're of unbreakable glass."

"Well, it isn't in the body."

"It must be. You can't shoot a man without a bullet!"

"Better search the rooms again." Dalton rolled down his shirt sleeves and adjusted his cuff links. "Not that it matters much. Clear case of suicide."

"Would a suicide have wiped Prickett's fingerprints off the gun?" Foyle was indignant. "Konradi talked to me this afternoon. He knew he was in danger and he warned me that the murder of a refugee might be mistaken for suicide. He said, *'No matter what happens, I shall not commit, suicide.'*"

"You can't go by what they say." Dalton shrugged his shoulders into his jacket sleeves. "Douglas Kerr mentions a case where a man discussed plans for a vacation with his family though he planned to kill himself the next day and did so. You can't prove Prickett's revolver was stolen this afternoon. He might have dropped it somewhere and Konradi might have found it and rubbed off Prickett's fingerprints inadvertently. Everything else points to suicide. It's May — May and June are the suicide months. Konradi was a refugee and every time you pick up your morning paper some refugee has committed suicide. A man is always more likely to kill himself when he's been overworking and everyone says that's what Konradi has been doing. He was a chemist and there's a high suicide rate among chemists."

"Surely a chemist wouldn't shoot himself?"

"Why not? A shot is as quick and probably as painless as any poison."

"He escaped from Germany and got a job over here doing work he liked — and so he killed himself?" Foyle was mocking Dalton.

"You don't need a rational motive for suicide. Ask Willing about the Freudian death-wish. Self-preservation can be inverted like any other instinct. Even courage in the face of danger may be a perverted desire for self-destruction. The same temperament that becomes a hero or a martyr in one situation may become a suicide in another. Suppose you take a look at the wound. It speaks for itself."

In the floodlights they could see the entrance wound — not a clean drilled hole, but a large, ragged wound shaped like a cross, scorched with flame, blackened with smoke and tattooed with unburned grains of black powder. But jaw, lips and teeth were uninjured except for a cracking of skin around the mouth caused by distention of the cheeks during the explosion.

"Obviously a contact shot," said Basil.

"In the roof of the mouth — one of the seven places always chosen by a suicide to shoot himself." Dalton was triumphant. "There's only one way you can make a wound like that: by putting the muzzle of the gun between the teeth in contact with the skin in the roof of the mouth. Then the high-pressure gases released by the explosion are concentrated in the hollow chamber of the mouth — a pressure of about 10,000 pounds to the square inch. Contact with the skin forces the gases into the wound with the bullet. They find a way out by shattering the top of the skull — as you see. Now tell me how a murderer could force the muzzle of a big .45 revolver between a man's teeth without bruising his lips and breaking his teeth? You simply can't shoot an unwilling victim in the roof of the mouth unless you use violence. That's why such a shot is considered clear proof of suicide when the lips and teeth are uninjured."

"If Konradi were bound—" began Foyle.

"But he wasn't!" insisted Dalton. "There are powder burns on his right hand — I took a nitrate test to make sure. That proves the gun was in his right hand when it was fired. You can't bind a man tightly without leaving some marks on his wrists and ankles. You can't strangle him without leaving some mark on his neck. You can't drug him without leaving some symptom. You can't even stun him without leaving some mark external or internal. Satisfied?"

"No." Foyle was unexpectedly stubborn. "We had a case once where a man was sandbagged and the medical examiner couldn't find any mark of a blow or any symptoms of concussion during the autopsy."

"Those freak cases are rare. There's no way a murderer faking suicide could make certain that the body would show no signs of concussion. He wouldn't dare take a chance on it. And there's another thing." Dalton shifted his gum to the other side of his mouth. "Come in here a minute."

He led them to Konradi's laboratory by way of the corridor. "When Konradi shot himself he was sitting in this chair near the side door leading to Prickett's lecture hall. The shape of these drops shows they fell from a man sitting or standing still." Dalton pointed to a spattering of blood on the floor around the chair — circular stains with an irregular edge all around. "As Konradi fell across the threshold the door must have been unlatched and he must have forced it open by falling against it."

"And why was the door unlatched?" cried Foyle. "It's usually locked. A murderer might have unlatched it and placed the body near it when he heard people in Prickett's room. He knew they'd stop to examine the body before going into the laboratory, and that would give him time to reach the janitor's window by way of the corridor. But there's no reason a suicide should place himself beside this door."

"Oh, yes, there is!" Dalton waved a hand toward the small, round mirror Foyle had noticed when he first entered Konradi's laboratory. "Get it? Konradi was sitting right in front of that mirror when the shot was fired. Would a murderer want to watch himself in the mirror? Hardly! But suicides often sit in front of a mirror so they can see where to point the gun."

Basil contemplated Dalton with interest. "In the dark?"

"What do you mean?"

"Foyle tells me Konradi was shot at eight o'clock — after Prickett had turned off all the lights in the building by tampering with the main switch."

Dalton expelled his breath slowly as a deflated balloon. Then he rallied. "Maybe there was moonlight."

"On the west side of the building? At eight o'clock? The moon still rises in the East, Dalton!"

"Maybe Konradi had a flashlight."

"Then what became of it?" As Dalton hesitated, Basil went on. "You may not be the first student of medical jurisprudence to enter this room tonight!"

"What do you mean?"

"Isn't it odd so many little details all point to suicide? In most criminal cases there's some uncertainty. But in this case every signpost shrieks: *Suicide!* Just as if a rather academic mind had studied the subject and determined to manufacture a classic case of suicide including every known clue. Things don't work out so neatly when they're unplanned. The perfect textbook case is as rare in criminology as in medicine."

"Well, that's a new kind of logic!" Dalton's scorn was massive. "It must be murder because there's too much evidence of suicide! How would that sound in court? And it isn't a perfect textbook case because there's no suicide note. When a murderer plans a fake suicide that's the first thing he thinks of!"

"There was a suicide note," cried Foyle quickly. "We found it here beside the body." He took a folded sheet of paper from his pocket. "We examined it for clues, but this murderer is too cagey to leave any. He typed it on Konradi's own machine — the Underwood here in the laboratory. It's on University notepaper, just like that in Konradi's desk. And Konradi's fingerprints are the only ones on the paper and the typewriter."

"And that proves Konradi didn't write it and it's just a plant?!" Dalton was rapidly losing his temper.

"The prints on the typewriter keys are smudged," explained Foyle. "Someone wearing gloves must have used it after Konradi."

"You never get clear prints on typewriter keys," retorted Dalton. "The typist smudges his own prints each time he touches a key."

Basil was reading the note. The heading was engraved:

Division of Biological Chemistry: Research Department,
Yorkville University,
East End Avenue at 86th Street, New York.

All the rest was typewritten — even the signature·

Sorry to involve the University in this rotten business, But life is hopeless if one loses friends ho;e country , , , everything, , , F Konrqdi.

"It was typed in the dark," explained Foyle. "I walked all around this building tonight just before eight o'clock, and when I passed this corncr I heard someone typing in here. I wasn't sure whether I'd heard it or imagined it because it only lasted a moment and there wasn't a light at any window. Now I feel sure it was the murderer typing this note on Konradi's typewriter. He couldn't risk using the typewriter during the day when the building was full of people. He had to do it at night and chose Saturday night because that's when the janitor goes to choir practice and the building is empty. Even then he didn't dare show a light for fear someone who knew Konradi wasn't in the laboratory would investigate. Of course he never dreamed I would be poking about."

Basil agreed. "If you heard Konradi typing, there would certainly have been a light in the laboratory. And Konradi wouldn't have typed his signature. The Viennese are nothing if not punctilious."

"Ain't psychology grand?" said Dalton sweetly. "If you study that note for ten minutes I suppose you'll be able to tell us just how a murderer can force a gun between a conscious victim's teeth without injuring his mouth. I'm going home! You don't need a medical examiner around here — you need a magician!"

"Wait, a minute!" Basil's voice stopped him. "Any old scars on the body? Any signs of ill health?"

"No. Why?"

"How long was Konradi at Dachau?"

"Four months." Dalton frowned. "I see what you mean. A concentration camp is not a health resort."

"I've heard they never release any prisoner whose body bears permanent scars," put in Foyle.

"But Konradi," answered Basil, "escaped."

"Every prisoner, released or escaped, is broken in health," added Dalton.

"And Konradi?"

"His body was in remarkably good condition. No sign of premature senility except a few scattered white hairs. No sign of ill health except a very slight lesion in the nose between the nostrils. Theoretically, that could be leprosy in its first stage — or cocaine inhalation. But he had no other symptoms of the cocaine addict and he never experimented with lepers. It's queer..."

Prickett, Salt and Halsey had been kept "on ice," as Foyle put it, in Prickett's office. Prickett constituted himself spokesman. "It's nearly midnight, Inspector. How much longer are we to be kept waiting?"

"Only a few minutes. This is Dr Willing. Tell him about your experiment this evening. He's the psychol — psychiatrist attached to the district attorney's office."

Prickett had taken pains to instruct Foyle in the difference between a psychologist, like himself, and a mere psychiatrist like Basil Willing. Psychologists were scientists who experimented with the normal mind. Psychiatrists were only doctors of medicine who got morbid ideas from observing the abnormal behaviour of mental patients. Foyle was a little disappointed when Prickett greeted Basil cordially. Even a Freudian psychiatrist may seem like a fellow human being to a behavioural psychologist who has just spent three hours in the hands of the Homicide Squad. Basil Willing might hold nonsensical theories, but at least he would have some idea what Prickett was talking about while the detectives had concluded that Prickett was either criminal or crazy.

"I feel sure Dr Willing will uphold me when I say there was nothing out of the ordinary about my experiment," announced Prickett. "It was planned to test the scientific value of the lie-detector—"

"What!" Ian Halsey was on his feet. "You told me it was a memory experiment!"

"Naturally. You were the subject, and a lie-detector test has greater significance when the subject doesn't know he is going to be tested until the last moment."

Halsey's face was congested, his fists clenched. He took a step forward.

Prickett retreated. "Really, Ian! You know the Department of Psychology expects active cooperation from all students in its research projects."

"Why, you—" Halsey's response should have been interesting, but he never finished it. He collapsed in a chair suddenly. His whole body was shaking, his breath as quick as if he had been running. He didn't seem to notice Basil's fingertips on his pulse.

"This boy is in no condition for questioning. He should be put to bed."

"The Dean's house is nearest," said Salt. "He's at the Alumni Dinner, but Mrs Lysaght will be there."

"Okay," agreed Foyle. "I'll send one of the boys with him and the watchman can show them the way."

"Do Halsey's parents know about this?" asked Basil.

"They're in Egypt at the moment," explained Salt. "I suppose the Dean will telephone to Cairo."

Prickett seemed to breathe more freely after Halsey had left the room. "I never expected to find such a completely personal bias in a boy who has had nearly four years of psychological training!"

Basil brought him back to the question. "Just what type of lie-detector did you plan to use?"

"A combination of the Marston systolic blood-pressure test and the Jung association time test." Prickett turned back to Foyle. "You see, there's more than one kind of lie-detector, but they're all based on physical and mental tests originally used to detect disease. They've proved equally useful in detecting guilt because a guilty conscience is a disease — at least it has a pathological effect on physical and mental functions such as blood pressure and association."

"Sure, I know all that!" Foyle was growing impatient. "I

want to know why you turned the lights off and locked the front door just before Konradi was shot."

"The lie-detector is used chiefly in criminal investigation." Prickett might have been addressing a classroom. "Now...to test a method of criminal investigation, what is the first essential? Why—" he smiled brightly. "A crime — of course!"

Foyle blinked. "Do you mean—"

"He's not confessing to a real crime," explained Basil. "He's talking about a sham crime."

"A *what?*" Foyle looked as if he thought it might be a short step from a sham crime to a real one.

But Prickett continued without appearing to notice. "Unfortunately it is not practical to have anyone commit a real crime for experimental purposes. Therefore we devise an act approximating a real crime and we call this a sham crime. After it's over the experimenter puts the sham criminal and a number of other people ignorant of the sham crime through a lie-detector test dealing with the sham crime. Their responses are analysed by a second experimenter who knows all the details of the sham crime but who does not know the sham criminal. If he can discover the sham criminal through his analysis of the tests alone, he has proved their value to criminal investigation. The sham crime I arranged for this evening was to have been the first in a series. I used my own students as subjects and I divided them into groups, each consisting of one sham criminal and nine people ignorant of the sham crime — controls, as we call them. Ian Halsey was selected as the sham criminal for Group No. 1."

Foyle fumbled in a pocket and dragged out a crumpled paper. "Then *you* wrote this cockeyed letter?"

"Y-Yes." Prickett's composure was shaken. "How did you get hold of it?"

"Found it on the campus this afternoon."

"How could Ian have been so careless! If one of the controls found that letter, he would have learned enough about the sham crime to ruin the experiment!"

"It doesn't say anything about a sham crime," drawled Foyle. "But it says a lot about murder."

Prickett tried to smile. "I couched my instructions in melodramatic terms purposely in order to intensify the emotional reaction of the subject."

"One moment," Basil interrupted. "Do you claim that there is no connection between the real crime and the sham crime?"

"None whatever!"

"And that this letter is nothing but a letter of instruction to Halsey outlining the sham crime?"

"Exactly."

"In that case why did it alarm Dr Konradi when he saw it this afternoon?"

"I don't know." Prickett's bewilderment seemed genuine. "Perhaps he was afraid of something else and mistook my letter for part of it. When you fear a thing you see it wherever you look."

"Why did you stage this sham crime in Konradi's laboratory?" demanded Foyle. "The letter says, *You will proceed directly to the laboratory.* You must have meant Konradi's laboratory because he's the only chemist with rooms in Southerland Hall."

Prickett laughed a little heartily. "I was referring to the psychological laboratory — the room you insist on calling the lecture hall. The rest of the letter makes that clear."

Prickett took a carbon copy from his desk. Foyle read it aloud:

"You will find various articles on the table including a candle which you may light after pulling down the window shades. Investigate the

objects on the table carefully. Eat and drink anything edible. Smoke some of the cigarettes and take particular notice of the brand. Help yourself to anything that may seem of value. Then turn to page 116 of the book you will find there and copy the first three paragraphs on the typewriter. This passage includes a rather gruesome description of an actual murder. While copying it endeavour to identify yourself mentally with the murderer.

"By this time it should be approximately eight-forty-five (8:45) and you must make haste to leave the building as surreptitiously as possible. If you follow these instructions exactly and if you can prevent the person who will test you afterward from discovering that you did so, you will receive a prize of five dollars ($5.00). Enclosed is a key to the psychological laboratory. The east door of Southerland Hall will be unlatched."

"Was that all there was to your sham crime?" Foyle was more baffled than ever.

"Oh, no. These instructions were devised to lure the sham criminal into the building at a certain hour and keep him busy for a while with objects that could be used for reference in the association test afterward. But I had to use more strenuous methods to make Halsey feel something of the panic and anxiety which play an important part in the emotional life of the real criminal. Such anxiety is greatly intensified when an unexpected hitch occurs in the commission of a crime, increasing the criminal's danger and forcing him to make unforeseen decisions quickly. Therefore I tried to introduce the surprise element as effectively as possible."

"And you certainly succeeded!" murmured Salt.

Prickett ignored the interruption. "I returned to Souther-land Hall this evening at 7:00 — just as Ezra was leaving. I set the burglar alarm, which hadn't been used for years, and nailed down all the ground-floor windows so they couldn't be raised. The basement windows are barred and the second-floor windows are too high for jumping. The west door is boarded up and Halsey had no key to the east door. Then I turned off all the electric lights by removing part of the main switch. The burglar alarm has a separate circuit of its own. Just as the library clock was striking 7:45, I left the east door ajar and took up my station in the shrubbery to the right of the entrance. Once Halsey had entered the building and started to carry out my instructions, I came out and locked the east door.

"In this way, I made it impossible for him to leave the building by 8:45 as instructed. When he tried the east door and found it locked, he would be sure to recall the *'very peculiar and unpleasant situation'* I had threatened in my letter if he were not out of the building by 8:45 — a threat all the more disturbing as it left so much to the imagination. He would certainly try to get out one of the ground-floor windows — only to find them nailed down. When he tried the switches, he would get no light. Of course he might suspect I had done this — but he couldn't be sure, and the uncertainty would make him all the more anxious. Locked in an empty building by an unknown agency, with only the uncanny flicker of a candle for light, he would experience something like the trapped feeling of a real criminal. And, as you all know now, he could break the window at the end of the passage where the janitor keeps his mops and pails.

"Do you get the idea?" Prickett's eyes were shining behind thick lenses. He seemed to have forgotten everything but his delight in his own ingenuity. "I turned Southerland Hall into a gigantic maze similar to those we use in animal experiments with only one exit which the animal is compelled to discover under the urge of fear, hunger or sex. It would require a somewhat long and complex train of thought for Halsey to recall that there was just one breakable window on the ground floor and still longer for him to conclude it was the only way out. I confess I never watched a rat in a maze more eagerly than I watched Southerland Hall tonight to see just how long it would take Halsey to work out the problem in his state of panic."

"So Halsey was just a rat in a maze!" Salt grinned. "You should tell him that some time."

"How could you be sure Halsey would try to break a window?" asked Foyle.

"There is a certain uniformity in human reactions to the stimulus of being locked in an empty building without adequate light. Blane found that nearly all his subjects broke a window and got out. I hoped the night watchman would hear the alarm and pursue Halsey when he broke the window. To make doubly sure, I told Woodman I had seen a tramp prowling around and he promised to keep an eye on the building tonight."

"You *hoped* the watchman would pursue Halsey?"

"Of course. The more vivid Halsey's experience, the more interesting it would be to see if he could conceal it during the lie-detector test afterward."

"And what about me?" grunted Foyle. "If you were watching the east entrance just before 8:00, you must have seen me go in. Why didn't you stop me?"

"I mistook you for Ezra. I couldn't see your face at that distance in the moonlight and I thought no one but the janitor would wander around the building the way you did. It was too late to stop you — Ian would be there at any moment and if he saw me it would spoil the surprise element. He would know it was I who had nailed down the windows and turned off the lights. Of course I thought a tip would compensate you — that is, Ezra — for being locked in with Halsey during the experiment. It made things even more difficult when Konradi entered the building. He was so quick I couldn't stop him without calling out. Halsey might have heard me and that would have ruined everything."

"I suppose it didn't occur to you the experiment might be postponed?" said Foyle.

"It did for a moment. But then I decided that Konradi, as a fellow scientist, should be willing to sacrifice a little time and convenience for the sake of a psychological experiment. As soon as I heard Halsey screaming, I hurried around the east corner of the building to the north side, where I could watch the janitor's window and see who was the first to break it and climb out. Incidentally, the fact that the murderer remembered the one breakable window and found it so quickly proves he is familiar with Southerland Hall and is quick-witted and resolute in emergencies."

"And he has no key to the east door," amended Salt.

But Foyle shook his head. "The man who broke that window couldn't go down the corridor to the east door without passing the open door of the psychological laboratory where Halsey and I were standing. But he could reach the janitor's window without passing us and that's why he chose it."

Prickett was indignant. "Are you suggesting that Salt or I—?"

"You each admit you were near Southerland Hall when the shot was fired, and you were each alone."

"You actually suspect me?" cried Prickett. "This is absurd! What possible motive could a professor of psychology have for such a crime?"

Basil smiled. "You might have thought it would intensify the emotional reaction of your subject."

Prickett looked as if such flippancy were beneath the

dignity of a psychologist but exactly the sort of thing you might expect from a psychiatrist.

"How many people besides yourself knew about this sham crime?" asked Foyle.

"Only two. As Halsey was the sham criminal, he knew everything in the letter of instruction — including the time and the place of the sham crime. But of course he didn't know about the nailed windows or the dead lights, the locked door or the burglar alarm, since those were contrived to surprise him. Dr Albert Feng Lo, our Professor of Abnormal Psychology, was going to analyse the responses to the lie-detector test, so he knew every detail of the sham crime except one — the identity of the sham criminal. Both Feng and Ian were pledged to secrecy. That is essential to prevent collusion between the sham criminal and the controls."

Julian Salt suppressed a yawn and glanced at a thin, plain gold watch that matched his cigarette case. "It would save time if you policemen put your questions more directly," he admonished Foyle with a lazy insolence. "Did the murderer know about Prickett's experiment and incorporate it in his plan? Or was the experiment a surprise element that upset his plan? That seems more likely. I can't see that the experiment was of any use to the murderer."

"Perhaps he thought it would explain his own presence at the scene of the crime." Foyle glanced covertly at Prickett. "Or he may have thought the sham crime would distract the night watchman from the real crime — as it did."

"On the other hand it brought a great many witnesses to the scene of the crime," argued Salt. "And I can't believe the murderer planned that. You've all been lavishing sympathy on Halsey and Inspector Foyle because they found themselves locked in an unlighted building with a murderer. But just think of the feelings of the murderer if he found himself unexpectedly locked in an unlighted building with two witnesses! I'm sure his emotional reaction would be intense enough to satisfy the most exacting psychologist!"

"My dear Salt! Why didn't I think of it myself!" Prickett turned to Foyle. "You've been wasting time, Inspector. This stupid fingerprinting and questioning and hunting for clues is so unnecessary!"

"Now look here, Dr Prickett—" began Foyle.

"Surely you see it, Willing?"

"I believe I do." Basil was cautious.

"The way to find Konradi's murderer is to carry on my experiment by applying my lie-detector to all the suspects!" announced Prickett. "I shall be only too happy to place my laboratory at your disposal if you will let me publish the results afterward."

Salt groaned. "I seem to have started something."

"What about it?" Foyle asked Basil.

"I'd like to try it," he answered. "It isn't legal evidence in New York State, but it might show us where to look for legal evidence — providing everyone involved will consent to take the test."

"Of course they will!" cried Prickett. "A refusal would be tantamount to a confession of guilt. Nobody would dare!"

"Oh, yes they would!" retorted Salt, imperturbably. "I'm refusing right now. I don't care to be a rat in a maze, and I don't care for voodoo."

"Voodoo?"

"You should go to Mexico, Prickett — you'd feel at home there. Last summer I found an village where they believed you could prove a suspect's guilt or innocence by cutting his arm with a sacred knife. If his blood flowed, he was guilty; if it didn't flow, he was innocent. Your lie-detector is just atavism. Some believe a guilty man can be forced to incriminate himself unconsciously. But most people prefer objective evidence obtained by legal methods."

"Methods as legal, civilised, and objective as the third degree?" Prickett spoke acidly. "Don't you understand the difference between police brutality and a scientific test? If the lie-detector proved successful in a case as important as this, it would replace the third degree."

"We can settle that later." Foyle rose. "Before you go, I must have your home addresses."

The murmur of voices, and the search for hats and coats reminded Basil of an audience dispersing after a play.

"I live in Henderson Place," Prickett said.

"I'll see Mrs Prickett tomorrow." Foyle scribbled the address in a small notebook he always carried. "And you, Mr Salt?"

"East End Avenue."

"Will Mrs Salt be at home tomorrow?"

Prickett pretended to be absorbed in brushing his hat, but he was watching Salt with sly amusement.

"I see no necessity for dragging my wife into this," said Salt curtly.

"The janitor says she came here to see you this afternoon when you were out," explained Foyle. "She was in the building for a few moments between 5:30 and 6:00 — the period when the revolver was taken."

"It's so damned silly!" Salt flushed under his sunburn. "Amy doesn't even kill moths. She opens the screen door and lets them out."

"Nevertheless, I must see her."

"You can't."

"Is she away?"

A grin hovered around Prickett's thin lips. There is always something comic about other people's tragedies. Indeed, comedy might be defined as something that happens to someone else.

"My wife left me six months ago." Salt's rigid face only half concealed the fury he felt at being forced to make this announcement publicly. "Our meeting at dinner was an attempt at reconciliation. It failed and I haven't the slightest idea where she may be now."

7

EXCEPTIONAL

Basil Willing lived in an old house on lower Park Avenue. The eastern sun made a cheerful guest at breakfast, ripening old white woodwork to the yellow of sour cream. Basil didn't even glance at letters and newspaper until his second cup of coffee and his first cigarette.

A special delivery letter on Yorkville University notepaper from the Dean of the College regretted that the Alumni Dinner had made it impossible for him to attend the scene of the unhappy occurrence last evening. Inspector Foyle had referred him to Dr Willing and he was anxious to discuss the matter. Would Dr Willing be kind enough to come to his house Sunday afternoon? If that was inconvenient, perhaps Dr Willing could take supper with him Sunday evening? Most informally, of course. He remained Dr Willing's very faithfully, Alan Lysaght.

Both *Times* and *Tribune* displayed photographs of Prickett and Salt leaving Southerland Hall — *Yorkville Professors Grilled by Police in Konradi Case* — and there were plenty of headlines.

Basil dropped the papers and went to the corner of his

bookshelves where he kept the German and Austrian criminologists. He took down a dog-eared volume he had purchased second-hand in Vienna and carried it to a window. He was absorbed in a study of suicide by JV Beck when the doorbell rang.

Waiting on the steps outside was a noticeably tall man dressed with a formality that was almost quaint — shapely, velvet-collared coat, hard felt hat, and silver-topped Malacca stick. A long, glossy Packard limousine was at the curb, and a chauffeur in bottle-green livery was just closing the door. Basil's glance shifted to the clock on the mantelpiece — 10:30 seemed rather early for a Sunday morning visit. A moment later Juniper, the Baltimore man who had grown grey in Basil's service, was announcing, "Mister Malcolm Southerland."

A hard, Roman face confronted Basil, its bleakness emphasised by cold blue eyes and the bluish tinge of steel-grey hair. But when Southerland spoke his voice was round and rich. It had warmth and colour. Its smoothness was almost caressing.

"Dr Willing? This is a most unseasonable hour to intrude on you. But the matter is urgent." He selected the most comfortable chair and waved away Basil's invitation to smoke. "I am one of the trustees of Yorkville University. I had your name and address from the Police Commissioner, my old friend General Archer. Before we go any further, just what is your function in the Konradi case? Archer was not very clear."

"I'm a medical assistant to the district attorney. I've specialised in psychiatry and the police consult me when any psychological question crops up."

Southerland's self-control was almost perfect, but his eyes flickered at the word *psychiatry.*

"Konradi was killed during a lie-detector experiment of Dr

Prickett's," went on Basil. "At his suggestion, I'm planning to try the lie-detector on all the suspects."

Southerland didn't allow his hesitation to lengthen into a pause, but it was the unmistakable hesitation of an adversary calculating his next move with care.

"Nothing could be more unfortunate for the University at this time." His face was as hard as ever but his voice was disarmingly confidential. "Our President is on a good-neighbour lecture tour of South America and Dr Lysaght is Acting President in his absence. I have the greatest respect and affection for Dr Lysaght, but he has not the President's gift for dealing with press and public. The University is scarcely in a financial position to stand a major scandal. Of course, a suicide would be less scandalous than murder — have the police considered the possibility of suicide?"

"Naturally."

Basil's curt response should have made it difficult for Southerland to continue. But his voice could not have been more easy and affable if he had received the warmest encouragement: "I've read the newspaper accounts of the case carefully. As I understand it, there were two spent shells in the revolver which Prickett identified as the blanks he had been using."

Basil nodded.

"And the bullet that killed Konradi has disappeared?"

"The police are still looking for it," amended Basil.

"Really?" Southerland ventured a smile. "May I suggest that they will never find it?"

Basil resisted an impulse to glance toward the treatise on suicide by JV Beck which lay on the table where he had set it down when Southerland entered.

"On what grounds?"

"There *was* no bullet."

85

"There's no doubt Konradi was shot."

"I dare say. But — have the New York police never heard of a man committing suicide with a blank shot? It's quite common in Germany and Austria. I suggest that there was no bullet and no murderer. Konradi used one of Prickett's blank cartridges to kill himself."

"You think that possible?"

"Of course!" Southerland hastened to explain. "If a bullet is fired when the muzzle of a gun is in contact with the body, gases from the exploding gunpowder are forced into the body with the bullet, making a large, ragged wound. These same gases shatter the gun itself if the barrel is choked when fired. In a contact shot it's not the bullet that does the damage but the gases. So you don't need the bullet. A blank shot will do just as well — so long as the shot is fired in direct contact with the body.

"That's the significant point. When a blank shot is used there can be no gap between the gun and the body. The muzzle must be pressed directly against the skin or placed between the teeth in order to concentrate the gases and force them into the body. A blank shot, to be fatal, must be a contact shot and it is considered impossible for a murderer to get close enough to an active victim to fire such a shot. Therefore, a blank shot is proof of suicide — unless the victim is stunned or drugged or bound beforehand. According to the Police Commissioner, there is no evidence that Konradi was stunned, drugged or bound.

"He was an Austrian, he was killed with a contact shot, the only shells left in the gun are blanks, and the bullet is missing. I can't imagine a clearer case of suicide. The Commissioner tells me there were even some grains of black powder on the wad. Blank cartridges are usually filled with black powder because it's supposed to make a louder explosion than cordite, and blanks are made chiefly for use on the stage where they want the shot loud to impress the audience."

"I did think of it," said Basil, as Southerland paused. "I even took the trouble this morning to look up the forty cases studied by Beck. But I'm rather surprised to find a man who is neither a police officer nor a criminal lawyer so familiar with these details."

Basil was startled by the look of pure rage that flashed into Southerland's eyes. But his carefully cultivated voice did not fail him: "I merely applied a businessman's common sense to the problem."

"And a little specialised knowledge."

They eyed each other with the wary hostility of boxers sparring for an opening.

"You're not convinced?" Southerland spoke sharply.

"No."

"But — good God! — Konradi was obviously killed with a blank shot. How *could* it have been murder? Don't you see it's mechanically impossible?"

"We make it a rule not to discuss a case with outsiders in the course of its investigation."

"Then I'm wasting your time." Southerland rose with decision. "I hope you'll consider my theory of suicide carefully before you reject it altogether."

"One moment. As long as you're here, I'd like to ask you several questions — if you can spare the time."

Southerland was not a man to refuse a challenge. He sat down, crossing his knees with an assumption of nonchalance that was not quite successful.

"If there's anything I can do to help you I'm entirely at your service," he said with beautiful insincerity.

And Basil answered with equal insincerity, "I'm sure you

are. That's why I venture to ask — just where were you at eight o'clock last night?"

"Driving from my club to the Waldorf where I was engaged to speak at the Yorkville Alumni Dinner."

"Alone?"

"Quite alone. I had given my chauffeur the evening — I usually do when I'm in town. I live at Greenwich and it's a little too suburban for his taste. I don't want to lose him, because he's a good mechanic."

Basil found all these explanations unnecessarily voluble. "What time did you reach the Waldorf?"

"Some time after 8:00 — 8:30 or even 8:45. You see, I was held up by traffic. Really, Dr Willing…" Southerland smiled. "Are you suggesting seriously that a trustee of Yorkville University would pause to shoot a professor of biochemistry on the way to a public dinner? And then appear at the dinner a few moments later to eat a hearty meal and deliver an address lasting half an hour?"

"Why did you wish to see Konradi yesterday?"

"No particular reason. I often dropped in to see him when I was in the neighbourhood. I went to Yorkville yesterday to see the Dean about this unpleasant deficit. I stopped afterward to see how Konradi was getting along with his work, but unfortunately he wasn't there."

"And while his secretary was looking for him, you went to his laboratory?"

"Mere curiosity. The door was ajar. I glanced at some books in the bookcase, but they were far too technical for me."

"Where did you go after you left Southerland Hall?"

"Directly to my club. I always stay there when I'm in town. I had a cocktail in the lounge. Then I went to my bedroom to change for dinner."

"I believe you financed Konradi's cancer research?"

"He was financed by a Foundation I endowed for such purposes."

"But you took a personal interest in his work?"

An undertone of strong feeling was in Southerland's voice as he answered, "Cancer is not just a word to me. My mother died of cancer when I was fourteen. We were very poor and lived in a small Maine village where there was no adequate medical service. By the time my father took her to Boston it was too late."

"Do you know what Konradi was working on at the time of his death?" asked Basil, more gently.

"I'm afraid I can't be definite."

"Doubtless the other officers of the Southerland Foundation can settle the point."

"I don't believe they can." Again Basil was conscious of an undertone — but it was no longer emotional. "We knew the general outline of Konradi's work — he was studying various chemicals that cause cancer by irritation. We supplied him with everything he needed, but we never bothered him for details of what he was doing."

"The answer to a chemist's prayer," murmured Basil.

Southerland's voice hardened. "Naturally we trusted a man of his reputation absolutely."

"Can you tell me why Konradi had no assistants?"

"The Foundation spent so much money equipping his laboratory that there was none left to pay the salary of an assistant the first year."

"Miss von Hohenems said it was because Konradi didn't want to break in a new assistant when he was repeating experiments he had made already in Vienna."

"Miss von Hohenems knows nothing about it."

"Then Konradi was not repeating experiments?"

Southerland didn't like that question. He sought refuge in a blunt answer. "I never asked him."

"Until last night I didn't even know he was in this country. I have friends who studied under him in Vienna. They didn't know it either."

"Really?" Southerland examined the polished toe of his boot. "Konradi was absorbed in his work all winter. Last autumn he slipped into the country Tourist Third. His name was not on the passenger list."

"Why not?"

"He didn't care for personal publicity."

"It was you who brought him to this country?"

"Yes. I discovered last June that he had escaped from Dachau and reached Geneva. He was looking for a chance to carry on his researches and I arranged for him to begin work at Yorkville this September. He was made a research professor of the Biological Division and the University paid his salary, but the Southerland Foundation paid his running expenses and equipped a laboratory for him in Southerland Hall as there were none vacant in the School of Medicine."

"You seem to have done a great deal for the University. Southerland Hall — the Southerland Foundation — Southerland expeditions and fellowships."

Southerland's smile was a little sad. "I have to do something with my money. My wife is dead, and I have no children or close relatives. I haven't even any hobbies or vices — a self-made man has no time for such things until he's too old to enjoy them. I worked my way through Yorkville, and I've been working ever since. I shall probably die in harness."

"One more question. Were you by any chance a track runner in your undergraduate days?"

Southerland laughed aloud. "I had no idea detective stories were so much like real life. Your questions are quite in the classic tradition of mysterious irrelevance. Yes — I was a track runner. But how did you suspect it? And why did you want to know?"

"Mere curiosity," answered Basil. "Like your entering Konradi's laboratory yesterday afternoon."

"You are discreet." Southerland's expressive voice was charged with meaning. "I hope I shall not have to change my opinion of your discretion. It's a most useful trait — in any walk of life."

"And I was on the point of asking you to be indiscreet," returned Basil. "As a trustee you must know most of the people at Yorkville and as you're not a member of the faculty you may see them objectively. I'd like to know your opinion of the professors in the case — Prickett, Salt and Feng."

Southerland had risen, but he paused. He decided on frankness — or at least the appearance of frankness.

"Feng is a Chinese scientist of international repute on leave from the University of Peking. That's all I know about him. Julian Salt is one of the most energetic and ambitious of our younger professors. I've offered him a job as anthropological member of the Southerland Expedition to Mexico next year because anything he undertakes will be a success. I can't say the same for poor Prickett." A frosty twinkle lighted Souther-land's cold, blue eyes. "Feng never has any trouble with students and they like Salt because he's athletic, good-looking and not much older than they. But Prickett is always appealing to the Dean to uphold his authority. He's a living example of Flügel's theory that some men become psychologists in order to compensate for a failure to understand their fellowmen. Have I answered your question?"

"Perfectly. Can you give me Feng's address?"

"He has an office in Southerland Hall. Number 3, I think, on the ground floor."

"But he may not be there on Sunday and I'd like to see him today. Can you give me his home address?"

Southerland's eyes lost their twinkle. "If I were you, I'd wait until tomorrow. It can't make much difference."

"I'd rather see him today."

Southerland was curiously reluctant.

"Of course I can telephone Dr Lysaght for it," went on Basil.

Southerland mentioned an address on the East Side below 14th Street.

"Rather far from the University—" said Basil.

"Yes." The utter absence of inflection was noticeable. "I don't see why you should attach such importance to seeing Dr Feng. Surely he and Prickett are eliminated automatically from your list of suspects."

"Why?"

"Because they planned the lie-detector experiment. Surely no one would plan a murder to coincide with a lie-detector experiment — too great a risk of the police taking a hint and using the lie-detector to find the murderer."

"That's just what Prickett wants us to do."

"Naturally — it's the obvious thing," insisted Southerland. "For that very reason, the murderer must be someone who didn't know anything about the experiment."

Basil accompanied his visitor to the front door. On the threshold, he asked suddenly, "Are there any other Germans in the University besides Miss von Hohenems?"

"Only a few German exchange students."

Southerland was obviously impatient to be gone, but Basil detained him. "Nazis?"

"Well, of course, they could hardly have left Germany if they had been actively opposed to the present regime. But they're only boys of eighteen or twenty. And they never came in contact with Konradi as he was a research professor. Are you suggesting—?"

"No. Our suspects are limited to the eight people who had access to Prickett's revolver Saturday afternoon. There's only one student on the list — an American named Halsey."

"Indeed?" Southerland's tone seemed to imply that a trustee could not be expected to keep track of undergraduates, American or German.

Only a few moments later, Basil's telephone rang.

Cynthia Willing had seen the morning papers. She might forgive Basil for leaving her dinner table so abruptly if he would tell her all about the murder.

Basil seized his opportunity. "What sort of man is Malcolm Southerland?"

"The sort that's a charter member of the Metropolitan Club but only got into the Union after the depression," answered Cynthia promptly.

Not for the first time Basil wondered why his cousin Paul had married a woman like that. "Very valuable information," he said dryly. "But not quite what I wanted. May I speak to Paul a minute?"

Paul was a broker. He knew all about Southerland: "Began in New York as a newspaper reporter and gravitated at once to the financial page. The crucial step in his career was his nimble leap from the newspaper to the presidency of the African Mining Company, which owns two of the largest chromite mines in Rhodesia. Rumours were that he had boomed the company's common stock on his financial page when it was over-capitalised. But nothing was ever proved, and he says he owes his success to thrift and hard work. He has a comfortable fortune now, all invested in the African Mining Company's stock — preferred, of course. He wouldn't touch the common stock with a ten-foot pole. The Mercantile

Bank owns the company and he's a director of the bank. He has enough money to make him a big man in a small town, but in New York he's only too glad to hold his little domain in fief to the bank in return for its protection.

"His newspaper affiliations make him useful to the bank. He's the only man in Wall Street who can say with any truth, 'I used to be a newspaperman myself, boys,' and he's the only one who brings out imported whisky and cigars during an interview. That's why the papers always give at least half a column to Southerland's views on war debts or the gold standard or credit inflation. Of course, they're just ideas the directors of the bank want to make public. And he never lets the papers quote him directly. They have to say: *'The consensus of Wall Street is...'* Or: *'A spokesman for a well-known banking house asserts...'*"

"But he's primarily a banker?" interrupted Basil.

"Banker nothing! He's a prefabricated super-streamlined press agent and errand boy for the Halsey interests. They own the bank and the African Mining Company and Southerland. I suppose he came to see you about Ian Halsey this morning?"

"No," answered Basil. "He said nothing whatever about his connection with Ian Halsey." .

"That's funny!"

"Isn't it?" agreed Basil.

8

EXTRANEOUS?

Julian Salt's house was one in a row of small houses on East End Avenue facing the East River. Basil rang the bell three times before the door was opened by a lean old crone in a soiled apron.

"Mis' Salt? She's gone for good. I thought everybody knew that. It was in the *News* this morning. Mr Salt? I dunno. Guess he's upstairs in the livin' room."

Basil turned toward a little gilt elevator dainty as a jewel box.

"Purty, ain't it? But it don't work now. I told Mr Salt he oughter get it fixed an' he says ter me, 'We'll let it go fer the time bein', Martha.'" She seemed to find this simple remark amusing. "So ye gotta walk up five flights." She opened a door that led to a narrow, enclosed stairway. "Why they gotta have the livin' room on the fifth floor, I dunno. 'Cause of the view, says Mr Salt. 'But I ain't walkin' up no five flights fer nobody,' says I."

Basil gathered that he was not to be announced. By the time he had toiled up five flights of steep stairs he didn't condemn Martha. He opened a door to find that it led directly into the living room. And then he understood why Salt couldn't give up this sky parlour — elevator or no elevator.

The whole fifth floor was one room. The front wall was all window — the back wall, all mirror. Facing the window from the centre of the room, you might be on board ship for you could see only a blue level of water dotted with little boats. Turning the other way, you could still see the river reflected in the mirror with the same little boats gliding across its surface.

Salt was sitting before an open typewriter talking to another man on the window seat. "You think, I'm lucky?" Salt was saying. "If you knew—" He saw Basil and stopped.

"Sorry to burst in on you. But Martha hinted it wasn't worth her while mounting five flights to tell you I was here, and I can't say I blame her."

"Neither do I!" Salt smiled pleasantly, and what might have been an awkward moment passed easily. "This is an old class-mate of mine, Mr Trevor," he added. "Dr Willing is from the district attorney's office. Too bad you had such a climb."

The morning sunlight brought out the contrast between Salt and his friend. Salt was exactly the right weight for his height. He moved with the flexibility of the athlete, and healthy red blood gave his sunburned skin a rosy tinge. His light grey flannels were impeccable, and he was completely at ease. But there was something awkward and slack about Trevor. His bones looked too big for his body, his skin was sallow, and his well-worn winter suit was too heavy for the warm spring day. If he were a classmate of Salt's he must be about the same age, yet he looked the older by several years.

"I must be going." Trevor rose and hesitated. "You really think there may be a chance for me?"

"There's always a chance, old man!" Salt's cheerfulness was

brisk and false. "Rely on me to do everything I can, I'll speak to the Dean about it Monday."

Trevor looked at his friend with a slight smile as if he realised the futility of all this. "You'll let me know as soon as possible?"

"Certainly...certainly!" Salt speeded the parting guest with a hint of impatience. "Too bad you have to walk down. You're sure to find something soon."

The door closed on Trevor. Salt was no longer smiling as he turned back to Basil. Their eyes met and Salt said, "There but for the grace of God go you or I."

"No job?"

"You know the symptoms?"

"I see them often enough at the psychiatric clinic. Anxiety isn't good for the mind."

"I suppose not." Salt offered Basil his cigarette case. "As soon as Trevor saw the news of Konradi's death he came running to me to ask if there were any hope of getting Konradi's place. Ghoulish, isn't it? But there'll be more like him tomorrow. I hadn't the heart to tell him there wasn't a chance. That job was made for Konradi because he was exceptionally gifted. Bill Trevor is quite as good at his job as I am at mine, but he isn't in Konradi's class. We started neck and neck — same age, same college, same degrees, and at first Trevor did pretty well as a lecturer in biochemistry at some western university. But when the depression hit, they preferred to drop a few people like Trevor rather than reduce the $30,000 a year they were paying their football coach. He's been doing odd jobs ever since — assisting other chemists temporarily, translating books on biology and chemistry from French and German.

"Sooner or later, he'll give up all hope of being a biological chemist and try to get some other sort of job. He'll be lucky if he gets it, but he won't be grateful. A specialised training makes it hard for a man to adapt himself to an ill-paid, unskilled job. God knows how many technicians are doing just that today. A chemists' club in New York maintains a permanent committee on unemployment for members and we've had a steady stream all winter applying for the job of assistant to Konradi." Salt shivered. "Let's talk of something pleasanter! I have the utmost sympathy for the sensitive fellow who couldn't bear the sight of a starving man watching him through the window as he ate dinner, so he rose impulsively and…lowered the shade." Salt smiled, but there was an undertone of feeling in his voice.

Basil gathered that Trevor had been a skeleton at Salt's feast for years. Such things could happen to the Trevors of this world — they must never happen to Julian Salt. Under his pleasant manner lay a tough core of egoism. Perhaps that was why his wife had left him. "Have you had any word from Mrs Salt this morning?"

"I thought I made it clear last night that I don't expect to hear from her."

"You did. But it occurred to me that when she saw your name in the papers involved in a murder case, she might communicate with you."

"The papers made much of my name this morning. A wasted effort, Dr Willing!" He smiled suddenly, teeth and eyeballs gleaming against his sun-browned skin. "They don't know Amy. She wouldn't come back if I were on my way to the electric chair!"

"If she doesn't the police will want to know why."

Salt swore under his breath. "Just because my marriage happens to crack up the same day that Konradi is killed I'm supposed to sob out my troubles on the sympathetic shoulders of the police! The absurd part is there's nothing to tell them."

"Nothing?"

Salt spoke impetuously. "Perhaps you can make them understand. They might believe you. There wasn't another man or another woman or anything like that. We — well — we loved each other." The words were spoken so unwillingly they seemed to burn his lips. "At least, I loved her. But, damn it, I love my job, too!"

"Teaching?"

Salt shook his head. "I thought Prickett would surely have told you. Did you see Lysaght's speech in the morning paper? *'We are even — most reluctantly — arranging to dispense with the services of certain junior members of the faculty next year...'* I was one of those who got the black spot last September, because, as our dear Dean was so careful to explain, the first to be sacrificed are those who have private means. I asked him what he expected me to do with the rest of my life? Take up tiddle-de-winks? And he replied with a sermon on self-abnegation in periods of economic crisis. I didn't quite see why I should let my brains and strength and training run to seed because I wasn't in actual want like poor Trevor. I tried other universi ties, but I've lived abroad too long to have many friends in this country, and I've published extremist views on anthropolog-ical questions. That's fatal. When jobs are scarce, they all go to the middle-of-the-road boys.

"Then I tried the Southerland Foundation. I suppose it was partly luck, as Trevor said, but someone had told me they were planning an archaeological expedition to Mexico and I had just spent a summer vacation there picking up data among the Indians. Southerland himself gave me a job as anthropological member of the expedition. I'll have a steady job for three years doing work I was trained to do at better pay than I'm getting now. But that isn't all. I'll probably get enough material for a book, and if it's any good I should land on my feet at some other university. I was drunk with joy about it. And then I told Amy." Salt looked at Basil quizzically. "Are you married?"

"No."

"Well, then I'll never make you understand. Still, I'll try." He paused to light another cigarette. "When I told Amy we were going to spend the next three years where there are no movies because there's no electricity, let alone theatres and night clubs, she — Well, do you see that dent in the ceiling? That's where she hit it. She loves parties and theatres and night clubs and I don't. My father was in the consular service abroad and I had enough pink teas then to last me the rest of my life.

"But I couldn't get Amy interested in Mexican Indians. She said there was nothing to do in Mexico — meaning no dances or cocktail parties. Finally I said, 'All right, I'll go alone.' That tore it. She didn't want to be anywhere without a husband to play host at her parties and escort at other people's parties and act the lapdog generally. But she didn't put it that way. She said that if I really loved her I wouldn't want to spend three whole years away from her, etcetera, etcetera. And why couldn't I get a job in America? As if jobs like that grew on every tree!

"I said things to her she couldn't or wouldn't forget afterward. She left me in November, but last Saturday evening we had a final meeting. I tried to make her understand that life can't go on without a great deal of forgetting — but unfortunately Amy is one of those people who don't know how to forget. I suppose she's halfway to Reno by this time. Now do you think you can explain all this to your friends the police? Or will that simple-minded Inspector wonder why I don't beat her up and drag her to Mexico by the hair of her head?"

"You've got the Inspector all wrong," answered Basil. "He

isn't simple-minded and he's thoroughly domesticated — the complete family man. Was your father's consulate in Austria?"

"No." Salt didn't like the implication. "Belgium, Switzerland and France. If you don't believe me, you can look up the State Department records."

Basil smiled at his vehemence. "I hardly think that necessary. There are far more French than German books on your shelves and unless I'm mistaken that typewriter is one of the Remington portables made for the French. Don't I see *bloqueur de majuscules* where it should read *shift lock?*"

"Maybe I planted the French books and typewriter so you'd associate me with France instead of Austria!" Salt had recovered his good humour. "There's really no limit to suspicion once it gets started." He stopped as they heard footfalls on the stairway. "Who on earth is that?"

"It may be the Inspector. He's rather worried about your wife."

Salt's cheerfulness faded as abruptly as an extinguished light. "Good God!" His voice was rough. "You don't mean Amy is in any danger?"

The door opened. Salt's face was the dull brown of a dead leaf as the blood drained away from his tanned skin. "Amy…" He was on his feet.

She came toward him. "Julian! I-I've come back."

For a long moment they stood looking at each other, still and unsmiling. Amy's lips were parted, her wide blue eyes were pleading. "Aren't you…glad?"

"Amy…darling!" shouted Salt.

Basil turned, wondering why other people's love affairs always seem silly and faintly disgusting. Or was he simply a little envious of Salt?

Amy spoke again, her voice joyful and unembarrassed. "Oh. Julian! I thought I'd never see you again and now — I'm almost glad poor Dr Konradi was murdered, for it's brought us together again!"

"Don't say that!" Basil was surprised at the note of horror in Salt's voice. He had not realised before that Salt was so deeply moved by Konradi's death. Their eyes met in the mirror and Salt released Amy. "This is Dr Willing from the district attorney's office."

"Perhaps I can come back later?" said Basil.

"You're just the person I want to see," cried Amy.

They came toward the window seat — Salt rather flushed and shamefaced; Amy serene and unabashed. They made a handsome pair — both fair and about the same height — the man brown and rugged, the woman with a fresh pink and white skin. A champagne-coloured dress of thin wool under-lined the rounded slenderness of her figure. Perhaps it was her very tall heels and very long nails that made her seem a little sharp and thorny to Basil, but most men would consider her seductive. One smoothly tapered hand was emphasised by the flash of a superb diamond, pure as a dewdrop. She perched on the window seat, crossing sleek, silken legs, and Salt sat beside her.

"Julian, why didn't you have the elevator repaired? You seem to have let everything go to pieces!"

"I'm not a good housekeeper," admitted Salt.

"You certainly aren't! I don't believe those ashtrays have been emptied for a week. The first thing tomorrow I must call the agency and see about getting a cook and housemaid. That horrible old hag downstairs smells of gin. Now—" she addressed Basil "—what's all this nonsense about Julian and Konradi? I could hardly believe my eyes when I saw Julian's picture in all the papers at breakfast! We hardly knew Konradi. When he first came here, I gave a little dinner for him because he was so famous, but he just didn't seem to fit in

— if you know what I mean. He was so...so preoccupied. It's amazing how often a famous man is the most awful dud at a party!"

"And it's amazing how often the life of the party is the most awful dud at everything else," murmured Salt.

"But the point is that I don't believe Julian exchanged a dozen words with Konradi after that party. Did you, darling?"

"No, but the police, in their inclusive way, suspect everyone who was in the building when Prickett's revolver was stolen. Even you, my dear."

"Me?" The wide blue eyes looked so startled all the time that it was hard to tell whether she was really surprised or not. "You mean just because I called to see you at Southerland Hall before dinner? How perfectly preposterous!" She laughed. It was honest merriment, not hysteria.

"Can you prove you were with someone else at the time of the murder?" asked Basil.

"Oh, dear, I don't believe I can!" Her cheeks lost some of their freshness. "I only came back to New York a few days ago and I've been staying at a hotel. Julian wrote me asking me to see him once more and talk things over before deciding on a divorce, so yesterday evening I went to Southerland Hall on impulse a little after five o'clock. Julian wasn't there, but the door of his office was open, and I left a note on his desk telling him I was going to dine at a little restaurant on York Avenue where we used to go last year. He got my note and reached the restaurant a few moments after I did. But it wasn't any use. I felt then that we could never patch things up. I told Julian I would leave New York Sunday but I wouldn't tell him where I was going, because I didn't want him tagging after me. I never wanted to see him again."

"And now?" Salt had drawn her arm through his.

She lifted shining eyes. "Now I'm even reconciled to three

years in Mexico — heat, dirt, and all! I knew that the moment I saw your name in the paper and realised what a mess you'd got into! We left the restaurant about half past seven," she went on. "I'd promised to meet some friends at a theatre and Julian got me a taxi. But it had a blowout and I couldn't find another taxi. I walked in my high-heeled slippers until my feet were nearly dead."

"Moral: don't desert your husband," put in Salt.

"At last I found another taxi, but there was a lot of crosstown traffic, so I didn't reach the theatre until nine and — I just haven't any alibi, have I?"

"Isn't all this rather extraneous, Dr Willing?" Salt lounged on the window seat. "Our only real contact with Konradi is that my office happened to be in the same building as his office and laboratory. It's the same with almost every other person under suspicion — Halsey, Feng, and the Pricketts. What connection had any of them with Konradi — except that their work took them to Southerland Hall Saturday afternoon? Konradi lived a solitary life here — the life of an exile. Only two people had any vital relation with him — Gisela von Hohenems and Malcolm Southerland. Those relations involved the two great motives for murder — the Freudian motive and the Marxian motive — love and money. I suggest you concentrate on Miss von Hohenems and Southerland."

Amy was surreptitiously admiring the big diamond on her left hand. She seemed the image of security as she murmured, "Haven't you forgotten Feng?"

"Feng?" Salt turned. "What do you mean?"

"There was something vital between Feng and Konradi. It wasn't just that they had rooms in the same building."

"How do you know? You haven't been here all winter! And neither of them was here last year."

"I saw them together Saturday afternoon. When I was

writing that note in your office, I left the door open and I saw Feng and Konradi go down the corridor toward Konradi's laboratory talking together. It wasn't small talk. They were terribly excited, and Feng was saying something about Southerland. I forget what it was, but it sounded as if they were all three mixed up in something together — something important."

"Amy, you're daydreaming!" Salt eyed her with affectionate mockery. "Don't pay any attention to her, Dr Willing. She'll be telling you it's her woman's intuition next! What possible bond could there be among an American banker, a Chinese psychologist, and an Austrian biochemist? One from Vienna — one from Peking — one from New York. Why, they never even met until this winter!"

9

EXOTIC

Basil followed the river south in his car. The sunlit, tree-shaded lawns and spacious buildings of the University gave way to dingy streets without a blade of grass. The narrow houses seemed squeezed out of shape; they were built so close together. He stopped before a building of bilious yellow brick. A fire escape zigzagged past open windows that bulged with bedding. On the flat concrete stoop a swarm of children played some game that required a great deal of screaming.

Basil turned to the children. "Does Dr Feng live here?"

The screams died away and they all stood staring at him. At last one thin little boy answered, "On de sixt' floor — right acrost from de stairs."

Basil climbed the stairs, passing through a variety of smells and noises. On the sixth floor he found a visiting card tacked to a door: *Dr Albert Feng Lo.* His knock was answered by a small, middle-aged Chinese man wearing white flannel trousers, a white shirt open at the throat, and tennis shoes.

"Dr Feng?" Basil introduced himself, "I had your address from Mr Southerland."

Feng could not have welcomed his unexpected visitor with more composure among the gilded lattices and vermilion walls of an old Pekinese palace. "You're just in time to share an early luncheon — or rather a late breakfast. Make yourself at home while I get some more water from the hall."

Basil glanced about the room. Gas jets were lighted, for the single window on a narrow shaft left the room as dark as if it were underground. It was spotlessly clean and frugally furnished — an army cot with a folding metal frame; table, chairs and desk of deal coated with varnish the colour of glue. A typewriter stood on the desk; beside it lay a squash racquet and the Sunday *Times.* Everything in the room was purely American except for a panel of silk thrown across the centre table. It was the purple shade the Chinese call "myrtle red". Watered in the silk were symbols of the Emperor Mu Wang. As Basil studied them a fat cockroach marched slowly across the Love Birds of Conjugal Peace.

"A visitor from next door!" Feng had re-entered the room without making a sound on his rubber-shod feet. He nipped the cockroach neatly between thumb and forefinger and dropped it out the window. "Unfortunately, no matter how clean I try to keep this room I can't clean my neighbours' rooms as well."

"If your landlord put running water in the rooms they wouldn't be so hard to keep clean," suggested Basil. "It's bad business to let the property run down."

Feng smiled — a slow, wise smile — as he set an aluminium kettle to boil over a small alcohol lamp. "Do you know who my landlord is?"

"No."

"Yorkville University."

Basil was startled. Was this why Southerland had been so reluctant to give him Feng's address?

"Theoretically, the University isn't in business," Feng was saying. "But practically, it's in a dozen businesses — real estate, utilities, railroads, industrials — everything. What can it do with an endowment except invest it? Living on capital is bleeding to death, whether you're an institution or an individual. When people give money to Yorkville, as a rule they give stocks and bonds and mortgages. Perhaps you saw in the morning paper that Malcolm Southerland has just given us a new endowment of $1,800,000? Of course, that doesn't mean a check for $1,800,000 or a bundle of crisp new banknotes. It means title to preferred stock in the African Mining Company now valued at $1,800,000. Southerland's gifts always take that form because the bulk of his private fortune is invested in the African Mining Company. This house and land were part of another estate willed to the University. The Dean tells me it is a profitable investment because taxes are comparatively low on old-law tenements and rentals don't fluctuate as capriciously as the income from stocks and bonds.

"So..." Feng's smile broadened. "Every time I go out to the faucet in the hall for water, I tell myself I am helping to finance the purchase of a new microscope for the Division of Chemistry or new bookshelves for the Department of Ancient Languages. You see, if the University put running water in every room the property would increase in value and its taxes would be assessed at a higher rate. The University would have to raise the rents to meet the increase in taxes. But the people living here couldn't pay more, so they would leave, and the University might have trouble renting rooms in such a neighbourhood to anyone else. The trustees argue that the University can't afford to take such a financial risk and that even if they could it wouldn't benefit the people living here."

"But why should you live here?"

"Why shouldn't I? At Yorkville visiting professors aren't given rooms rent free. I'm sending every penny I can spare to China to buy guns and planes. It's the only thing a man of my age can do. I have an office in Southerland Hall for receiving students — it doesn't matter where I sleep and eat. Our poor people in China would regard a faucet on each floor for a dozen families as the last word in modern convenience. I think the kettle is boiling now."

Feng set the centre table with a bowl of salad and a plate of bread and butter before he poured the tea.

"Green tea! All the way from China?"

"No, I got it at Macy's." Feng was blandly innocent of any incongruity. "The water should be boiled in an iron pot to bring out the flavour, but I can't get an iron pot in New York, so I add a pinch of salt to the water. That does almost as well. Won't you join me?"

"Thanks, but I had a late breakfast."

The smile disappeared. "So you suspect me of murdering Dr Konradi?"

"What makes you think so?"

"I have read that police investigators do not eat or drink with those whom they suspect."

"And you think I am a police investigator?"

"My dear Dr Willing! You forget that I'm a professor of abnormal psychology. I've read all your books on criminal insanity and of course I know you're a medical assistant to the district attorney."

"The western mind just doesn't associate abnormal psychology with the Chinese," admitted Basil.

"You've been told that psychoneuroses are due to the strain of your western industrial civilisation," said Feng, "but it isn't true. I could show you agrarian villages in the heart of China with as ripe a crop of psychoneuroses as any in New York or Chicago. And yet there are almost no qualified psychiatrists in Asia. That's why I specialised in abnormal psychology. I had hoped to train young men to meet that need. But now..." He shrugged. "My best students are dead. You see, Dr Willing, all my interests are in China. Why should I be suspected of killing anyone as foreign to me as Konradi?"

"Was he entirely foreign to you? We've been told that you knew Konradi rather well. You were seen talking to him very earnestly in the corridor at Southerland Hall shortly before his death."

"Oh, we used to talk together sometimes." Feng's eyes were suddenly blank as black marbles. "I suppose we did look as earnest as conspirators, for our subject was serious enough — international politics. Not that either of us knew anything about it, but we had similar points of view as we were both exiles from invasion. I can't say honestly that I knew Konradi well. He never discussed his private life with me, and our work lay in different fields. We weren't even in the same department of the University and we came from opposite ends of the earth. I don't believe you'd suspect me at all if I didn't happen to be Chinese!" He smiled once more. "The sinister Chinese person is a familiar figure in your western detective stories."

"All that was changed when Charlie Chan superseded Fu Manchu," returned Basil. "Today it's one of the rules of the game that the murderer must never be a servant, a madman or Chinese."

"How consoling! But do the police realise that this is only a detective story? I'm afraid they'll forget the murderer must never be Chinese when they find that I have no alibi. I got my own supper here Saturday evening and ate it alone — about eight o'clock. You probably noticed that there's no doorman downstairs — not even a telephone operator. I can come and go at any hour without attracting attention. That's why I'm taking such pains to point out that I had no motive…"

Basil tried another tack. "Where were you and Prickett when you planned the sham crime?"

"In the psychological laboratory."

"Could anyone have overheard you?"

"The doors and windows were closed."

"Did you ever mention the sham crime to anyone besides Prickett and Halsey?"

"Certainly not. Prickett pledged me to secrecy."

"Then only you and Prickett knew all the details of the sham crime before the real crime occurred?"

"I'm certain of it. And I should think that would eliminate us from the list of suspects."

"Why?

"According to the papers, Konradi went straight to his laboratory last night without pausing to switch on the lights in the corridor. But if he had tried and found them dead, he would surely have suspected a trap and he wouldn't have gone on into the laboratory alone. Therefore the murderer didn't know the lights would be out of order. Both Prickett and I knew that was one of the surprise elements in the sham crime."

Basil felt that he was dealing with a mind at once firm and supple. But it was not a candid mind. No question Basil could contrive succeeded in prying any real information from Feng. He answered each one fluently and courteously — and he said exactly nothing.

At last Basil rose to go. "Prickett suggested last night that we try a lie-detector test on everyone involved. Could you take it tomorrow?"

"I'm afraid not." Feng's hand slid into his trouser pocket

and produced a bit of amethyst quartz carved to represent a lotus.

"Tuesday then?"

Feng studied the jewel held between thumb and forefinger and then smiled disarmingly at Basil. "This is a fingering piece. I think we are the only people who have evolved an art appealing to the sense of touch alone." He stroked the smooth surface of the quartz, which looked as if it had been polished for generations by sensitive fingertips. "I'm sorry, Dr Willing." His eyes were on the quartz again. "But I must decline to take this lie-detector test — at any time."

"I thought you had something to conceal," said Basil without rancour.

"But I haven't!" Feng's eyes were round with reproach. "I don't share Prickett's trust in the infallibility of the lie-detector. It's been successful in detecting sham criminals, but that doesn't prove it would be equally successful in detecting real criminals. Some emotional states can't be reproduced artificially in a psychological laboratory, and the criminal's emotional state is one. Prickett tries to create a criminal state of mind by getting his subjects to commit a sham crime. In real life it's the other way round — the crime doesn't create the criminal mind; it's the criminal mind that creates the crime. The sham criminal knows that no matter how many unpleasant things happen to him he is in no danger of arrest, imprisonment or death. Do you think he can experience the feelings of a real criminal any more than a rich man's son who takes a job at $20 a week to show how 'democratic' he is can experience the feelings of a boy who is dependent on $20 a week and nothing else? He—"

There was a thunderous clatter of feet on the stairs.

Feng stepped to the door and opened it a few inches.

"I must see you, Dr Feng!" Basil could hear a boy's voice shaken by quick, panting breaths. "Something awful has happened!"

Feng stepped into the hall and closed the door, leaving Basil alone in the room. But he could still hear that shaken voice, muffled by the flimsy partition.

"...in the laboratory...just before dawn...everyone had gone except one policeman..."

Feng murmured something so low that Basil could not hear it. Then the boy's voice rose. "Willing here? Now? My God, I have put my foot in it!"

Basil went to the door and threw it open. "Good morning, Halsey. Will you come in here a moment?"

He came reluctantly. Feng followed, closing the door.

"You snooping police spies are all over the place!"

Feng intervened. "There's no occasion for rudeness."

The boy whirled. "Throughout my life it has been my policy to speak the absolute, unvarnished truth in any circumstances!"

Basil fought a temptation to laugh. "How long has your life been going on?"

"I'm twenty-one — if it's any of your business!"

"Why did you come here to see Dr Feng?"

"I—" Halsey opened his mouth and closed it.

"Remember..." Basil smiled. "The absolute truth."

Again Feng intervened. "Halsey knows I'm interested in the psychology of hallucination—"

"I'd like to hear Halsey's own explanation."

"That's right!" Halsey looked gratefully at Feng. "He's a hound for hallucinations and I've just found a pippin for him. Ezra — the janitor at Southerland Hall — thinks Konradi's ghost walked last night. Swears he heard the noise of a typewriter in Konradi's laboratory after everyone had gone, though all the doors were locked, and a policeman was on guard at the entrance. It's obviously an auditory hallucination and I thought it might interest Dr Feng."

"But it never occurred to you that it might interest me?"

Halsey surveyed him uneasily. "What do you mean?"

"You said you'd put your foot in it when you heard I was here. It sounded as if you didn't want me to hear about this…hallucination."

"How could that be? You were sure to hear about it anyway. It's all over the college."

"Then it was something else you wanted to hide? Your own interest in the hallucination, perhaps?"

"Why should I want to hide that?"

"Just what I was wondering." Basil studied the sulky, young face until a slow, red flush darkened it. "Why should a student of psychology be so frightened by an auditory hallucination?"

"I'm not frightened!"

"And why did you come to Dr Feng instead of Dr Prickett?"

"Abnormal psychology is Dr Feng's subject. Hallucinations don't interest Prickett much."

Basil rose. "I'm driving back to the University. Can I give you a lift? Or are you at home now?"

"I'm still at the Dean's. I'm perfectly able to go home and I'd be more comfortable there, but he insists on my staying. Says I need rest and quiet. I'm supposed to be resting now. I had to sneak out the garden door."

"I don't want to intrude," said Feng diffidently, "but I was just going to the University and if there is room…"

"Plenty of room."

Feng slipped into a light overcoat and picked up his squash racquet. Halsey eyed it curiously.

"Those basement courts at Southerland Hall are hot this time of year, sir. Why don't you try tennis?"

"I'm not really playing," explained Feng. "Just practicing a few strokes by myself."

As the car halted at the first red light, Basil turned to Halsey. "How did you happen to lose Prickett's letter of instructions?"

"I don't know."

"You followed those instructions to the letter?"

"Sure. Why not?"

"Did you add any…improvements of your own?"

"No."

"Your memory is quite clear on that point?"

"My memory is as good as anybody's!"

A green light shone, and they sped forward. Halsey remained silent until Basil halted the car at East End Avenue and 84th.

"There's something I might as well tell you right now, Dr Willing. I'm not going to take that lie-detector test Prickett is talking about. It can't make much difference if only one person backs out."

"It makes a lot of difference," retorted Basil. "If all suspects take the test, their responses can be compared. If only a few suspects take the test you may pick out a lie here and there, but you have no basis for a statistical comparison."

"Well, I can't help that. I'm not taking the test. I object to lie-detectors on principle!"

"And yet you agreed to be the subject of Prickett's experiment?"

"He never told me it was going to be a lie-detector test!" cried Halsey indignantly.

"Oh, yes, I remember. You said that last night."

Halsey turned his head slowly as if Basil's intent gaze was

drawing his gaze against his will. "Why are you looking at me like that?" His lips twitched. "Haven't I a constitutional right to refuse to answer questions — with or without lie-detector trimmings? I won't take that blasted test! Do you understand?"

He flung open the door on his side of the car away from the curb. Brakes squealed and horns blared. Basil breathed a sigh of relief as the bare-headed figure in the shaggy plaid jacket and crumpled trousers reached the curb and plunged under the archway of the School of Mines.

Feng got out and closed the door which Halsey had left swinging open. "Don't judge that poor boy too harshly."

"Poor?"

"He's an only child. He never went to any sort of school or college until he came to Yorkville. He had tutors at home. His family is exceptionally wealthy, and he is spoiled. He has no sense of other people's feelings. It's a sort of moral colour blindness."

"Would you call it 'emotional stupidity'?"

Feng's eyelids dropped. He said nothing.

"Why didn't you want me to drive back here alone with him?"

"You're mistaken. I had no such idea."

"Can you tell me how many people have keys to the psychological laboratory besides yourself and Prickett?"

"The Dean, of course, and Ezra, the janitor. Prickett sent Halsey an extra key so he could enter the laboratory during the sham crime." Feng fingered the handle of the door as he had fingered the amethyst quartz. "Thank you for the lift, Dr Willing and good afternoon."

Basil didn't see the piece of paper on the floor of the car until he reached for the gear shift and something white caught his eye. It was folded twice and soiled along the creases as if carried in a pocket for days. There was no mark on it except a crude drawing in black ink of an apparently meaningless symbol — a cross surrounded by a circle. The paper was white with green lines — like the paper in Konradi's notebooks.

Basil knew it had not been there when he drove to Feng's house. Had Feng dropped it? Or Halsey?

10

EXTRAORDINARY

As Basil crossed the campus, he found it hard to believe that this was the scene of a crime. The uniformed policeman basking in the sunshine at the door of Southerland Hall looked like an ordinary patrolman loitering on his regular beat.

Basil stopped to speak to him. "What's this about a ghost, Grady? Were you here last night?"

"Sure I was and I'm on again tonight." Grady rolled uneasy eyeballs toward the building behind him. "I just come on about five minutes ago. I don't believe in ghosts, but when you hear a voice like that…"

"Voice? I thought it was a typewriter."

"First a typewriter and then a voice, screamin' something horrible. Honest, doc, I heard him."

"How do you know it wasn't the janitor?"

"'Cause *he* was standing beside me when it happened. He couldn't sleep last night, he says, so he gets up just before dawn an' makes some coffee. He asks me if I'll have a cup an' we was drinkin' it in the basement when we hears this noise upstairs. First tap, tap, tap — real quick — that was the type-writer. An' then came the voice screamin' an' screamin'. I was that upset I dropped my cup an' broke it. We run upstairs together — Ezra an' me — an'…" Grady swallowed "…there weren't nothin' there. The boys tried Konradi's typewriter for fingerprints this morning, but they didn't find none — except Konradi's. Ezra says he won't sleep here no more an' I can't say I blame him."

"Are you sure the ghost used Konradi's typewriter?"

"The sound came from his laboratory."

"It's difficult to identify the direction of sound."

"That's what the Inspector said. He had the boys try all the typewriters in the building for prints, but there wasn't no prints that hadn't oughta be there."

"Was the front door locked all the time last night?"

"Well, Ezra had to unlock it when he let me in the buildin' for the coffee an' it don't seem worthwhile to lock it again while I was in there. I was only gonna be inside a minute an' I knew I'd hear anyone who came in — Ezra's kitchenette is right at the foot of the basement stairs. But that door stays locked tonight!"

"If I were you, I'd leave it unlatched and watch it from the shrubbery."

Grady's massive jaw sagged. "You think he's coming back tonight?"

"I shouldn't be surprised."

"Would a guy risk comin' twice to the scene of a crime bein' watched by cops just to type somethin'?"

"Perhaps he had some other reason."

Basil left Grady staring after him.

Boards had been nailed across the broken window at the end of the janitor's passage. But in Konradi's laboratory there was no sign of anything unusual. Glass and metal sparkled cheerfully in the late afternoon sun. The long, stained work bench and the dripping faucet made the room as commonplace as a kitchen. The intermittent hum of a lawnmower came through the open windows. Even the typewriter was a standardised Underwood machine — desk size and a little shabby — exactly like thousands of others in New York. The man in shirt sleeves and rubber gloves who busied himself among Konradi's slides and test tubes looked more like a graduate student working for a PhD in chemistry than a toxicologist of the chief medical examiner's staff examining evidence in a murder case. It was only when Lambert lifted his eyes from the decapitated mouse in his hand that Basil knew something was wrong.

The two men had studied medicine at Johns Hopkins together long before one became a psychiatrist and the other a toxicologist. Basil knew that Lambert had a tough mind and a thick skin, insensitive to atmosphere or innuendo. Lambert didn't believe in ghosts.

"The Inspector's not here yet," he said briefly. "I can't imagine what's keeping him. He's an hour late."

"I came to see you." Basil produced his cigarette case. "I don't care what you say about smoking in a laboratory. I need this."

"Well, don't throw lighted matches on the floor."

Lambert began to dissect the headless mouse, paying particular attention to lungs, stomach and bladder.

"We drew nothing but blanks at Konradi's apartment this morning," he informed Basil. "I went along to look for the missing laboratory notes, but there was neither hide nor hair of them. Just the sort of place an exile would live — small, furnished suite in an apartment hotel on East End Avenue. No personal belongings. The living room was like something from a furniture manufacturer's catalogue — there are rooms just like that all over the world."

"Was there a black crystal ashtray?"

"There was! And a floor lamp with a phoney parchment shade. Sort of place where they throw in a radio with your room and don't allow children. Konradi didn't bring anything from Europe except a certificate of identification from the Swiss government which he had to use in place of a passport. Even his toothbrush was new and bought in this country."

"A prisoner escaping from Dachau doesn't carry an overnight bag." Basil's glance went to the desk piled high with the remainder of Konradi's laboratory notes. "Find anything there?"

It was not like Lambert to hesitate. As a rule he was headstrong. But now he paused to choose his words.

"When Foyle asked me to go through the papers of the great Konradi, I expected to find something startling and original. But so far as I can see these notes are simple routine stuff. They run from September 15 to February 23, and are concerned largely with work done by other men in the same field."

"What field?"

"The study of irritant chemicals that cause cancer. He was particularly interested in the fact that chromic acid may cause anaemia and cancer, while ferro-chromium — the metallic form of the same element — appears harmless to living tissue. But I don't see what bearing all this can have on the murder. Nobody's going to kill a man for discovering just which arrangement of atoms in the chromium molecule causes cancer of the lungs, and nobody's going to kill a man for proving that aniline dyes do or do not cause cancer of the bladder. Everybody knows that chromic acid and aniline dyes are irritating.

The only debatable point is the degree of irritation. Do they cause cancer or only simple lesions? However you answer that question, it would hardly be a world-shaking discovery. The laboratory notes I've read don't suggest anything worth stealing.

"Of course, it may be I'm just a bottle-washer not competent to appreciate the work of genius. I've seen enough here to realise that Konradi's laboratory equipment is to mine what a 1940 Rolls is to a 1925 Ford. I haven't got Southerland and the Mercantile Bank behind me — I have only the City of New York, so I have no micro-balance, no spectrograph, no photo-electric colorimeter. Let alone an electric furnace with amperage stepped up to produce high temperatures without wasting current!" Lambert waved his scalpel toward a squat furnace at the far end of the room.

"That makes it all the more curious," said Basil. "Elaborate equipment and simple, routine experiments." His glance wandered to the bookshelves. "No chemical text books?"

"Not a book in the place except the Manhattan telephone directory. And that's not the only thing that needs explaining! These mice, for one thing."

"What's wrong with them?"

"That's just it. There's nothing wrong with them."

Lambert turned from the dead mouse on the bench to the living mice in the cages. "They've been brought over to Konradi's laboratory from the School of Medicine almost every day since last September. The mice in the cage with the red tag are control mice bred selectively for an inherited tendency to cancer. According to the tag these were bred for susceptibility to cancer of the lungs. The cage with the green tag contains ordinary mice. The idea is to expose both types of mice to some condition that may produce cancer and use the inbred mice as a check on the ordinary mice to eliminate hereditary factors as far as possible. I've examined all the mice in both cages and dissected several of each lot. There's nothing the matter with any of them and yet — Konradi has had them in his laboratory for eight months."

"I suppose whatever chemical Konradi was testing proved either harmless or slow to act," suggested Basil.

"I might think so — if it wasn't for this chart business." Lambert reached for a roll of thick paper and spread it across the work bench. "When you experiment with disease in mice you keep their daily charts more meticulously than if they were millionaire patients in a swank hospital. But the last entry on these charts is dated February 23 — two months and nine days before Konradi's death."

"Perhaps the charts for March and April were stolen."

"Did Konradi complain about any missing charts?"

"No, but they might have been stolen after his death."

"Can you tell me why anyone should wish to steal charts recording the pulse, temperature, blood count, or basal metabolism of a bunch of laboratory mice?"

Basil shook his head.

"And can you imagine anything that would induce a biologist to stop recording the condition of laboratory mice for a single day — let alone two months — when an experiment was in progress?"

"It seems as if something must have interrupted that experiment on February 24," responded Basil.

"Then why did he have the mice brought over nearly every day in March and April — when he was no longer experimenting with them?"

"There's another question even more curious. What has Konradi been doing in his laboratory all during March and April? Crossword puzzles? And just what was he doing here at the time of his death?"

"The worst of it is, there's no way of finding out." Lambert looked at Basil uncomfortably. "His laboratory notes for March and April are gone. He had no laboratory assistants. And his secretary doesn't know anything about chemistry."

Lambert studied the mice in the two cages. Their small, shiny, black eyes returned his gaze. "Pity you little brutes can't talk! You were in the laboratory when Konradi was shot and you've been here every day for two months. Whatever he did you saw and heard. Whoever stole the laboratory notes you saw and heard."

"Southerland believes Konradi was studying the effect of alum on the stomach," said Basil.

"Then why didn't he use control mice bred for susceptibility to cancer of the stomach?" retorted Lambert. "These mice bred for cancer of the lungs suggest an experiment with carbon monoxide or chromic acid. But I can't find any evidence of it."

"What was the condition of the mice in February, when the last entries were made?"

"He was working on chromic acid then," answered Lambert. "It was too soon to expect signs of cancer, but the mice had begun to show a few pulmonary and nasal lesions. All the lesions have healed. These mice haven't been exposed to chromic acid for a long time."

"Did you say nasal lesions?"

"Chromic acid fumes cause a characteristic lesion in the septum of the nose between the nostrils. You find it in workers who make pigments or batteries or blueprints or anything that involves handling the oxides of chromium."

"At last, two pieces of this puzzle fit together! Laboratory notes or no laboratory notes, you've proved Konradi was working with chromic acid up to the moment of his death. For he had just such a lesion. Dalton found it when he examined the body. If Konradi had stopped working with chromic acid in February, the lesion would have healed by this time."

"That only makes it more baffling," retorted Lambert gloomily. "If Konradi was still at work on the experiment, why haven't these mice any lesions of the septum or the lungs? Especially the control mice who were bred for susceptibility to lung irritation?"

"And why did Southerland suggest that Konradi was working on cancer of the stomach?" added Basil. "He must have known it was cancer of the lungs!"

"Ask me another!" Lambert looked at his watch and began to peel off his rubber gloves. "Foyle must have forgotten he was going to meet us here."

Just then they heard Foyle's step in the corridor.

He looked tired. He took a bundle of black cloth out of his briefcase and dropped it on the work bench.

"Will you see if that's human blood?"

Lambert was indignant. "It's after five o'clock and I've been waiting an hour and a half for you!"

Basil moved to the work bench. "That looks like an academic gown."

"It is." Foyle's voice was as weary as his manner. "Worn by the murderer to protect his clothes from bloodstains. Perhaps that explains why Salt mistook the figure in the moonlight for a woman."

Still grumbling, Lambert began to soak one of the dried bloodstains in a solvent for testing purposes.

"Whose gown?" asked Basil.

Foyle smiled. "The Dean's. He kept it in the Administration Building in a locker that was never locked. He's quite upset about it."

"Human blood all right," Lambert was examining a slide under one of Konradi's microscopes.

Foyle didn't seem surprised.

"Where did you find this?"

"In an incinerator — in Garden City."

"Garden City! Is that where you've been?"

Foyle nodded. "One of the German exchange students has been living in a hotel in Garden City and commuting to Yorkville. A boy named Kurt Dietrich. He committed suicide this morning — sometime between midnight and six o'clock. As he always slept late on Sundays his body wasn't discovered until this afternoon."

"Suicide?"

Foyle looked as sceptical as Basil felt. "None of the details are being given to the newspapers. They're just being told it was suicide with a revolver. The Nassau County sheriff says it's the clearest case of suicide he ever saw. The boy was shot with his own gun — Mauser left over from the last war, belonged to his father. That's what he used to tell people who asked about it.

"The muzzle was placed between his teeth, and the top of his head was blown off. But his lips and teeth were uninjured. No sign he had been stunned or drugged or bound. They couldn't find any bullet and that worried them at first. Then their ballistic man discovered that Germans and Austrians often commit suicide with a blank shot."

Foyle was taking a photograph out of his briefcase. It had a glossy finish as if intended for publication, but it was no studio portrait. A dried rivulet of blood ran down one cheek from the top of the head.

"Dietrich?" queried Lambert.

"Yes, I waited until they developed one for me."

Basil was studying the smooth, immature face. Death had relaxed it, and the harsh glare of a police photographer's flash bulb had flattened and whitened it. But it was the angel's face of the boy Basil had seen talking to Gisela von Hohenems the night of Konradi's murder — the boy whose existence she had denied.

HENDERSON PLACE IS an appendix to 86th Street. Its double row of dolls' houses face each other across a quiet, empty space that knows no traffic beyond an occasional delivery wagon or family sedan. An enterprising real-estate speculator had turned one of the dolls' houses into a two-family house and rented the top floor to the Pricketts. The vestibule was so dark Basil had to use his cigarette lighter to see which door-bell belonged to Prickett.

The door opened with a mechanical click. He mounted stairs covered with worn linoleum.

The second-floor hall was even smaller than the hall below. A fan of light came through a door standing ajar. A small boy with large, serious eyes was swinging on the doorknob.

"Tell your mother Dr Willing would like to see her."

They stepped directly from the hall into a shallow living room cluttered with odd pieces of furniture. There was a faded green carpet on the floor and several small rugs scattered at random. Between the two windows stood a table covered with a white cloth and set for supper. Basil almost stumbled over a pair of roller skates in the exact middle of the floor. There was no place to sit. One armchair was occupied by a huge sewing bag stuffed with socks and rompers; the other by a pile of books. He picked up the first volume. *Sex Behaviour of the Albino Rat,* by Raymond Prickett... Dedicated to Malcolm Southerland, Esq... Yorkville University Press.

"Dr Willing?" Marian Prickett entered the room brushing a

damp lock of hair from her eyes with her forearm. "You're from the district attorney's office?"

She looked as old-fashioned as a portrait by Monet or Renoir. Her colouring was sentimental and her outlines vague. Her wispy, light brown hair turned to a golden mist against the lamplight, but her figure was neglected and shapeless.

"You've come to see Ray? He's only just gone out to get some milk for baby — he'll be back in a moment. Did you get his telephone message?"

"No, I've been out all day. Did he call me?"

"Oh, yes! He's been trying to reach you at your home all afternoon. Won't you sit down? I'm afraid things are a *little* untidy." She snatched a stray sock from the floor, stuffed it in the sewing bag and thrust the bag into a bookcase. "Jim, do pick up your roller skates as I told you! Oh, don't bother to move those books, Dr Willing."

"Let me!" Jim cleared the chair by the simple method of pushing the books on the floor.

"You see, I wasn't expecting anyone here this evening — I was just giving baby his bath! Isn't it dreadful about Konradi? And so awful to think that Ray's revolver was used! I could hardly believe it when he first told me. We had dinner early Saturday night because Ray had to be at Southerland Hall by 6:30 to prepare for the experiment. When the children were in bed, I sat here sewing and listening to the radio. But I was so tired I fell asleep in my chair. That was before eight o clock so I must have been asleep at the time of the murder. I woke when Ray came in after midnight and the first thing he said was, 'Konradi's been shot — with my revolver!' It was like a nightmare."

"If you had let me stay up until eight o'clock Saturday night you'd have had an alibi." Jim came of a generation weaned on radio thrillers.

"Oh, dear! Do I need an alibi?" Marian looked at Basil helplessly. "I don't see how I can get one. The children were all sound asleep and we haven't any maid. But I really don't know a thing about Konradi. Why don't you question that Hohenems girl? She was with him all the time and there's something very…well…very *foreign* about her, if you know what I mean. I don't see how she can afford those clothes she wears. I can't afford stockings as sheer as that — and yet she's supposed to be a penniless refugee! I wonder if Konradi — but I suppose I ought not to say that. I—"

A sudden splash from the next room was followed by the uninhibited yell of a young child.

"Oh baby!" Marian ran out of the room as Prickett came in, carrying a milk bottle in a brown paper bag. He was not surprised to see Basil.

"You got my telephone message?"

"No. I came to talk over plans for the lie-detector test. Will your laboratory be free tomorrow?"

"Oh." Prickett looked at his son, who was listening to every word. "Take this milk to mother, Jim," he said with military sharpness. "And then go to your room. Dr Willing and I don't wish to be disturbed."

"Yes, sir," responded Jim with flawless courtesy. "Good night, Dr Willing."

Prickett's gaze followed him with paternal pride. "I've brought Jim up scientifically," he explained. "In him, we have a glimpse of the children of the future. Will you have a drink? I have some Scotch somewhere…" He went to the sideboard and opened a door — only to be confronted with a glass jar of hard candy and a baseball catcher's mask and glove. "It doesn't seem to be here," he remarked unnecessarily.

"Never mind," said Basil. "I'm dining with the Dean and I really haven't time for a drink."

"But it must be somewhere." Prickett was rummaging in the desk, seizing each pretext that presented itself for postponing any talk about the lie-detector.

"Will the laboratory be free tomorrow?" persisted Basil. "I could stage the show at my own office, but of course your laboratory would be more convenient if you really wish to lend it to us."

"Here are some cigarettes and — damn!" Prickett stumbled over the roller skates. "This place is getting to be a pig sty! Any statistician will tell you that a man with my income should never have more than one and a half children, but..." he shrugged and lit a cigarette.

"Has it occurred to you that the man you saw in the moonlight last night could have been Southerland?"

"Southerland?" Prickett's astonishment sounded genuine. His face was in shadow, but his glasses caught the lamplight.

"He's tall and large. He wears a felt hat. He was a track runner."

"It never occurred to me for one moment! I-I'm afraid I was...er...a little carried away by the excitement last night." Prickett drew on his cigarette before he went on. "It seems to me, on sober second thought, that it is fundamentally unfair to apply the lie-detector to a real crime. Asking suspects to incriminate themselves savours too much of the third degree."

Basil could hardly believe his ears. "Last night you said the lie-detector should replace the third degree. What's made you change your mind so suddenly?"

"I was upset last night. I hardly knew what I was saying."

"You said that if a suspect refused to take the test it would be tantamount to a confession of guilt."

"Did I really?" Prickett's smile was all teeth. His eyes were screened by the blind glitter of his glasses. "I've had time to reflect and I've begun to realise that things which may be interesting and valuable in a psychological laboratory are not always adapted to real life. That's why I tried to reach you by telephone this afternoon." He dropped all pretence of dealing with theories and came down to facts. "My wife and I have talked over the matter carefully and we've decided not to take the test."

11

EXTEMPORANEOUS

By Dean's house NIGHT the was even more quaint than by day. A ship's lantern hung to the right of the fanlight, casting a golden glow on the spotless white door and the blue spruce trees. The hall was dark. Through the plate-glass door to the garden Basil could see the riding lights of boats at anchor in the river.

A maid showed him into a drawing room bright with flowery chintz and a driftwood fire. Malcolm Southerland was sitting in a wing chair before the hearth.

"Ah, good evening, Dr Willing!" His rich voice rolled smoothly. "Lysaght told me I might be fortunate enough to find you here."

"You have something to tell me?"

"Yes. Would you care to try one of my cigars?"

Basil shook his head, wondering if these were the famous cigars Southerland kept for newspapermen.

"I had a talk with my lawyer this afternoon." Southerland pared the tip of his cigar with a tiny cutter attached to his watch chain. "He insists it would be inadvisable for a man in my position to expose himself to this lie-detector test which the Dean tells me you're planning. The mere fact that I had taken such a test in relation to a murder charge would be bad for the Mercantile Bank if the thing leaked out — and such things always do leak out."

"Is that your only reason for declining?"

"What other reason could there be?"

"That's what I'm wondering. You know that Dr Prickett and Dr Feng have also refused?"

"Have they indeed?" Southerland's voice was bland. "That shows psychologists themselves have little faith in the accuracy of the test."

"Or too much faith." Basil was watching Southerland closely. "Have you heard about Dietrich?"

"Dietrich? I don't know anyone named Dietrich."

"One of the German exchange students you mentioned yesterday. He was shot early this morning — apparently with a blank cartridge."

It was difficult to read Southerland's eyes. But he was not indifferent to the news of Dietrich's death. He frowned at the fire and expelled a puff of smoke. He leaned forward as if he were about to say something confidential, but at that moment Dr Lysaght entered.

"So sorry to keep you waiting, Dr Willing! I was immersed in the proofs of our *Anthology of Greek Inscriptions* and I lost all sense of time. It is rather a job to collect all known Greek inscriptions."

Basil saw why Alan Lysaght had been made Dean. He had a talent for preserving the smooth, conventional surface of life. His brow was broad and noble, his chin square, and his wide mouth was stamped with the stubborn serenity that usually means Quaker blood.

A woman in white lace that matched her hair came

placidly into the room. Southerland rose and tossed his cigar into the fire as the Dean performed introductions.

"Dr Willing — my wife." He kept up a flow of banalities that made any awkward pause impossible. "Quite summery today — more like June than May. I even noticed some buds on the magnolia rose bush. Ah, here's Ian. Will you ring for cocktails, my dear boy?"

The dear boy scowled as he turned to the bell and came face to face with Basil. "I didn't know you were going to be here!"

"Didn't you?" Basil answered equably as he took a cocktail from the maid's tray.

"Why should I?" Halsey waved her away. "Don't shove that stuff under my nose! I never touch it!"

"They're quite mild," called the Dean from his station by the fire. "Do try one."

"Thank you, sir, but I don't like cocktails."

"No?" The Dean smiled reminiscently. "Your father was not so abstemious. I remember one particularly poisonous cocktail he invented when I was at Harvard with him — Stinging Lizard, it was called. It was pale green — chartreuse, lime juice and absinthe."

Something in Basil's expression seemed to disturb Halsey. "What are you thinking about?" he muttered under his breath.

"Dr Konradi's ghost."

"Do you mean to say you take that seriously?"

"Perhaps." Basil drew a folded slip of paper from his waist-coat pocket — white paper marked with faint green lines. "Did you drop this in my car this morning?"

Halsey looked with apparent indifference at the crude sketch of a cross surrounded by a circle. "Never saw it before. Feng must've dropped it. He's writing a book on the psychology of symbols."

"Do you recognise the paper?"

"No. Why should I if it's Feng's?"

Basil had thought the supper party complete. But now a slight figure in filmy black slipped into the room silently as a moving shadow, and the rather dull domestic meal in prospect suddenly seemed charged with possibilities as exciting as they were vague.

"You're late, Gisela," said Mrs Lysaght. "But I saved a cocktail for you."

"Thank you." Gisela saw Basil and smiled at him over the rim of her glass. A quick movement drew his attention back to Halsey. The boy was eying Gisela as a child might eye a box of candy.

Supper was served in a room overlooking the garden that sloped to the river. Mrs Lysaght allowed them to choose their places at the round table. Halsey promptly put himself beside Gisela. Southerland watched them with guarded eyes and spoke little. That left the burden of conversation to the Lysaghts and Basil.

On the surface it was all very pleasant and home-like and informal without anything to suggest that extraordinary circumstances had brought them together. Two maids served a delicious Sunday night supper of cold salmon and cold chicken, hot asparagus and hot bread. The Dean strove to make things seem ordinary, but everyone was conscious of something abnormal under the surface. Basil heard it in Mrs Lysaght's rather shrill laughter and saw it in Halsey's hot, unsteady eyes. Gisela's smile was too fixed. The Dean was too voluble. Malcolm Southerland crumbled bread beside his plate and left his chicken untasted.

Was it simply a case of conventional people determined to avoid all mention of anything unconventional? Or were there deeper forces at work, building a wall of silence around something the police must never learn? There were moments when that reticence wore thin. So many avenues of thought led back to Konradi — it was difficult to avoid them all. Mrs Lysaght told a story about some member of the faculty — only to realise too late that he was a biochemist. The Dean plunged to the rescue with politics — and in a moment someone was talking about the Nazis. Basil thought French art would surely be a safe subject — but mention of Fragonard's drawings evoked Vienna. Finally Southerland began talking about the car made to his order last winter. This miracle of engineering was an inexhaustible subject. The piston rings alone lasted from salad to dessert.

Coffee was served in the drawing room with French windows open to the spring night. Southerland had succeeded in detaching Halsey from Gisela. Basil glanced about and saw that she was gone. He put down his coffee cup and stepped through one of the windows into the garden. The moon was full that night. It bleached the open stretches of lawn and blackened the shade under the trees. A slender figure was huddled against a balustrade above the river. With her moonlit face, her shadowy hair and cloak, she seemed part of the night. She heard his step and turned her head.

"I couldn't stay in there another minute!"

"Not interested in Southerland's car?"

"How can they? They've been kind — but I wish they wouldn't try to make me forget. That will come soon enough. I want to remember and be unhappy a little longer."

"Halsey seems determined to make you forget as soon as possible."

She shivered in the warm air but said nothing.

"How long has it been going on?"

"Ever since October when Ian first began coming to Southerland Hall to help Dr Prickett."

A sudden breeze from the river swept her hair back from her ears, exposing the firm young lines of chin and throat. Her cloak fluttered like a flag and brushed his hand — black velvet lined with silver.

"Paris?"

"Vienna." The bright lining disappeared again as she wrapped herself closely and leaned her arms on the balustrade. "We who left Austria at the last moment were only allowed to take 200 schillings of Austrian money and 500 of foreign money — $140 altogether. My father and I had a small sum — a few thousand in your money. None of our relatives were remaining in Austria. Should we leave the money we couldn't take with us? We thought not. So we squandered it. My father bought books and phonograph records; I bought clothes. We were afraid jewels or anything negotiable would be confiscated at the border.

But they could hardly object to our taking our clothes — or our books and records. The only valuable thing I got was a fur coat which I sold in Prague to pay my passage to America. Everything else was quite frivolous. The sheerest stockings that run if you look at them — the palest suede gloves that become soiled if you wear them ten minutes — the finest handkerchiefs that any public laundry will tear to ribbons. In short, everything that I had never had."

"What a very Viennese thing to do! Mrs Prickett will be disappointed."

"Mrs Prickett? What do you mean?"

"She noticed your stockings and hoped for the worst. To the pure all things are impure."

"But whom did she think...? Not Konradi?" Gisela's laughter rang out light and clear. "He would rather have spent his money on an improved colorimeter than on a woman."

"Did Halsey ever show jealousy of Konradi?"

"How could he?" She spoke with unnatural calm. "He had no cause. The humiliating truth is that Franz Konradi scarcely noticed my existence. All he cared about was his work. I was no more to him than a piece of furniture and much less than a laboratory instrument."

Basil realised how dim the deceptive moonlight was when he tried to read her expression. He could see nothing but the pale contour of one cheek and the glitter of her eyes under the heavy shadow of her hair.

"You don't believe me? And yet it's the truth! You're as bad as Mrs Prickett."

"Perhaps he loved you without saying so. That can happen."

"But it didn't."

"You can't be sure."

"I am sure." Her voice was low and bitter. "I made him kiss me. A kiss doesn't lie."

"Then you loved him?"

"Perhaps." She drooped against the balustrade, her whole body yielding to grief as to a lover.

This was the moment the Inspector would have chosen to ask a great many questions: *If you loved Konradi, why won't you help us find his murderer? How did you know he was in danger before you learned of his death? Why did you deny talking to Dietrich on the pathway that night? Do you know Dietrich was shot and killed early this morning?*

But Basil was not the Inspector. He gave her a handkerchief. "I don't say you'll get over it — but you will."

"I never—" The words choked her.

"Oh, yes, you will!" Her mouth was near, and he kissed her. The soft shock of her lips scattered his thoughts and it was only afterward that he wondered if she had "made" him kiss her.

As they came through the French window, the room looked like a stage set for an amiable domestic comedy. Mrs Lysaght, her profile to the fire, was knitting a sweater. The two elder men sat facing her as they finished their after-dinner cigars. A low table set with tumblers, ice, soda and whisky, sparkled invitingly in the mellow lamplight. Halsey was fiddling with the radio:

"Germany is desperately in need of raw materials essential to war such as tin and rubber..."

"Will you please turn that off?" cried Gisela.

Halsey complied with a sullen glance at Basil. Had he been looking out the window a moment ago?

"Dr Willing?" Mrs Lysaght gestured toward the table.

"Thank you." Basil mixed his own highball. As he set down the decanter, Halsey snatched it from him and filled a tumbler half full of whisky.

"Ian!" Southerland was on his feet.

Halsey met his stare defiantly. "Well, why not? I'm getting pretty sick of your leading rein!" He lifted the glass to his lips. Before he could drink, Southerland struck it out of his hand.

It crashed to the tiled hearth. Splinters of glass flew, and the air reeked with alcohol. Something had gone wrong with the amiable domestic comedy.

Halsey glared at Southerland. "God damn you!" he said softly and venomously. He seemed unconscious of the blood running down his face. A jagged piece of glass had laid open his cheek bone, just missing his eye. But Southerland was more shaken that he.

Basil plucked the clean handkerchief from Halsey's breast pocket, sterilised it with whisky and staunched the wound. "That'll need three or four stitches."

Halsey turned on him. "You leave me alone!" He ran out of the room and they heard his feet on the stairs.

"Will you call Dr Parrish, Gisela?" Mrs Lysaght hurried after the boy.

"I'm extremely sorry, Lysaght," muttered Southerland, his hand at his forehead. "I-I'm afraid I lost my temper. It was unpardonable, but please forgive me."

"I quite understand." The Dean was determined to pretend that nothing had happened. "We are all under a great strain since the…er…unfortunate occurrence of yesterday. If you'll ring for Delia she'll clean up that mess. Please don't go yet, Dr Willing. I've been looking forward to a little talk with you all evening. Won't you come into my study?"

To step into Dr Lysaght's study was to step into the 19th century. The most amazing item was the velvet carpet — large, vivid pink roses against a background of pale turquoise blue, almost as fresh as they must have been 60 years ago. Rather grudgingly, Basil recognised that it had a certain decorative value in this small, white room with its black walnut furniture, inlaid with mother-of-pearl. On the mantelpiece stood a pair of candelabra — a fringe of prisms hung below the candles and then came bas-reliefs in brass on small marble pedestals.

"Dr Willing, I think you must have guessed the reason I was anxious to see you. I know the police can't talk freely about an unsolved crime — even to someone they have no reason to suspect. But surely you can answer this one question: Do you suspect any member of this University of murdering Dr Konradi?"

Basil stood looking down at the cold hearth. Then he turned deliberately toward the Dean. "The murderer of Dr Konradi is someone with an academic mind."

"Academic?" The Dean caught his breath in dismay.

"Perhaps *pedantic* is the word I want. Only a pedantic

murderer would have faked such a perfect textbook case of suicide."

"But…Southerland says the evidence of suicide couldn't be faked."

"Of course that's what the murderer intended us to think — in Dietrich's case as well as Konradi's. I think the idea of shooting Konradi came to the murderer when…" Basil's eyes wandered toward the French windows that led to the garden. They were screened by drawn curtains of heavy turquoise damask and those nearest Basil were swaying slightly.

"May I close that window?" He crossed the room and parted the curtains. The window was barely ajar. He opened it and stood looking across the moonlit stillness of the lawn to trees that shuddered in the wind and sent the shadows dancing in shifting patterns. He latched the window and drew the curtains before he returned to the Dean.

"I believe the idea of shooting Konradi came to the murderer when he heard Prickett firing his revolver during the startle-pattern experiments. As long as Prickett was conducting those experiments no one would pay much attention to a shot fired in Southerland Hall, and if the murderer used Prickett's revolver, he would not have to risk buying a gun that might be traced to him afterward.

"The fact that it was a revolver Konradi himself could have obtained would suggest suicide.

"That fitted neatly with the fact that the suicide rate is high among refugees from the Nazis. Of course, some of these refugee suicides are believed to be Nazi murders. So much the better. If the police saw through the fake suicide, the very fact that suicide had been faked would suggest murder by a Nazi agent and distract attention from the real murderer. That was his second line of defence. When he got that far, I suspect he did a little intensive research on suicide. With truly academic thoroughness, he amassed all available data, including those details which so impressed Southerland and the medical examiner — possibly because they have academic minds themselves.

"The most useful point the murderer discovered was that many Germans and Austrians have killed themselves with blank shots. If he could kill Konradi with one of Prickett's blank shots he would be spared the risk of buying cartridges to fit Prickett's revolver. If he could do it without leaving any evidence that Konradi had been drugged, or stunned, or bound, the police would consider the blank shot proof of suicide because you can't kill a man with blank shot unless it's a contact shot and you can't kill a man with a contact shot unless he's disabled beforehand.

"It was the murderer who telephoned Gisela von Hohenems' apartment when Konradi was there and induced him to return to Southerland Hall at eight o'clock — provided she's telling the truth. In any case, the murderer must have entered the building when Prickett was in the basement working on the lighting system and the burglar alarm — unless the murderer is Prickett himself — for that seems to be the only time no one was near the front door.

"When Konradi got there he found his laboratory door locked and he presumed the laboratory was empty. It never occurred to him that the person he had come to meet was provided with a key to his laboratory made from an impression of his own key. He unlocked the door and stepped across the threshold, groping for the light switch in the dark. He must have been thinking that the person he had come to meet was late — and that was his last conscious thought.

"The murderer was waiting in the dark laboratory. He had been there long enough for his eyes to grow used to the faint glimmer of light from the streetlamps outside. He could see better than Konradi, who stepped into the dark room from the candle-lit hall. The murderer stunned Konradi by striking him on top of the head. When Konradi was unconscious it was a simple matter to prop him in a chair, place the muzzle of the gun between his teeth and aim it at such an angle that the explosion from the blank shot would pass through his skull at the point where it had been struck — thus shattering skin and bone and blood vessels and destroying any medical evidence of the blow that stunned Konradi. Of course, the murderer put the gun in Konradi's hand, holding his own hand over it when he fired the shot, so there would be powder burns on Konradi's hand and fingerprints of Konradi's on Prickett's gun. Result — a perfect textbook case of suicide."

It was a long time before the Dean spoke. "An unconscious man is so defenceless. How could anyone be brutal enough…?" The Dean sighed. "Are you asking me to believe that this man is a member of the faculty of Yorkville?"

"Why not? Webster, the Harvard professor, murdered to avoid paying a debt. Schopenhauer, one of the world's greatest minds, crippled and nearly murdered a woman who was a complete stranger to him, in a fit of sexual antagonism. Scholarship doesn't always mean emotional maturity. It — what was that?"

It was a small sound — a muffled thud. They would scarcely have noticed it if the house had not been so still. They couldn't identify its nature or its direction.

Basil went to the door first. The lower hall was empty, the front door closed. A single light burned near the stairs. The other ground-floor rooms were dark.

He returned to the study and opened the window he had shut a few moments before. The moonlit lawn was as still and empty as ever. He went out on the lawn and looked up at the Dean's house. The upper floors were in darkness, but he could see white curtains belling in the breeze. Some of the windows were open.

"What was it?" The Dean was waiting on the threshold of the French window.

"I don't know. Everything seems all right. But…there's something tantalising about a sound you can't identify — especially when it's nearly midnight."

Southerland had gone and the household was asleep. Basil spent some moments trying to discover what Delia had done with his hat and coat, until the Dean remembered the cupboard under the stairs.

"Didn't you say you were at Harvard with Halsey's father?" Basil was near the front door, buttoning his coat. "What sort of man is he?"

"The sort of man who would invent a cocktail called Stinging Lizard. He used to boast that his guests could ask for any kind of drink in his rooms and be sure of getting it, though I believe some explorer caught him out once by asking for some brew made from goats' blood in Central Asia."

"And yet he's the President of the Mercantile Bank?"

"He inherited the job. Southerland and the other directors do all the work — if you call running a bank work."

"I don't want to cast any reflections on Yorkville — but why didn't this boy go to Harvard as his father did?"

"I don't know. Perhaps Southerland recommended Yorkville. Or perhaps Ian's parents chose a college in New York so he could go on living at home. He's an only son and heir and they fuss over him. They telephoned him from Cairo this morning after they saw the news of Konradi's death in the Egyptian papers."

The Dean paused, frowning, one hand on the doorknob. "I do wish my wife had not chosen this particular moment to ask Gisela to stay with us. Of course, we did know her in Vienna, and it was dreadful for her to be living entirely alone after the shock of Konradi's death. Perhaps I'd better let Ian go home tomorrow. If a…situation should develop, his father wouldn't like it at all."

"If I were Count von Hohenems I don't believe I'd like it either," suggested Basil.

"You're looking at it romantically." The Dean's smile was old and tired. "I'm looking at it practically. She's five years older than Ian. Even 'matrimonial bargain-hunters' are no longer interested in a coat-of-arms. And Ian is scarcely a matrimonial bargain-hunter."

The moon was drifting through a pool of its own light in the cloudless sky. As Basil walked down the gravel path, the crunch of each footfall sounded unnaturally loud in this still, pale empty world.

He passed between chapel and library and crossed the quadrangle opposite Southerland Hall. All the buildings were dark. He took a short-cut across the grass to the campus where he had left his car.

"Hey!"

A flashlight blinded him. "Oh, it's you." The voice was relieved. "You sure had me scared, Dr Willing. I'm Woodman — night watchman. Remember?"

"Why should I scare you?"

"Don't you know where you are?" Woodman's voice sank to a whisper. "This is where I saw the murderer running last night after Konradi was killed."

"Is it?" Basil turned to look back at Southerland Hall. Its slate roof was iridescent in the moonlight, but the shadows clustered thickly around the ground-floor windows.

"Yes, sir. This is the very spot," Woodman was saying. "You see that window that's boarded up now? That's the window he broke."

"Woodman, did it ever occur to you that the man you saw was Dr Prickett?"

"But—" Woodman gasped. "He come up right behind me a minute later."

"Panting, as if he'd been running?"

"Dr Prickett's no killer," insisted Woodman. "Maybe he is short an' thin an' maybe he does wear a soft felt hat, but — My God! Wossat?"

An inhuman scream cut the stillness, holding a high note as persistently and senselessly as a jammed motor horn. The two men were halfway down the hill before it quavered and sank into silence.

The great front door of Southerland Hall was wide open. The corridor was dark and empty. But Prickett's laboratory was brilliantly lighted — all the ceiling lights and the big flood lamps Prickett used for taking moving pictures. The door was unlatched. The room was empty. But there was a smell of fresh tobacco smoke and one of the windows on the south side had been raised.

"I-I don't get this," muttered Woodman.

The strawberries, the California sherry and the Butterthin biscuits were gone. So was the book and the candle. But the other things — the candlestick, the glass bowl and ashtray, the wine glass, the Chesterfield cigarettes, the matches and the Corona typewriter were still on the table. Basil noticed that the typewriter was open. His deliberate glance took in two cigarette stubs and one burnt match in the ash tray — two more burnt matches on the tiled floor.

"What happened, Grady?" shouted Woodman.

Basil turned. The massive policeman who had been guarding Southerland Hall stood in the doorway.

"I dunno…honest! I left the door unlatched — like you said, doc — an' then I waited in the bushes — like you said.

But nothin' happened. I got cramps an' I pretty near fell asleep. Mebbe I did sorta doze like — it's awful hot in those bushes. Then about ten minutes ago, I was wide awake an' the thing that woke me was the tap-tap-tappin' of a typewriter — just like last night — comin' from this building so I knew somebody got inside while I was dozin' off like. I thought, 'I'll just stick right here in the bushes an' get this bird when he comes out.' An' then…" Grady paused and swallowed "…an' then I heard that scream again — just like last night. Don't get me wrong, doc. I don't believe in ghosts. But that scream — it wasn't human."

"What was it then?"

The policeman's eyes strayed from the moving-picture camera to the typewriter on the table — anywhere to escape Basil's unsympathetic stare. "Sounded like a lost soul cursin' the devil an' callin' on God to let him out of hell. You see, doc, I could catch some o' the words tonight, an' that's what they sounded like. An' then — nobody passed me. I waited there in the bushes beside the path an' I saw you an Woodman go in. But nobody came out. An'…there's nobody here now."

"The window's open," Basil reminded him.

He looked at it and gasped. "I left all the windows shut an' latched when I left the buildin'. I don't believe in ghosts, but…"

Something glittered on the floor. Basil picked up a small glass phial. He held it gingerly in his gloved fingertips to avoid blurring the prints of other fingers and unscrewed the aluminium top. Some capsules fell into the palm of his hand. There was no label on the phial, but all psychiatrists know those capsules.

"Do you ever have insomnia?"

"Who — me?" Grady was taken aback. "No, sir! I sleep like a top."

"And you, Woodman?"

"I sleep all right. I've been working at night and sleeping during the daytime for years."

Basil smiled as he wrapped the phial in a handkerchief and stowed it in his breast pocket. "This is the first time I've ever heard of a ghost who took sleeping medicine." Then he added, more thoughtfully, "Perhaps you're right, Grady. Perhaps it was a lost soul we heard just now."

EXTERMINATION

Monday's dawn was misty, but by the time Basil reached his office in the psychiatric wing of his hospital, the sun was out once more. A messenger from Foyle greeted him with a copy of the autopsy report on Kurt Dietrich:

...We find it difficult to estimate the age of deceased. Superficially, his appearance is that of a boy of 18 or 20. But this appearance may be explained by the fact that the thymus gland was unusually large for an adult, weighing 32 grams and measuring 6¼ inches long, 1 inch wide and 1 inch thick. We venture the hypothesis that deceased was what is known as a thymus type. In such cases, the thymus gland of childhood, which shrinks and finally atrophies in the normal adult, remains as large as ever and its chemical action on the body, especially on the face, skin and hair, preserves a false appearance of youthfulness well into the middle age.

Therefore, we cannot even hazard a guess as to the actual age of deceased. But we may add that such a temporal dwarf usually has difficulty adjusting himself to any normal social environment. The fact that others regard him as immature long after he has ceased to be anything of the sort may be a considerable handicap economically as well as emotionally. Perhaps for this reason the thymus type is not infrequently driven into the criminal class where he is generally known by some such nickname as "Pretty Boy" or "Baby Face."...

Clipped to the report was an envelope containing a hastily scrawled note from Foyle:

Can you make anything of the enclosed suicide note? This isn't a copy, but the original found with Dietrich's body. The Nassau County people are so sure it has no significance they lent it to me without a protest. The paper is from Dietrich's desk and the only fingerprints are his. It was written on a portable he bought after reaching this country.

Basil examined the enclosure. Even the signature was type-written:

To those it concerns: No one is responsible for this suicide but the undersigned. Kurt Dietrich.

What could be deduced from such a brief, perfunctory message? Why had Foyle bothered to send it? Basil turned the sheet over and discovered something on the other side — a crude pencil outline of a cross surrounded by a circle.

Basil went into the outer office. "Miss Price, will you please telephone Dr Albert Feng Lo at Yorkville University and make an appointment for this morning at his office in Southerland Hall. And send these capsules upstairs for a quantitative analysis."

He gave her a small glass phial with an aluminium screw top. There was no label.

He was in the psychiatric clinic half an hour later when an orderly brought him a report from the hospital's analytical laboratory. He glanced at it and handed it to his chief assistant. "What do you make of that?"

"'Each capsule contains 2½ grains of phenobarbital in powder form.' Rather large dose for ordinary insomnia. One of your patients been taking it?"

"No." Basil smiled. "Sleeping medicine is the last thing I'd prescribe in this case!"

ALBERT FENG LO greeted his visitor gravely. He sat at his desk, his back to the light. Basil facing the window had a clear view of the grassy slope crowned with trees where the man in the moonlight had disappeared the night of the murder.

"Dr Feng, I understand that you're writing a book on the psychology of symbols. Do you happen to know anything about a symbol that consists of a cross surrounded by a circle?"

"Curious that you should ask me that."

"Why?"

"Because Dr Konradi asked me the same thing in almost the same words the day of his death. He knew I was studying symbols and he made me a rough drawing of the thing on a sheet of paper torn from one of his notebooks. I wonder what I did with it?" Feng pulled out the drawer of his desk and began to shuffle the papers there.

"Is this it?" Basil produced the drawing he had found on the floor of his car.

"Why, yes. Did I drop it somewhere? How careless!"

Or how careful, thought Basil. Aloud, he was asking, "Why didn't you mention this before?"

"I didn't attach much importance to it."

"Can it be you share Halsey's passion for the absolute truth?"

"Perhaps I do," returned Feng calmly. "If everyone told the absolute truth, life would be much simpler."

"To say nothing of criminal investigation! What did you tell Konradi?"

"There wasn't much I could tell him. The cross in a circle is one of the oldest known symbols, found all over the world. The cross represents the four points of the compass and therefore earth, space or nature. The cross and circle combined are supposed to symbolise two aspects of nature and therefore any duality, including sexual duality, fertility and good luck. According to a Chinese tradition, the cross in a circle was made first by barbarians far beyond the borders of China who scratched it on soft surfaces such as sandstone and clay, When the symbol reached China, long before the Han Dynasty, the sculptors of that day tried to carve it upon slabs of jade. But they found it too difficult to make a curve — let alone a perfect circle — on such a hard surface with their primitive tools. So they compromised. They drew the cross and added a short, straight line at a right angle to each arm of the cross to suggest the surrounding circle they could not engrave.

"That was the first swastika — the hooked cross that seems to revolve if you stare at it long enough. It spread in many forms to many countries where jade was unknown. The Irish shamrock and the French *fleur-de-lys* appear to be derived from it as well as the Chinese *yin yang* sign. In Sicily and the Isle of Man it became the *triskeles* — a cross made of three or four human legs. In Tibet it became a symbol of good or evil according to the direction in which the arms appear to be revolving. And in Germany today it has become the *haken-kreuz* of the Nazi Party. Perhaps they were drawn to it unconsciously because it was a fertility symbol. Their cult of a high birth rate as the prelude to war has a certain resemblance to the orgiastic fertility rite of primitive man which also culminated in human sacrifice." Feng ceased speaking and looked down at his hands clasped on the desk before him.

"Then the cross in a circle is a primitive swastika?"

"Precisely."

"How many people in the University know that?"

Feng shrugged. "I don't know. I believe I mentioned it to a number of people."

"Where had Konradi seen this primitive swastika?"

"He said he found it on a slip of paper in his laboratory among his notebooks. He had not put it there himself and Miss von Hohenems knew nothing about it. You believe this symbol is related in some way to Konradi's death?"

"It seems probable."

"But couldn't it be what you call a plant? A misleading clue designed to confuse the police?"

"That would make it all the more valuable."

"I'm afraid I don't understand."

"A real clue is objective," said Basil. "Like a photograph, it's a product of external circumstances — accidents of time and space, force and matter, light and shadow. But a false clue is subjective. It's like a Chinese painting, a product of internal circumstances — the imagination and personality of the murderer himself. In these days of mass production a button or a cigarette stub found at the scene of a crime can rarely be traced to a single individual. But a trick contrived by a murderer's mind and executed by his hands must always be a clue to his mental processes and manual training. Like all creations, it's stamped with the traits of its creator, and therefore it may be a clue to his identity."

"I see." Feng's thumb and forefinger slipped into his waist-coat pocket and the fingering piece of amethyst quartz appeared. His nerves were beginning to feel the strain of this interview.

Basil attacked again. "Dr Feng, I have a feeling that something secret and unpleasant has been going on at Yorkville — something that culminated in murder. That's the only way I can explain the reluctance shown by every member of the faculty to help the police. What is this secret? I think you could tell me — if you would."

"I can tell you nothing." There was a note of fatalism in Feng's voice.

"Would it surprise you to learn that Prickett the man who first suggested we use the lie-detector test, has now refused to take it himself?'

"I can only suppose that Prickett concluded, as 1 did, that laboratory tests are not always adaptable to real life. Prickett has lived so exclusively for his laboratory work that this sudden encounter with reality must have been a revelation to him."

Basil was unconvinced. "I can understand a man of Southerland's stamp declining to take a psychological test on principle — or rather on prejudice. But when two professors of psychology and a psychological student refuse to take their own medicine — there's something queer somewhere. What's the real reason you're refusing?"

"I've already told you." Feng's voice was so low Basil could scarcely hear it.

"Everyone says you were a friend of Konradi's. Do you really want the man who killed him to go free?"

"I don't believe anyone killed him. I believe he killed himself. Doubtless his experience in the concentration camp at Dachau undermined his mental health and induced a melancholia which was intensified by exile until it led to suicide. I think the exchange student, Dietrich, killed himself in the same way after reading about Konradi's suicide in the Sunday morning papers. Suicides are always imitative." Feng's voice trailed into silence as he saw Basil's face harden.

"How did you know Dietrich was killed in the same way as Konradi? That hasn't appeared in any paper. The reporters were told Dietrich had shot himself — nothing more."

To Basil's amazement, Feng smiled, and it was obviously a smile of relief. "I can demonstrate my answer more easily than I can put it into words. Will you come down into the basement for a few moments?"

Like the ground floor, the basement was cut in two by a central corridor. On the right was the suite of rooms occupied by the janitor. On the left were three painted steel doors with chromium-plated handles. Feng unlocked the third and pressed a light switch.

They were standing on the threshold of an underground squash court — a hollow cube with plaster ceiling, cream-coloured concrete walls and hardwood floor. There were no windows — the only light came from powerful electric bulbs in the ceiling protected from stray balls by hoods of wire mesh. The high tones of ceiling, wall and floor refracted every ray of light with dazzling intensity and made the place look hot and airless. But it wasn't. A moist, unnatural coolness played upon their faces. A thick furnace pipe enclosed in asbestos crossed the ceiling at one end of the room. There were other pipes less easily identified, with openings like ventilators, in the wall near the ceiling.

Feng closed the door. "We are now directly under Konradi's laboratory. Next door under Prickett's laboratory there is another squash court. Between the two is a small room where the furnace and the air-conditioning machinery are. Those openings you see near the ceiling are not old-fashioned ventilators, but outlets for the air-conditioning system so that—" Feng stopped speaking.

Basil heard Lambert's voice, remote and muffled yet fairly distinct: "Were there any prints on the typewriter in Prickett's laboratory this morning?"

Inspector Foyle's voice answered, "Just a few old, blurred prints of Prickett's and Halsey's."

"Then Grady must've been dreaming. After all, he admits dozing."

"Yeah, but he says Dr Willing heard the scream, too, and found a bottle of sleeping medicine on the floor."

"Willing dreams all the time!" returned Lambert, mixing the finical distaste of a chemist for a psychiatrist with the hearty contempt of one medical school fellow for another. "The sleeping medicine might have been dropped there days ago without anyone noticing it."

"We-ell…" There was the sound of a chair creaking as someone rose. "You'd better come with me for a last look at Konradi's apartment. The hotel manager wants to redecorate it before he rents it again."

Foyle's voice receded. They heard footfalls, the noise of a door closing, the click of a lock. It was like a radio play with extraordinarily realistic sound effects.

"You understand?" Feng was smiling his slow, wise smile. "I came here yesterday afternoon to practice my forehand stroke. To my amazement I overheard every word of your conversation with Dr Lambert and Inspector Foyle in Konradi's laboratory — including the Inspector's announcement of Dietrich's death from the same sort of wound that killed Konradi. Perhaps it is fortunate that I was alone at the time."

"What is it? The air-conditioning system?"

Feng nodded. "Anything that can carry air may carry sound — unless elaborate precautions are taken. For instance, the air-conditioning pipes may be adroitly curved to block sound waves or there may be a sort of sound filter similar to the Maxim silencer that reduces the loud report of a gun to a sibilant whisper. But the principles of acoustics are very tricky. Every now and then a lecture hall or theatre is built only to prove quite useless because of an unforeseen echo. Something of the sort seems to have happened in this air-conditioning system — some miscalculation of an engineer — some blunder of a mechanic. It may be simply that it was difficult to adapt a modern air-conditioning system to such an old building. But whatever the cause, the fact remains that down here in this basement squash court you can overhear everything said in Konradi's laboratory directly above it now the air-conditioning system is in use."

"How long has it been in use?"

"It was turned on May 1 — five days ago."

"Then anything said in Konradi's laboratory during the last five days could have been overheard by anyone playing squash on this court?"

"I suppose so. I only discovered it yesterday. That was the first time I had used the court since April."

"Did Konradi know this?"

Feng shrugged. "I hardly think so. Konradi didn't play squash."

"What about the court under Prickett's laboratory?"

"I don't know. We can test it if you like."

Feng switched off the lights and relocked the door. The second court was an exact replica of the first except that the pipes in the ceiling were at the opposite end of the room. They stood there a few moments without hearing a sound.

"I don't believe there's anyone in the psychological laboratory," explained Feng. "I'll go upstairs and—"

Prickett's unmistakable voice came to them, clear and

weirdly disembodied: "...My work will still be experimental. Only I'll be experimenting with consumers instead of rats."

"A fine distinction," murmured Feng at Basil's ear.

The child of the future answered his father: "Can I have a bicycle and a police dog and an air rifle?"

"I see no reason—"

"But you just said we were going to be rich! You said they'd pay you three times as much for watching consumers as they pay you now for watching rats!"

Feng, one hand on the light switch, looked inquiringly at Basil.

"You can be noble if you must," responded Basil. "I wouldn't miss this for anything!"

"I don't understand how it happened," Marian Prickett's voice was plaintive and bewildered. "For years and years you've been trying to get some advertising agency interested in your theories, but none of them would even listen to you. Why should these Argus people come rushing to see you just now?"

"I see nothing strange about that," answered Prickett. "No man can expect recognition immediately, but if his ideas are any good it will come eventually. The President of this agency has just read my study of the *Sex Behaviour of the Albino Rat*. He was deeply impressed with my preface and its discussion of the three basic drives — fear, love and anger. As he says, fear and love have already been exploited in advertising everything from life insurance to toilet paper. But what about anger? He wants me to work out some method by which advertising can draw upon the rich, untapped resources of the third great basic drive, anger, which is now completely uncommercialised."

"And just for that they'll pay you $15,000 a year!" Marian sighed the words. "I think I'll stop to see Amy Salt on my way home and tell her all about it. She's always been so sympathetic about my living in a three-room apartment with three children. That's one thing I won't put up with any longer — dear Amy's sympathy! Ray, if ever we become really rich please don't let me sympathise with anybody who has trouble making both ends meet. It'll be all right if I snub them and patronise them and insult them. But whenever you see any signs of my sympathising with them, just whisper 'Amy Salt' and I'll remember."

"Amy can be pretty poisonous when she's being sweet," Prickett's voice sounded more human than usual. "But see here — I don't think you'd better say anything about this to anybody just yet. Not even to the Salts or the Dean."

"Why not? It's all settled, isn't it?"

"Ye-es. But I don't want it talked about. We'd better wait until June when I hand in my resignation. By that time all this Konradi business will have blown over and the police will have gone."

"But...why...what have the police and Konradi got to do with us?"

"Nothing...nothing at all. Only the police are so infernally curious. I must insist that you don't mention this to anyone, Marian. And that goes for you, too, Jim. You won't get that bicycle if you talk."

The voices were farther away — an indistinct murmur.

Basil looked at Feng. "What day was it that you and Prickett planned the details of the sham crime?"

"May 1." Feng's smile broadened. "And we were in the psychological laboratory all the time! If Prickett had published an account of his lie-detector experiment he would have solemnly affirmed that there was no way the sham criminal could have learned about the surprise elements in the sham crime. But actually if Halsey had happened to play squash on this court while we were talking in the laboratory he would have heard the whole thing."

"Is any record kept of the people who use these courts?"

"In winter, when there's a demand for them, they're reserved in advance and the janitor keeps a record. But not at this time of year when most people prefer tennis outdoors. I suppose that's why the flaw in the air-conditioning system hasn't been discovered. I'm probably the only one who's used a squash court since May 1."

Feng turned to the door. As he fingered the gleaming chromium-plated handle, he cast a sidelong look at Basil. "Pretty stuff, isn't it? And it comes such a long way over land and sea before it reaches the American house and the American car! That's what I believe you call the romance of business. 'Romance' is not precisely the word I should use — but possibly I miss some of the finer shades of meaning in English."

Of course there wouldn't be a record of people using the squash courts, Basil argued as he crossed the quadrangle. No murderer with an orderly, academic mind would overlook such an obvious clue to his identity — if it were a clue. How had he managed all these manoeuvres without leaving a trail? He had probably prepared a neat synopsis of the crime beforehand. If such a murderer were to be caught at all he would have to be caught by something that a prim, precise, rational mind would not foresee — something erratic, mischievous and irrational. In one word, something unconscious.

Basil stopped at the Administration Building and borrowed a telephone to call Police Headquarters. He got Foyle's office and asked for Sergeant Samson.

"Could you find out about the Argus Advertising Agency? I'd like to know the names of all the directors and stockholders — particularly the big stockholders."

In the golden light of a May morning it was hard to believe that the University grounds could seem bewitched by moonlight. Students going from one class to another loitered, their heads bare to the sun. As Basil walked toward the car he had left on 79th Street he wondered if he had been "dreaming" when he heard that inhuman scream last night.

The ping and thud of tennis balls sounded close. He looked over a stone wall beside the river and saw a drop of 20 feet to the embankment. The University had built tennis courts on an old pier. An iron fence topped with an inclined border of wire mesh was to keep balls from falling into the water. Only one court was in use this morning and the players were Gisela and Halsey.

Running for the ball in the sunshine, both seemed younger than they looked last night. Halsey was a quick, competent player. His boyhood had probably included professional coaching and winter practice in Florida. Or perhaps he played squash in winter — that was always a help with tennis. Gisela was quick, but she hadn't enough muscular strength for modern tennis.

"Oh, hell!" grunted Halsey. The ball sailed over the wire mesh toward the water. Basil's glance followed it. He began to run down the concrete steps to the pier.

Gisela pressed her face against the fence as she tried to see into the water. Halsey had just reached the exit of the court when Basil met him. The cut on his cheek bone was covered with surgeon's plaster. He looked as if he hadn't slept well.

"My car's just above, at the end of 79th Street. Drive over to Konradi's hotel and get Inspector Foyle."

"But—"

"Tell him there's a dead body in the river at the foot of the tennis courts."

"I'll telephone." Halsey started for the steps.

Basil's voice halted him. "Not through the University exchange! Do you want to start a panic?"

"Then I'll walk." Halsey held out the ignition key Basil had thrust into his hand. "I might miss the car."

"You can't. It's the only one there — a Buick convertible — black."

With a sudden gust of rage, Halsey hurled the key down the steps. "If you must know — I don't know how to drive a car! I've got to walk!"

Basil watched him take the steps two at a time. He hadn't stopped to ask who lay dead in the river. Almost anyone else would have done so.

"What's wrong? Has Ian gone to get more balls?" Gisela had come to the exit, racquet in hand. A faint rose colour in her cheeks made her eyes seem darker.

"Do you mind staying where you are?"

The colour fled from her cheeks. "Something is — wrong?" Her lips formed the words almost soundlessly.

"Stay where you are — please!"

"No. I'm coming with you."

"You'll be sorry."

"I-I don't want to be alone. There's something uncanny about this place now — even in the sunlight."

A narrow boardwalk ran down to the river between two tennis courts like a corridor without roof or walls. At the end, Basil found a bit of the original pier — thick logs of rotting timber coated with slime. Below, he could see a shoulder of rock embedded in mud. The river was not beautiful at close range. Half a grapefruit, an empty packet of Camels and the stray tennis ball floated on its greasy surface, caught against the timber, gurgling in me swift current that flowed around them. And something else was caught there. Something Basil had seen from a height, though it could not be seen from the tennis courts on the same level.

"Is it safe?" Gisela set foot on the timber.

Basil blocked the way, hiding the water from her.

"You stay here. I'm going out on the pier. But I can swim."

He moved cautiously along to the water's edge and bent on one knee. It would have seemed less horrible at night or at dawn or even on a dull day. But a day like this — with blue water and white boats and green shore sparkling in the sun, and the warm, fragrant breath of Spring promising new life.

"Oh." Gisela had come behind him without making a sound in her rubber-soled shoes. She swayed perilously above the water's edge. He rose and caught her.

"But why?" Gisela was sobbing. "What had she done? Poor Amy!"

EXPLORATION

Amy Salt's body was taken to the autopsy room in the School of Medicine for a preliminary examination.

"No question of robbery," muttered Foyle, staring at the superb diamond on her left hand.

"She looks sort of — surprised," said Dalton.

"Doesn't mean a thing," answered Foyle. "Those round, pale blue eyes set wide apart made her look surprised all the time."

"Died early this morning." Dalton bent over the body. "Say between seven and ten. I may be more definite when I get at the contents of the stomach. Water in the lungs, so she must've been alive when she went in the river. But probably not conscious…" His rubber-gloved fingertips explored the crown of her head. "The bone is fractured and depressed here."

"That part of Konradi's head was blown to pieces," said Foyle to Basil. "Dietrich's, too. If the shots were fired so they would destroy evidence of a blow, the murderer must have used the same blow to fell Mrs Salt."

"Most killers have a favourite method of killing," Basil

reminded him. "Just as most boxers have a favourite knockout blow. Any violently emotional act tends to become a ritual."

"But why didn't he destroy evidence of the blow in Mrs Salt's case?" demanded Foyle. "As it is, we have a practical demonstration of your theory."

"We weren't expected to see the evidence of the blow," responded Basil. "We weren't expected to find the body at all." He was examining Amy's jacket and skirt of thin grey wool. On the jacket he found what he was seeking — a rust mark. "Something heavy — perhaps an iron chain — was fastened to her waist. This part of the river isn't called Hell's Gate for nothing. Its currents are deep and strong, and they hold what they have. There's a treasure ship sunk offshore that no one's ever been able to re-float. Amy Salt would simply have disappeared — if the weight that held her hadn't worked loose. As she'd already deserted her husband once without leaving an address we'd have thought she'd done the same thing again, and so would her husband. Perhaps he's thinking that now."

"Unless he killed her himself," put in Dalton.

"Nuts, he was crazy about her," answered Foyle. "I never saw a guy more broken-hearted that night in the restaurant when she was going to divorce him. Besides, she had the dough. He has nothing but what he makes."

"Does he inherit?"

"No. I looked up the financial standing of everybody in the case yesterday. Nobody had any real dough but Southerland and Amy Salt. His is all gilt-edged stuff — African Mining Company stock. Hers is in her father's hardware business and it's all tied up in a trust fund that will revert to her brother in Missouri now she's dead without issue. Halsey gets an allowance from his father, but no capital of his own until his father dies. All the rest are living on salaries, and not big salaries either. Feng did have some money, but he gave it all to the Chinese defence fund when the Japanese moved in. I can't see why anyone should kill Amy Salt unless—" Foyle turned slowly toward Basil. "Do you suppose she was onto something about Konradi's murder? Or Dietrich's? Something so important she couldn't be allowed to live?"

Basil frowned. "That seems to be the only motive Konradi's murderer could have for killing Amy Salt. But what could she have known? She hasn't been living here since October. She did tell me that something Feng said to Konradi Saturday afternoon sounded as if Feng and Konradi and Southerland were all involved in some common enterprise."

"You've no real proof that Mrs Salt was killed by Konradi's murderer," interpolated Dalton.

"No, but I'm morally certain of it. This crime bears the same psychological signature as the first. The victim is killed when she is unconscious and unable to defend herself — as Konradi was. The circumstances of her life are used ingeniously to disguise the fact of murder — as his were. If Amy had just disappeared we'd never have been able to prove it wasn't a case of a capricious woman leaving her husband again — exactly as the murderer hoped we'd never be able to prove that Konradi's death wasn't just another refugee suicide."

"How could a murderer carry a woman's body down to the river without being seen?" demanded Dalton.

"Perhaps she carried herself," suggested Basil. "The murderer who enticed Konradi to Southerland Hall Saturday night could certainly find some way of inducing Amy Salt to walk down to the tennis courts early this morning. Someone she knew and trusted — just as Konradi knew and trusted the person who called him on the telephone at Gisela's apartment. Once Amy had brought herself to that old pier it was the work of a moment to strike her down, fasten a weight to her waist and push her into the water while she was unconscious. A clean, quick, silent murder — no scream, no shot, no blood on the murderer's hands or clothing."

"But it was risky," objected Foyle. "Even early in the morning, someone might happen along — someone might look over the wall and see the whole thing."

"Oh, yes," agreed Basil. "This is more reckless than the carefully planned killing of Konradi and Dietrich. The murderer is taking chances now. He's kept his nerve — but he's beginning to lose his head."

Gisela and Halsey were waiting in the corridor.

"See here, Inspector," cried Halsey. "I'm going home and so is Miss von Hohenems!"

Foyle's glance measured the boy. "Why?"

"Do you think we both want to be killed like Amy Salt? This place isn't safe!"

"Well, don't leave the city—" began Foyle.

But Basil interrupted. "Miss von Hohenems will be much safer at the Dean's house than alone at her own apartment. If it's safe enough for her, don't you think it's safe enough for you?"

Halsey's mouth hardened, but he said nothing.

"Is there any other reason why you wish to leave Yorkville so suddenly?" Basil's voice was dispassionate, but his words seemed to infuriate Halsey.

"Of course not! I'll stay! But I don't see the point in so much fuss over the murder of Amy Salt. She was an idle, extravagant, empty-headed woman of no value to society! I don't see why we should pretend she was anything else just because she's dead."

"So you didn't like her?" Foyle was interested. "Where were you this morning between seven and ten?"

"Where would anybody be between seven and ten in the

morning? I was taking a bath and shaving and eating breakfast and reading the morning paper. We started playing tennis about quarter of ten."

"Why tennis this morning?"

"Would you spend a day like this in a stuffy lecture hall if you could help it? Gisela looked white as a ghost at breakfast and I thought it would do her good."

Foyle started forward. "What have you been doing to yourself?"

The boy's gestures had loosened the top buttons of his open-necked shirt. His breast was criss-crossed with deep red scratches. They had been treated with iodine and they were not bleeding. But they were fresh. They must have been made within the last few hours.

"Nothing!" Halsey jerked the two halves of his shirt together. But not before Basil had seen that at least one of the scratches was a series of minute punctures very close together, like the scar left on a horse's hide by the rowel of a spur.

The boy's face was dark with anger. "Aren't you through with me yet?"

"No," said Foyle, imperturbably. "I want you both to remain here with Sergeant Samson until we've notified Mr Salt of his wife's death." He studied Halsey for a moment and then added, "I shall ask the medical examiner to pay particular attention to any skin or blood he may find under Mrs Salt's nails. I noticed that she wore them rather long and pointed."

At the Administration Building Foyle learned that Julian Salt had no lectures to deliver on Monday mornings. If he were not in his office at Southerland Hall he was most probably at his own home.

Martha answered the doorbell, yawning prodigiously. "Mr Salt? I guess he's upstairs. I only got here five minutes ago an' I ain't seen him. But he's had breakfast. I found dishes in the sink. Mis' Salt? Naw, I ain't seen her either. Her bell ain't rung once an' that means she's still asleep. When she's awake it rings every five minutes. I only stayed here to oblige Mr Salt but now she's back I dunno if I'll stay."

As they mounted the fifth flight of stairs, they heard Salt's typewriter. "Let me handle this my own way," muttered Foyle to Basil. "It's no time for kid gloves."

"Come in!" The voice that answered Foyle's knock was cheerful. As they entered the living room, Salt looked up with a smile, but went on typing until he had finished his sentence. The sheet of paper in the typewriter was headed:

Southerland Archaeological Expedition to Rio de Flores —
Executive Committee.

"I'm pretty busy this morning, Inspector. Can't you come back this afternoon?"

Foyle kept his voice casual. "I'm afraid this can't wait, Mr Salt. Have you any idea of your wife's plans this morning?"

Salt looked as if he didn't know whether to be annoyed or amused. He decided to be amused. "She said something last night about going to an employment agency to get a cook and housemaid."

"Haven't you talked to Mrs Salt this morning?"

"No. She was asleep when I got up at seven and I didn't wake her."

"Can you think of any reason why she should go down to the tennis courts before ten o'clock?"

"Certainly not!" Salt's amusement yielded to annoyance. "If anyone was seen down there doing anything suspicious before ten it was not my wife. She's never up that early." He glanced at his watch. "She's probably just waking now. If you must see her, come back at noon."

There was a moment of grisly silence.

"Mr Salt, your wife is not here," began Foyle.

"But she must be here!" insisted Salt. "If you didn't see her downstairs she's in her own room."

"Would you have heard if she'd left before ten?"

"No, I've been up here ever since eight. What is this anyway? Has — something happened?"

Foyle hesitated.

Suddenly, Salt was frightened. "She must be here!"

He sprang to his feet and ran to the stairs. They followed close on his heels, but he didn't seem aware of them. On the floor below was a narrow hallway with two doors opposite the stairs. He tapped on the first door and listened. Then he rapped smartly.

"Amy!" He opened the door and they followed him into the room. It was large and light and luxuriously feminine in hyacinth blue and citron yellow. There was a low, wide bed with tumbled sheets and pillows. A white satin nightgown lay on the bed in a heap. On the rug a pair of blue kid mules lay heel to toe as if kicked off hastily. But the room was empty.

Salt ran to the other doors — a dressing room walled with mirror, a clothes closet, a bathroom, his own bedroom — all empty. He whirled on Foyle. "You — you knew!"

Foyle nodded.

"Is she—?"

Their eyes answered him.

"Oh, God!" He threw himself on her bed and sobbed aloud, his cheek against the nightgown she had worn only a few hours ago.

All that day detectives from the Homicide Squad searched in vain for some clue to the murderer of Amy Salt. There were no recent fingerprints in the house except her own, her husband's and Martha's. The papers in her desk revealed nothing. No one had met her when she walked down to the tennis courts. Apparently the University grounds had been deserted until nine o'clock, when the first lectures began, and even after nine no one had gone near the tennis courts — except Gisela and Halsey. No sailor could have seen the pier from a boat offshore because of the mist early that morning.

After the first few moments Salt recovered his self-control. But he seemed too dazed to answer questions coherently. All during the examination of the house he remained passive in the living room, scarcely conscious of what was going on. He spoke only once — to Basil when they were alone a few moments.

"Did she…suffer?"

"No. The blow was quick, and she went into the water unconscious."

Salt turned toward the great window. "The river?"

"Yes."

His mouth twitched. "She loved the river. That was why we took this house." His eyes, usually the colour of smoked crystal, grew dark as amber. "It would never have happened if the police hadn't let Konradi's murderer slip through their fingers! That Inspector was on the spot when Konradi was killed and yet he let the murderer get away while he was fooling around with Prickett and his lie-detector experiment. Of all the stupid, silly, pseudo-scientific hokum…"

At five o'clock, Foyle came back to the living room where Salt and Basil were talking. "We've found nothing," he admitted. "But perhaps you can help us, Mr Salt."

"Want me to do your job for you?" Salt had worked himself into a cold and bitter fury. "Just what have you been doing to find Konradi's murderer in the last 48 hours? If you knew your business, you would have got him, and Amy would not be dead! Why didn't you protect her?"

Foyle was patient because he had been saying the same things to himself. "Have you no idea why Mrs Salt got up so much earlier than usual this morning? Or why she went down to the tennis courts?"

"No."

"Do you think she might have gone there on the trail of some clue to Konradi's murderer?"

"What utter rot!" cried Salt. "If she were on the trail of anything, she would've told me. She never would have gone there alone."

Foyle refused to be perturbed by Salt's truculence. "I'm not so sure. Dr Willing tells me you took her ambitions as an amateur detective rather lightly yesterday. You're probably the last person she'd tell if she were on the trail of Konradi's murderer."

"Konradi's murderer!" Salt was in a mood where he seized upon anything as a pretext for rage. "Why should Amy care who killed Konradi? Why should any of us care who killed Konradi? Good God! If Konradi had never come here Amy would be alive now! Why did he have to come here? Why should a damned foreigner have a job like that when Americans like Trevor are wearing out shoe leather tramping in search of a few days' work to keep body and soul together?"

"You said yourself that Konradi was exceptionally gifted," Basil reminded Salt.

"Did I?" He couldn't sit still. He paced the room lengthwise. "Perhaps I was wrong. Konradi certainly doesn't seem to have accomplished much since he's been here this winter." Salt halted his pacing and fixed his gaze on Foyle. "How do we know that the man murdered at Southerland Hall Saturday night really was Franz Konradi, the famous Austrian biochemist?"

Twilight had crept into the room — slyly at first, then

openly, dissolving outlines. The Inspector's face looked lifeless as a *papier-mâché* mask, the eyes dim hollows without eyeballs or lashes. Salt's blunt profile was just visible, dark against the pale mirror. A phantom Sound steamer moved silently across the mirror with every porthole lighted and vanished into the wall. Basil put an end to magic by switching on the reading lamps.

"What the devil do you mean?" demanded Foyle.

Salt blinked in the sudden glare of lamplight. Shock had destroyed the spurious youth he owed to health, exercise, and buoyant spirits. His eyes were bloodshot, there were pouches under them and his whole face was sagging and sallow. But there was vitality in his voice — vitality and pugnacity.

"Don't you see it yet, Inspector? No wonder you've made such a botch of the whole case!"

Foyle couldn't be drawn. "I still don't see it."

"Did anyone in this University ever see Konradi in Vienna? No! Are there any photographs of him in newspaper and magazine files at the library? No! I took the trouble to look yesterday. The man whom we knew here as Konradi *claimed* to have escaped from Dachau. He appealed to our facile sympathy. But it was the way he first roused my suspicion. Have you ever heard of anyone escaping from a Nazi concentration camp? I never have! Konradi was a Jew, and Jewish prisoners are segregated and watched more closely than others. At Dachau there is a high wall, a ring of barbed wire and a ring of electrified wire guarded by machine-gun squads. How could anyone get through that?"

"Then," Foyle groped for words, "who was the man who lived here all winter and spring as Konradi?"

"Suppose the real Konradi died at Dachau as so many prisoners do. Couldn't the Nazis have allowed one of their own men to 'escape' and come over here posing as Konradi to introduce a Nazi agent into this country? A refugee from the Nazis would be welcomed without suspicion everywhere! It would be far easier for him than for an avowed Nazi to obtain information. At Yorkville, many significant facts about industrial conditions and rearmament might be learned through Malcolm Southerland and the Mercantile Bank. Southerland would say things to a foreign professor of biochemistry that he wouldn't think of saying to a foreign banker.

"Of course, the false Konradi would have to know enough to pass as a chemist superficially. But it wouldn't be possible to get a chemist of the real Konradi's ability to take such a dirty job, so he couldn't carry on the real Konradi's experiments and he wouldn't dare to have a laboratory assistant who might see through his pretensions. He couldn't even risk having a secretary conversant with biochemistry. He would avoid his form students and the other biochemists at Yorkville. He might even pretend that his laboratory notes had been mislaid or stolen in order to delay publication of his researches.

"He'd have to have some rough resemblance to the real Konradi in height and colouring. Then if he happened to meet any old friends in America, he could claim that Dachau had altered his appearance. The man we knew as Konradi need not have been Jewish. He was dark and aquiline but no more so than many who are not Jews. He had a few startlingly white hairs. That might be due to shock — but it might also be due to artificial bleaching. He spoke German like a Styrian, and Styria was one of the pro-Nazi provinces of Austria.

"Doesn't this theory explain a lot of things that can't be explained in any other way? Why was Konradi never seen with other German and Austrian refugees? Because he was afraid of meeting someone who had known the real Konradi in Vienna. Why did he destroy all the letters he got from Austria and Germany? Was it really to protect anti-Nazi friends in the Reich, as he claimed? Or was it because those letters were confidential communications from the Nazi Party? Why was he solitary and preoccupied and apprehensive? Because he was playing a damned dangerous game and knew it. Why was he alarmed when he saw Prickett's absurd letter to Halsey about the sham crime? Because such a phrase as 'murderer for Group No l' wouldn't sound absurd to a Nazi agent. It would suggest some anti-Nazi terrorist organisation."

Salt sank into a chair, shivering with excitement.

"It does explain things," admitted Foyle soberly. "There were no marks of flogging on Konradi's body. If he were a Nazi agent allowed to 'escape' from Dachau, that's easily understood. But if he were really a prisoner at Dachau, it seems inexplicable."

"Two things you haven't explained," put in Basil. "If Konradi was not Konradi, who murdered him — and why?"

"There's only one person here who would want to murder a Nazi agent masquerading as an anti-Nazi refugee!"

"Who?" snapped Foyle.

"Why, the real refugee! Gisela von Hohenems. No one had a better opportunity to find out the truth about Konradi than his secretary, and how would she feel if she discovered that he was an agent pretending to be a refugee while actually working for the Nazis. Perhaps she killed Dietrich, too — perhaps he was sent here to work with Konradi. German exchange students have their own organisation, distinct from the exchange students of all other nationalities, and that organisation is in close touch with the Nazi government. No student would be allowed to leave Germany if he were anti-Nazi, so Dietrich must've been pro-Nazi. If Konradi was really an anti-Nazi refugee, why should he be killed at the same time and by the same hand as Dietrich, the pro-Nazi? But if they were both Nazis, it's only logical they should be killed by the same person."

"It's possible," admitted Foyle.

"Possible?" shouted Salt. "What other explanation is there? Amy must've worked this out for herself. She always liked Gisela and she'd be sure to give the girl a chance to clear herself before going to the police. They must've arranged to meet near the tennis courts early this morning and…" Salt couldn't finish the sentence. "You've got to arrest Gisela von Hohenems. Tonight."

"We can't do that," protested Foyle. "We've nothing to go on."

Salt turned to Basil. "Won't you do something? Can't the district attorney's office get a warrant for her arrest?"

"Not without evidence."

"Evidence!" Salt's grimace was contemptuous of criminal law and its slow procedure. "There's really no point in prolonging this interview. I'm going to engage private detectives. They'll get evidence and they won't be fussy about the methods they use."

Foyle rose. "If you should have any further information or suggestions—"

"I'll save them for the private detectives! Why should I work with either of you when you both refuse to arrest the murderer of my wife?" Salt's gaze shifted to Basil "You can tell the district attorney that as soon as I've got a case, I'll put it in his hands. Meanwhile, I'll thank you both not to trouble me again!"

NIGHT HAD CLOSED in on the city, bringing a sudden drop in temperature. Basil suggested dinner at his own home and the Inspector accepted.

On cold evenings the living room was at its best. The warm red of old Italian damask drawn across the windows shut out chill and darkness. White-panelled walls blushed pink whenever the fire quickened its pace.

Foyle helped himself to a glass of brandy and looked at it as gloomily as if it were castor oil. "He sure had me fooled."

"Who?".

"Konradi. That afternoon I talked to him on the campus. Why, I liked the guy!"

Basil considered Foyle through the blue haze of an after-dinner cigarette. "Aristotle said it. There is no drama like a change in fortune or identity."

The Inspector was not interested in Aristotle. "God knows I don't want to believe Konradi was an impostor. But how else can we explain those points Salt raised? If only we could get hold of someone who knew the real Konradi in—" Foyle turned toward Basil. "Why, you said *you* knew him in Vienna! Saturday night — I called you on the telephone — you were at some party somewhere. You—"

Basil's eyes were on the fire. "I heard him lecture twice in 1925. I was at the back of the hall near the door taking notes. As a student I was paying more attention to the lecture than the lecturer. All I remember is a well-shaped head and an extraordinarily vivid face. The head I saw Saturday night was crushed with a frightful wound, the face was bloodstained, still and dead. How could I identify him? I have no more idea whether he was Konradi than you have." Basil's voice died away. When he spoke again, he was thinking of something else "If a man were playing what Salt called a damned dangerous game, he'd avoid entanglements with women, wouldn't he?"

"He might," said Foyle cautiously.

"I'm sure he would," insisted Basil. "One form of excitement kills another. If you watch gamblers when they're playing for really high stakes, you'll notice that they're indifferent to the women around them."

"But Konradi wasn't indifferent to women," protested Foyle. "He was in love with Gisela."

"She says he wasn't."

"She's crazy! He said something about her when he was talking to me Saturday afternoon. The moment he spoke her name I knew he was in love with her."

Basil weighed Foyle's words for a moment. Then he tossed his cigarette stub into the fire and rose. "Nearly ten o'clock. I must get back to Southerland Hall."

"Again? Tonight?"

"Yes." Basil took a flashlight from his desk drawer and tested it. "I have a rendezvous with a ghost."

"You don't think this…this invisible typist will be on the job again tonight?"

"I'm sure he will."

"But why is it so important for this message or letter or whatever it is to be typed on some typewriter at Southerland Hall?"

"Partly because the moon is only past the full and there are no clouds."

"What's the moon got to do with it?"

"Better come along and see for yourself."

Foyle looked about the warm, bright room as if reluctant to leave it. "Okay. But no one in his senses would repeat a stunt like that three nights running. I didn't even leave a guard there tonight."

They went by subway because a man from Basil's garage had picked up his car while they were at dinner.

On York Avenue he stopped at a small grocery. "I want to get some cigarettes."

Foyle waited outside until he reappeared carrying a large brown paper bag. "Just cigarettes?"

"And a few other things."

On the campus, the night seemed to be alive. The leaves whispered in a gentle breeze from the West. Every now and then a faint rustle reminded them of humble lives that populated the darkness unseen and generally unheard — gulls and rats by the river, sparrows and pigeons and squirrels among the trees, insects everywhere. So close to nature it was impossible to feel fear because it was impossible to feel isolated.

But the moment they stepped inside Southerland Hall everything was different. The moon limned their shadows on the tiled floor at their feet and left the far end of the corridor in half light, still and empty. But it was a haunted, indoor emptiness that made the Inspector feel something had passed along the corridor so recently that if he had only looked a moment sooner, he might have seen a door closing. For the first time Foyle understood why ghosts prefer to haunt houses rather than open fields and hills.

His hand groped for the electric switch.

"No lights!" said Basil. "And leave the front door ajar. Got your keys?"

He unlocked the door to Prickett's laboratory. Moonlight poured through the east window and cast on the floor an oblong of light cross-barred with shadow. Methodically, he emptied his paper bag on the table — a basket of strawberries, a bottle of California sherry, a box of Butterthin Biscuits, a tin of Chesterfields, and an old-fashioned wax candle.

"Where's the five bucks?" muttered Foyle.

"I'm not as extravagant as Prickett — one will do." Basil put the strawberries in Prickett's glass bowl and tucked a dollar bill underneath it. He stuck the candle in Prickett's green china candlestick and set Prickett's wine glass beside the bottle. Prickett's tin of cigarettes was nearly empty. Basil replaced it with the one he had bought. From Prickett's desk, he took some sheets of yellow paper and a pencil. He carried the Corona portable from the desk to the table. Finally, he went to Prickett's bookshelves, took down a book and weighed it in his hand. He returned it and hefted another.

"Always pick your books by weight?"

"Invariably!" Basil added the book to the other things and stood back to contemplate the effect. "Is that the way it looked the night of Konradi's murder?"

"The ashtray was on the right of the typewriter."

Basil rearranged the ashtray. "Anything else?"

"The book Prickett had was about murder and that—" Foyle peered at the title in the moonlight. "That's Locke's *Human Understanding*."

"But the size and weight are all that matter."

"What's the idea anyway?"

"You wouldn't believe me if I tried to tell you. And now all we can do is to wait. I think the best place is under the stairs. We can take a couple of chairs."

Foyle's mind went back to that other vigil he had kept under the stairs only two nights ago. Almost everything was the same — the ill-assorted objects on the table in the laboratory — the moonlight filtering through the front door as it stood ajar — the long, dim corridor with its closed doors on either side.

The sudden, deep voice of a bell shattered the silence. Once again, he began to count the strokes of the library clock — six...seven...eight. His heart was pounding. He would hardly have felt any surprise if he had heard a quick, resolute step. But the clock went on...nine...ten. And nothing happened.

The craving for tobacco gave way to a craving for sleep.

The moon passed its zenith and the psychological laboratory grew dark except for a faint glow from the southwest windows.

"Lissen, doc — why can't we smoke?"

"Better keep our hands free."

Suddenly, Foyle was wide awake. *Better keep our hands free — for* what? "See here, do you—?"

He stopped in mid-sentence. The front door was opening slowly. He stood up, automatically doubling his fists. Then he felt Basil's touch, light on his arm, and Basil's voice whispering in his ear, paraphrasing his own words: "Suppose you let me handle this my own way. It's no time for strong-arm stuff!"

Something white was glimmering on the threshold. It made no sound as it came toward them. Something in its slow, even pace suggested the fatalistic passivity of a machine set in motion by forces independent of itself. There was no hint of the wilful irregularity that distinguishes the human from the mechanical.

14

EXORCISM

Just as Foyle decided he couldn't stand it any longer if the thing came nearer, it swerved toward the psychological laboratory. There was a scratching sound and a match flared, clung to the candlewick, wavered and grew steady picking out the bosses of the face above and leaving its hollows in shadow.

"Halsey!" whispered Foyle. "What on earth—?"

The boy wore loose white trousers — apparently part of a pyjama suit. His torso was bare and so were his feet. But his hands were encased in the same heavy gauntlets he had worn the night of Konradi's murder.

The match fell from his listless fingers to the floor. The flame crept along the matchstick until it licked his bare foot. But he did not wince or move his foot.

Once again, a candle flame stood straight as a spear in the still air of the laboratory, and Halsey's shadow towered monstrously against the wall, moving only when he moved. Once again, he gravely sipped a glass of sherry and ate strawberries one by one with gloved fingers. When he had finished, he pushed the bowl aside. He picked up the dollar bill with fingers that trembled slightly and went through the motions of putting it in a breast pocket. But as there was no breast pocket, the bill fell to the floor unheeded. He lit one of the cigarettes from the tin, dropped the match and trod on the flame. Then he began turning the pages of *Human Understanding,* pausing every few moments as if he were reading.

"God!" muttered Foyle. "His eyes are closed!"

Halsey held his wrist before his closed eyes — there was no watch on his arm. Still moving slowly and mechanically he crushed his cigarette in the ashtray and lit a second one — dropping the match in the tray. The cigarette hung limply from his lower lip as he sat down at the table and began to type. His head turned toward the open book from time to time as if he were copying something. In spite of his gloves he typed swiftly by the touch system.

"He's doing everything he did Saturday night," said Foyle. "Even the matches — two on the floor and one in the ash tray."

"Just as I found them last night," added Basil.

Halsey dropped his second cigarette in the ash tray and ripped the paper from the typewriter. Going to the other side of the table, he sat down, picked up a pencil and began to mark the page he had typed as if he were correcting typographical errors.

"I'm going in there," said Basil. "You can come — if you like."

"But—"

"You needn't whisper — he won't hear. He's withdrawn into a world of his own — a safe, subjective world where his memory is absolute master and there are no intrusive stimuli from other people. He didn't feel the match that burned his bare foot tonight because he is reliving the events of Saturday night when he wore shoes."

Halsey did not look up as they approached. The curious scratches on his breast which they had seen for a moment that morning were plainly visible now — very deep, narrow scratches parallel with the ribs. His eyes were not entirely closed — there was a slit between the upper and lower lids where the white of the eyeballs gleamed. The pupils were dilated, the upper lids fixed and unblinking.

Foyle looked at the paragraph Halsey had typed. He had not copied a passage from *Human Understanding;* he had typed from memory the same words he had typed the night of Konradi's murder — words from the murder story which Prickett had provided to "intensify the emotional reactions of the subject."

Basil faced Halsey across the table. Gently he laid a fingertip on the typewritten page and drew it away. Then he slid a blank sheet of paper into its place. The change made no difference to Halsey. Gravely he went on marking the blank page with the pencil as if still correcting the typewritten page. When he finished, Basil drew away the blank page and laid it under the typewritten page. Then he held them up to the light, one over the other. Foyle felt the skin crawl on the back of his neck. For the spacing of the pencil corrections on the blank page coincided exactly with the errors on the typewritten page.

"How in God's name did he do that? He made those corrections on the blank page!"

Basil shrugged. "It may be an abnormally vivid visual memory — or it may be something like an after-image caused by brilliant light."

"What's wrong with him anyway?"

Basil made a gesture for silence.

Halsey had started as if he heard something they could not hear. Now he was running toward Konradi's laboratory. He wrenched the door open. The laboratory was empty. But Halsey faced that emptiness with a look of unspeakable horror on his blind face and screamed — an inhuman scream that clung to a high note, wavered, and fell a long way into silence.

For a moment he stood still, his gloved fist pressed against his mouth. Then he turned and spoke for the first time. "H- How did you get in here?"

"Why, we—" Foyle stopped.

Halsey's head was not turned toward Foyle or Basil. It was bent toward the floor as if he could see someone kneeling there. He walked to the nearest switch as if he were wading knee-deep in water. He fumbled for the button. Every movement was slow and heavy with the conscious effort of a man fighting against drunkenness or sleep. There was a click — and Foyle blinked as the great floodlights in Prickett's laboratory blazed into being.

But Halsey cried in a voice that cracked, "The lights won't go on! Let's get out of here .. Locked?" He ran to the window and put forth all his strength trying to push it up. The sash rose at once, but he cried, "It's nailed down!" He was gasping for breath and beating his fists against empty air. "Let me out! You devil! Let me out! Oh, God, I forgot!" He sank to his knees with a sob. "Unbreakable glass in all the ground-floor windows! What are we going to do? We're locked in with a murderer!" His voice was shrill. "You…you won't leave me alone in the dark?"

A violent spasm passed through his body. Then all feeling seemed to flow out of him. He lay on the floor under the window, crumpled and relaxed. His eyes closed naturally, his breathing grew slower and more regular. He was in a normal sleep.

"Whew!" Foyle wiped cold sweat from his forehead with a handkerchief. "That was too damned realistic! What now?"

"Let him rest a little while."

Basil moved the limp body into a more comfortable position and covered it with his own overcoat. His fingertips lingered for a moment on the boy's pulse. Then he rose, lit one of the cigarettes from the tin on the table and drew on it thoughtfully.

"Was this Ezra's ghost?"

Basil nodded. "Many a ghost and many a werewolf is really a sleepwalker. As you said, no one in his senses would risk coming back to the scene of a crime three nights in succession — but it's just what a sleepwalker would do. I felt sure we were dealing with one when I realised that every night Ezra's ghost appeared the moon had been full or nearly full. Most sleepwalkers walk when the moon is full. Moonlight shining through a bedroom window seems to provoke the transition from ordinary sleep to the hypnoidal state of sleepwalking just as a bright object may provoke the transition from the waking state to ordinary hypnosis. That's why Austrian peasants call it moon-walking. When Hitler's mother said he was moon-struck — *mondsüchtig* — she meant that he walked in his sleep, and he is still beating his fists against empty air and screaming that the lights won't go on when they will."

"How did you know the sleepwalker was Halsey?"

"Whoever he was, he had been in Prickett's laboratory last night, so he had a key to it — Prickett, Feng, the Dean, Halsey or Ezra. Ezra was with Grady when Grady heard the ghost scream. It couldn't be Prickett or Feng as both sleep outside the University grounds. A sleepwalker in night-dress couldn't walk through city streets to the University without being seen and stopped. That left the Dean and Halsey, who were both sleeping at the Dean's house inside the grounds each night the ghost appeared.

"The fact that Halsey attended a small university in his own city as a day student instead of going away to his father's university suggested some reason for his sleeping at home. His horror when he first heard of the ghost suggested that he recognised the ghost as himself. His sudden visit to Feng, the professor of Abnormal Psychology, suggested that he was seeking some remedy for an abnormal mental state. Of course he was annoyed when he found me there for fear I would put two and two together — as I did. Last night, after the ghost visited this room, I found all the lights blazing, a window open and a disposition of cigarette stubs and burnt matches that corresponded with Halsey's actions here the night of Konradi's murder. When Grady said the ghost had cursed the devil and called on God to let him out of hell, I recalled the words Halsey had screamed at Prickett the night of Konradi's murder 'You devil!' and 'Oh, God! Let me out!' Then I was certain that Halsey was the sleepwalker, re-enacting a shocking experience as you or I might re-enact it in a normal dream without leaving our beds.

"You see, Ezra was right. It really was a ghost — the ghost of a dead experience haunting a tortured mind. A shock is an emotional experience you can't assimilate. You keep going over and over it in your mind as you go over and over French verbs you're trying to assimilate. If your mental constitution is weak, you repeat your shocking experience in action as well as thought — realistically in a sleepwalking state or symbolically in a neurotic state."

Basil extinguished his cigarette and walked back to Halsey, sleeping peacefully now — lips parted, one arm under his head — very young and defenceless.

"It isn't just sleepwalking…is it?"

Basil looked up quickly. "How did you know?"

"Why should Halsey want to hide it if it were just sleep-walking. Lots of people do it."

"And that makes it perfectly natural?" Basil smiled. "I've often wondered why sleepwalking is the one symptom of mental disorder that doesn't frighten the layman."

"Is this sleepwalking of Halsey's a symptom of something else?"

Basil weighed his response. "You remember Prickett's saying that the various forms of lie-detector are all based upon tests first used to detect disease and later adapted to the detection of lies?"

"Sure."

"Hasn't it occurred to you that at least one of our suspects might be refusing to take the lie-detector test because he feared it would reveal an illness he wished to hide? When anyone goes around insisting that he always tells the absolute truth, you may be sure he's lying about something. Halsey's whole life is a lie because he is always trying to hide that he is an epileptic."

"Epilepsy!" The Inspector recoiled from the sleeping boy with sudden physical repugnance. "And when I first heard he was the son of John H Halsey I thought: 'Boy, what wouldn't I give to be in his shoes!'"

"Property isn't the only thing that can be inherited from a father who makes a habit of absinthe cocktails. Alcoholism affects the motor nerves. That's probably why alcoholic parentage is associated so often with sleepwalking, epilepsy and sadism — all diseases of the motor nervous system."

Halsey stirred and opened his eyes. "What…where…?" His gaze wandered around the brilliantly lighted room and came back to the two men who stood looking down at him.

"You're in Prickett's laboratory," said Basil.

Halsey looked down at his pyjama trousers and gloved hands. His face whitened in the glare of the floodlights. The surgeon's plaster on his cheek bone quivered as the cheek muscles contracted. "I-I must've been walking in my sleep."

"Better put on that coat." Basil extended a hand to help him, but he seized Basil's arm in both hands and clung to it. His lips moved and no sound came at first.

Then he said thickly, "You…saw me tonight? When I came in here? Tell me…what did I do?"

"You repeated everything you did the night Konradi was killed."

Basil could feel Halsey's fingers bite through the sleeve of his jacket. "And…what was that?"

"You don't know?"

"No!" Halsey shook the arm he held. "I don't know whether I murdered Konradi or not! I don't remember anything that happened Saturday night from the moment I entered Souther-land Hall until I woke up in Salt's office with the Inspector and Woodman. But you must know! You must have seen me go through the whole thing again tonight. For God's sake…tell me…what did I do? Did I kill Konradi?"

"You did nothing to suggest you had killed anyone. That wouldn't convince a judge and jury of your innocence, but it goes a long way with a psychiatrist — provided you were in a genuine sleepwalking state."

"Thank God!" Halsey didn't seem to hear Basil's last words. But they startled Foyle. He searched Basil's face with a long, level look.

Halsey was struggling into Basil's overcoat. It was too big for him, so he wrapped it around his body without attempting to button it and stumbled to a chair.

"Suppose we turn off these flood lamps." Basil flipped two

of the switches and the white glare of light subsided to a clear, moderate illumination. "And now..." He returned to the table where Halsey was sitting. "What is the last thing you do remember just before Konradi's murder?"

Halsey helped himself to a cigarette from the tin on the table. The flame of the match wavered in his shaking hand. He dragged the smoke into his lungs with a deep inhalation and expelled it before he answered.

"I was walking toward this building in the moonlight. I was pretty excited. Prickett had said the psychology of the sham crime must be as much like the psychology of a real crime as possible, so I tried to do all the things a real murderer would do and think all the thoughts a real murderer would think. I put on rubber-soled shoes that evening so I wouldn't make any noise. Just as I was starting out I remembered that most murderers wear gloves to avoid leaving fingerprints. I never wear gloves if I can help it, but I had an old pair of winter gloves in my locker, so I put those on. I kept in the shadows so I wouldn't be seen. When I passed people on the campus, I turned my head away so they wouldn't recognise me. It wasn't all put on. I tried so hard to imagine how a real murderer would feel on his way to commit a murder that I really did succeed in feeling...well, criminal. And I wasn't a bit frightened. I felt reckless and bad — really bad. And then...well, that's the last thing I remember."

Halsey had forgotten the cigarette between his fingers. As the burning ember reached his skin, he winced, and the long ash fell on the floor. He crushed the cigarette in the ashtray.

Foyle, sitting squarely opposite Halsey, missed none of this. But Basil, perched on the edge of the table side-saddle, didn't appear to be watching Halsey.

"Is that all you have to tell us?"

Even his voice was impersonal. But Halsey lifted his eyes and, confronted Basil with a hard hostility.

"Isn't that enough?"

"I think not."

Suddenly the hardness went out of the boy. His gaze dropped, his shoulders sagged, his whole body slumped in the chair. "I told Southerland it was no use trying to bluff a psychiatrist." One elbow rested on the table. He covered his eyes with a hand.

"What happened Saturday night?" persisted Basil.

"I came up the steps of this building Saturday night. The next thing I knew I was in Salt's office with Woodman offering me whisky, blissfully ignorant of what would happen if I took any. And you, Inspector, were talking to Police Head-quarters on the phone about...murder. By listening to you I got an idea what had happened. I remembered all too clearly how reckless and criminal I felt just before I lost conscious-ness. You said I had walked into a bottle of wine and even wine has a very odd effect on me. I began to wonder if Prick-ett's sham crime had turned into a real crime and if I had become a criminal in the epileptic state without knowing anything about it. When you asked me why I was wearing gloves, I didn't dare tell you I had worn them because I had been trying to reproduce the mental state of a murderer in my own mind."

Foyle had listened in growing bewilderment. "I saw you go up those front steps!" he cried. "But you didn't fall down in a fit."

"Of course not — I never do!" Halsey was beginning to recover his combative spirit.

Basil explained to Foyle. "An epileptic attack isn't neces-sarily a fit. It's a sudden lapse of consciousness not caused by a blow or a drug, and not comparable to ordinary sleep. It may last a few seconds or several hours. It may be an active convulsion, or a passive semi-conscious state. But it is always a sudden fading of consciousness for no external reason — like the sudden fading of an electric light when the current is short-circuited. The sleepwalker only enters the sleepwalking state during his natural sleep. But the epileptic may enter the epileptic state waking or sleeping — at any moment in any circumstances."

Halsey gripped the edge of the table and leaned forward. There was a hard, hot light in his agate-grey eyes that disconcerted the Inspector, accustomed though he was to the criminal and abnormal.

"Do you know what that means?" Halsey's voice had the timbre of a wire stretched almost to breaking point. "I have money to buy all the liquor I want...but I can never take a drink, not even a glass of sherry, because one drop of alcohol acts on an epileptic like a flaming match on a keg of gunpowder. I have money to buy all the cars I want...but I can never drive a car for fear I'll kill someone. I'm brought here every morning by a chauffeur and called for at night as if I were a kid going to kindergarten. My mother and father don't want anybody to know — they're ashamed of it. They would never have risked sending me here to college if our doctor hadn't told them I must lead a normal life or I'd get worse. They chose Yorkville because Southerland is a trustee and they thought he could hush things up if...if anything went wrong. That's one reason Southerland has given so much money to Yorkville — so he'd have a big pull here in case I got into a mess. Sometimes things happen. There was that spaniel."

Halsey shivered and drew Basil's overcoat more closely about him.

"Of course there's nothing really the matter with me." His hard, hot eyes darted from Foyle to Basil and back again.

"Epilepsy isn't like…like insanity. All the textbooks say that. I'm perfectly normal in the daytime. When I entered college the medical officer never guessed anything was wrong with me and Feng is the only professor of psychology here who guessed the truth. Prickett never guessed. He isn't interested in abnormal psychology, and he isn't a doctor of medicine. He even wanted to use me as a subject in some of his startle-pattern experiments. I couldn't let him because epilepsy destroys the normal startle pattern and he would have realised the truth as soon as he saw a slow-motion picture of my failure to react. I suggested I act as cameraman during those experiments so I'd never be in the picture myself."

"But you weren't so cautious when Prickett asked you to take the part of the sham criminal," put in Basil.

"I thought I'd take a chance on it. I'd never done anything like that, and I thought it would be fun. The hour was set for eight and my attacks don't come as a rule until eleven or twelve. Mother and father were in Egypt so they couldn't interfere. Sometimes I get so sick and tired of never doing anything I want to do that I just have to break loose — the way I did last night when I tried to drink that whisky and Souther-land knocked it out of my hand.

"Of course I knew I oughtn't to take a chance on the sham crime. I think it was a subconscious impulse to chuck the whole thing that made me lose part of Prickett's letter of instructions. If I'd known about the 'surprise elements' for 'intensifying the emotional reaction of the subject' I'd never have risked it. Or if I'd known it was a lie-detector experiment. Prickett's lie-detector includes the Jung association test, and the association test detects epilepsy as well as lies because certain word associations are peculiar to epileptics."

Foyle whistled softly. "No wonder you collapsed Saturday

night when Prickett told you the experiment was really a lie-detector test!"

"That was nothing to the way I felt Sunday morning when I woke up at the Dean's house and the Dean told me that Dr Willing was planning to use Prickett's lie-detector on everyone involved — including me."

Halsey lit another cigarette. His hand was steadier.

"What did you do?" asked Basil.

"I got hold of Southerland. Whenever there's any trouble in our family we call on Southerland. He knows all the skeletons in our cupboard because it's his job to keep them out of the papers. He's the only person who knows about me — besides my parents, the nurse I had when I was a baby and our doctor.

"I didn't dare tell Southerland I had no conscious memory of anything that happened when Konradi was shot, and no idea whether I had murdered him. But I did say the police would be sure to suspect me if they found out I was an epileptic, and they would be sure to find out because they had a psychiatrist on the job — a Dr Willing — who was going to give us all a lie-detector test that would detect epilepsy. Southerland said I must refuse to take the test. I answered, 'Then they'll know I'm the murderer!' But Southerland is really smart because he'd thought of that. He smiled grimly and said, 'Not if several other people refuse to take the test at the same time!' I said, 'You can never wrangle that!' And he answered, 'I've secured Dr Feng's refusal already.'"

Basil's cool voice cut across Halsey's feverish volubility. "Are you sure Southerland made his bargain with Feng before he talked to you?"

"He said so."

"But why should he want to obstruct the lie-detector test *before* he knew it would betray your epilepsy to the police?"

"Search me!" Halsey moved restlessly. "I was too busy worrying about myself to worry about Southerland."

"How did he get Feng to refuse the test?"

"I don't know. I'm like my father. I don't care how Southerland does things, so long as he gets them done."

"Then the only reason you refused the test was because you didn't want the police to learn about your epilepsy and lapse of memory during the murder?"

"That's what I'm telling you." Halsey was growing impatient.

"You had no other motive?"

"Of course not. How could I?"

"In that case — now that we know all about the epilepsy and the lapse of memory — you should be perfectly willing to take the test."

Halsey's impetuosity was checked abruptly. He measured Basil with a look that was sidelong and sly. "Of course I'm willing. But there doesn't seem much point in it. Now you've seen me re-enact everything I did Saturday night you know I'm not the murderer."

"Miss von Hohenems is taking it tomorrow morning at ten," said Basil. "Can you take it at twelve o'clock?"

"Okay. Why not?" But Halsey's bravado was plainly counterfeit. He shivered again.

"It's cold and it's late." Basil looked at Foyle. "What do you say, Inspector?"

"Sure." Foyle turned to Halsey. "Your lips are getting blue, young man. No wonder, with bare feet on this tiled floor. We'll take you back to the Dean's and you'd better have a drink—" He stopped.

"You see?" Halsey's eyes had a hard glitter. "There are so many things I can't do, sometimes I think it'll drive me mad!"

It was nearly 3:00 am when Basil and Inspector Foyle

parted at the deserted 86th Street subway station — Basil taking the downtown local and Foyle going to the lower level for an express to Brooklyn. Just before Foyle went down the stairs, he caught Basil's arm.

"Forgot to tell you we got the dope on Argus Advertising Agency! Mercantile Bank owns seventy-three percent of the stock — Southerland and Halsey's father are both directors!"

15

EXPERIMENT

On Tuesday a leaden sky masked the sun and diffused a weak daylight evenly. Mist from the river drifted across the campus in ragged white streamers.

There was no sound of young voices and quick footfalls hurrying to classes. The Dean had decided to close the University and already most of the students were gone, leaving an uncanny stillness behind them. The three men waiting in Prickett's laboratory for Gisela von Hohenems were startled by her light step in the corridor.

She smiled as Basil introduced Bartlett, his bored young assistant from the psychiatric clinic, and Duff, the stolid police stenographer. Something in that brief smile made Bartlett less bored and Duff less stolid. The morbid elegance of black tweed and white angora suited her black and white beauty.

Her glance rested on the centre table. There were pencils and paper and three simple instruments — a stethoscope, a pressure gauge attached to an inflatable bandage like that used for taking blood-pressure tests, and something like an electric clock with a great many digits on its dial and only one hand.

Her eyebrows lifted. "Don't tell me that's all there is to Prickett's famous lie-detecting machine?"

"A lie-detector is a test, not a machine," explained Basil. "Lies are detected by watching for minute, involuntary changes that occur in the functions of a witness whenever he lies — a rising of his blood pressure or a slowing of his association time. It can be done with a lot of awe-inspiring machinery bristling with impressive gadgets such as markers that plot polygraphs mechanically on smoked drums. But it can also be done quite as accurately with inexpensive instruments found in any doctor's office. If you'll sit in this armchair..."

Gisela looked delicately sceptical as Bartlett pushed up her sleeve and wrapped the inflatable bandage around her upper arm. He slipped the flat end of the stethoscope under the lower edge of the bandage just over the brachial artery.

"Don't move your arm — just let it rest comfortably on the table."

Gisela's eyes challenged Basil. "Do you honestly believe that if I don't tell the truth my blood pressure will give me away?"

He smiled at her candid incredulity. "Systolic blood pressure is the maximum pressure of blood in an artery during the contracting phase of the heartbeat. The pressure rises when anyone lies because the creative effort of mental invention strengthens the contraction of the heart. The same thing happens when you lie to yourself, so the same test can be used to unmask a neurosis which is simply a form of self-deception. Someday blood-pressure tests may replace the older, less objective methods of psychoanalysis altogether."

Bartlett adjusted the stethoscope to his ears and sat down near Gisela where he could see the figures on the pressure gauge. In his left hand he held a rubber bulb attached to the bandage by a rubber tube. His right hand rested on the table, holding a pencil over a large sheet of paper divided into columns. Duff sat at the same table with his own notebook and fountain pen. Basil stood beside Bartlett. At his nod, Bartlett pressed the rubber bulb and the bandage swelled until the flow of blood in the artery stopped. Then Bartlett released a small lever with his thumb and there was a faint hiss of air escaping from the bandage. As the first sound of blood flowing back into the artery reached his ears through the stethoscope, he looked at the pointer on the pressure gauge and jotted down the figures it indicated.

Basil's face was grave as he read the figures. He had been right in suspecting anaemia. But he could not help admiring the fineness of wrist and ankle, the brittle narrowness of waist and flank, and the jasmine-white of the blood-starved skin. Those anthropologists who believed that our idea of beauty was based upon health just didn't know what they were talking about.

She was leaning back in her chair now — her brows drawn together and her lips compressed. Was she regretting already that she had consented to take the test? Yet as Konradi's devoted assistant she could hardly have refused to help the police.

"It's very warm in here," she murmured.

"The air-conditioning system has been turned off," answered Basil. "We've discovered a fault in it by which people in the squash courts downstairs can overhear everything said in this laboratory or Konradi's. I don't want anyone to overhear us now."

He waited until Bartlett had taken enough tests to established 112 as her normal blood pressure under excitement.

Then Basil spoke quietly as if taking up a conversation they had dropped a few moments earlier.

"I'd like you to repeat the story you told Inspector Foyle the night of Konradi's murder."

Gisela's voice sounded small and thin. She did not change her story, but she condensed it and hurried through it so breathlessly that it only took two pages of shorthand in Duff's notebook while Bartlett did not have time for more than a dozen blood-pressure readings before she stopped speaking.

As Bartlett jotted down his column of figures, Basil watched them closely. In his mind he was translating them into the convenient, pictorial graph with a blood-pressure curve. His voice was expressionless when at last he spoke: "Did you know Dr Konradi in Austria?"

"No." The question surprised Gisela. "I told you that before."

"Did you ever see him there in any public place? At one of his lectures perhaps?"

"I never went to his lectures. So far as I know I never saw him in a public place."

"Do you know anyone in New York, Austrian or American, who knew him both here and in Vienna?"

"No. He knew so few people here. Why do you ask?"

"Someone suggested that we have no proof the man who died Saturday night was Konradi, the biologist. Do you think he could have been an impostor? Perhaps even a Nazi agent?"

"But — that is monstrous!" Her hands gripped the arms of her chair. Then she remembered the blood-pressure apparatus on her arm and relaxed. "It couldn't be," she whispered, more to herself than to Basil. "It couldn't be." Was there doubt in her voice?

"How did Konradi escape from Dachau?"

"I don't know. He would never talk about it."

"Have you ever heard of any other prisoner at Dachau who escaped successfully?"

"No. But Konradi could always do things that other people couldn't do. He had exceptional courage and strength and intelligence."

Duff's face, ordinarily as mobile and expressive as a side of beef, had lighted with interest during the colloquy; This was not like the "questioning" that went on sometimes in the "back room" at Headquarters. Merciless floodlights did not beat against the suspect's eyeballs, and the examiner did not drink a glass of water or light a cigarette while his victim went thirsty and smokeless. Gisela's voice might falter anxiously at one moment or quicken impatiently the next, Basil's voice remained equable and even friendly. He made no accusations and he set no traps. But Duff admitted to himself, almost grudgingly, that the impersonal, clinical procedure was having an effect on the witness. Her eyes never left Bartlett as he repeated the simple blood-pressure test every few seconds without paying any attention to the questions and answers except to time them so they could be correlated with the time of each test.

"Did Dr Konradi ever speak of his arrest by the Nazis?"

"Sometimes."

"When did it happen?"

"In March 1938. I don't know what day of the month, but it was late at night."

"Who arrested him?"

"Some SS men — that's the *Schützstaffeln*. He said there were about a dozen. He had no warning. He was working in his laboratory with an assistant."

"How did they behave?"

"How do they usually behave?" She shrugged. "They put all his papers in a big bag to take away. Apparently they hoped to find letters or something."

"Did they?"

"No. I asked him once if there were anything compromising in those papers, but he said no, just records of his biochemical experiments. Of course they wrecked his laboratory — smashed all the instruments, killed all the animals, and spilled all the liquids on the floor. He knew they were doing it to make him angry, so he managed to keep his temper. But it was hard, for he was not a rich man and some of the instruments were valuable. When they took him away the building was in flames. He was never sure whether they burned it intentionally or accidentally. Several of them were smoking cigarettes and apparently they didn't realise how inflammable some of the chemicals were. He said they were very young — schoolboys running amok — and incredibly ignorant. They didn't seem to know what any of the apparatus was for but they enjoyed smashing it almost as much as if it had been a living thing that could feel pain. He thought they hated the learning, skill and labour the instruments represented — perhaps because learning and skill were things they had never been able to achieve and even labour was denied them when work became so scarce in Austria after the war.

"Once Konradi talked to Feng about it and Feng compared them to the boys who used to make up the armies of the war lords in China. He said, 'When a country reaches a state when some of the people must starve it's never the young men who do the starving. It's the old men and the women and children, for the young men will always take the law into their own hands and rob everyone else.'"

Basil touched Bartlett's shoulder lightly as a signal that he wanted a blood-pressure reading taken at the very moment he asked the next question.

"Did you meet Kurt Dietrich, the German exchange student, on the campus last Saturday evening about nine o'clock?"

"No."

"Was there any particular reason why Konradi should go to your apartment Saturday evening just before eight o'clock?"

"No. He simply…dropped in, as I told you."

"Did he accuse you of having taken his missing laboratory notes?"

"Never!"

"Weren't you the only person besides Konradi with access to his notebooks?"

"I don't know."

"Is there anyone else you suspect of having taken the notes?"

"No."

Basil touched Bartlett's shoulder again. "Was Konradi in love with you?"

"No."

"Did you love him?"

"These questions are impertinent. I won't answer."

"There are no more questions."

Basil turned to the table and began adjusting the object that resembled an electric clock.

"Have you ever taken an association test?"

"No, but I've read about it. It's a sort of psychological shorthand for questions and answers. You speak a single word and I answer with another single word — the first that comes into my mind. If my word comes more slowly than usual it means that your word has roused a feeling of guilt in me."

"Exactly. And if the first word that comes to your mind is

one that gives away something you want to conceal you can't substitute a second word for it consciously without causing the same tell-tale delay in your rate of response. I'm going to ask you to use this voice key attached to an electric chrono-scope so the time it takes you to respond can be recorded in thousandths of a second. Ready?"

"Yes."

"*Notebook.*"

Gisela knocked over the voice key and its stand as she sprang to her feet. "I told you I know nothing about the note-book. I don't know who took it or why! I don't know enough chemistry to know what was in it! I've had enough — I can't stand it — I can't!"

Tears stood in her eyes and her thin fingers plucked desperately at the bandage on her arm. Bartlett never shifted his glance from the pressure gauge and Duff stolidly sat still, waiting for the next word. But Basil loosened the bandage without a word.

Bartlett looked up in surprise and even Duff was bewildered.

"Thank you." Gisela looked at her arm as if she expected to see a wound. But it was only faintly pink from the constric-tion of the bandage. She lifted eyes bright with tears that did not fall. "Is that all?"

"Yes."

She looked at the instruments and Bartlett's column of figures. "Does it say I told the truth?"

Basil evaded a direct answer. "We can't tell much about it until we make a graph."

"Oh. You'll let me know the result, won't you?"

"Certainly."

"I'm sorry I was so upset." She had reached the door. "I

don't know anything about the notebook — really I don't!" Again she smiled briefly and was gone.

Bartlett seemed annoyed with his chief. "What did you let her go for? Just as it was getting interesting! She lied when she said there was no particular reason for Konradi's going to see her Saturday evening. She lied when she said he didn't accuse her of stealing the notebook — when she said she didn't meet Dietrich Saturday evening — when she said she didn't suspect anyone of stealing the notebook. If that doesn't mean she *and* Dietrich stole the notebook — I'm a Nazi myself! She's in this up to her neck. She's probably a Nazi agent sent here to spy on Konradi. She stole his notebook for the Nazis and shot him when he accused her."

"Yeah, but what would the Nazis want with a lotta laboratory notes about cancer prevention?" demanded Duff. "And why did she suspect Konradi of being a Nazi? She lied when she said she didn't suspect him, but if she'd been a Nazi herself, she'd've known."

Basil stood looking down at the blood-pressure record. "She lied when she said Konradi did not love her. She may have been lying to herself since self-deception has the same effect on blood pressure."

Bartlett grinned. "So that's what's worrying you?"

It was not necessary to explain the technique of lie-detecting to Halsey. On the contrary, it was Halsey who explained it to Basil and Bartlett. As Bartlett said afterward, "You'd've thought that pup had discovered the lie-detector himself!" He entered Prickett's laboratory and sat down in the armchair without waiting for an invitation. As he supervised the fastening of the bandage around his arm he criticised Prickett's equipment and Basil's procedure with equal frankness. Wasn't there any pneumograph? Surely a bp record should be checked by a breathing record! Wasn't Basil going to take a continuous bp test with a mechanical pen recording each fluctuation on a graph paper? Halsey didn't think much of the discontinuous method himself.

"The discontinuous method is better for my purpose today," answered Basil, more sharply than usual. "I don't want to stop every few minutes while someone changes a graph paper and I don't want to confine myself to questions that have to be answered yes or no."

"But—"

"Will you keep quiet until Bartlett has got your normal blood pressure under excitement?"

"I'm not excited!" returned Halsey. "You don't expect a man who's had nearly four years' psychology to be excited by an amateurish test like this, do you? Marston's claims for the discontinuous bp test are grossly exaggerated!" He turned to Bartlett. "Aren't you ready yet? You've had time to get twenty readings."

Bartlett nodded to Basil. "This time we'll begin with the association test." Basil adjusted the voice keys.

"Notebook."

"Article."

The response came slowly — 3.986 seconds by the chronoscope.

"Warm."

"Warm — too hot — sultry." (4.001)

"Only one word at a time, please," said Basil.

"Recover."

"Condition." (6.258)

"Car."

"Wheel." (8.001)

"House."

"Steer." (7.102)

"Offense."

"Fensid." (6.887)

Duff looked up from his notebook. "Did you say *offensive?*"

"It sounded like *fensid*," replied Basil.

"But there's no such word!" Duff was outraged at being forced to invent shorthand symbols for word's that didn't exist.

"Isn't there?" Halsey looked uncertain.

"If there are any words you don't understand write them in longhand as they sound and put a question mark on the margin," Basil advised Duff.

"Blank."

"Paper." (4.031)

"Book."

"Article." (5.492)

"Bright."

"Brilliant-glittering-shining." (3.642)

"Blood."

"Stone." (3.975)

"Sham."

"Crime." (5.983)

"Quick."

"Fast — rapid — swift." (4.001)

"Sweet."

"Sweetness." (6.258)

"Blue."

"Condition." (8.001)

The blood-pressure record kept simultaneously by Bartlett showed none of the big peaks that would have occurred if Halsey had tried to cheat. The occasional increases in blood pressure were so slight that even words as unpleasantly suggestive as *blood* could not have disturbed him emotionally.

At last Basil switched off the chronoscope, put the voice

keys aside and began to ask questions. "When did you first realise that you had been sleepwalking?"

"When I woke Sunday morning I knew I'd been dreaming about walking in the moonlight toward Southerland Hall, But I thought it was just a dream — until I heard Ezra talking about a ghost. Then I knew. It's years since I've walked in my sleep — I used to do it when I was thirteen and fourteen whenever the moon was shining brightly through the window. Especially if it were shining on water. I used to feel that I'd like to walk up the path of the moonlight on the water and crawl inside the moon. I had that same old feeling Saturday night when I saw the moon shining on the East River from my room at the Dean's house."

"Why didn't you tell me or Inspector Foyle that you were the ghost?"

"How could I? The ghost had haunted the scene of the crime. That meant I had gone to Southerland Hall in a sleepwalking state and that I had probably re-enacted all the things I had done when Konradi was killed. I couldn't remember what those things were. I had no way of knowing whether I'd killed Konradi and…well, you know it isn't just superstition that a murderer returns to the scene of his crime. It's a form of remorse — a deep, irrational impulse, quite likely to come to the surface in a sleepwalking state. *Vide* Lady Macbeth. Had I returned to Southerland Hall in my sleep because I had killed Konradi? Had I re-enacted the killing in a sleepwalking state? If I'd told you or the Inspector you might have followed me the next night and seen me re-enact the murder of Konradi — a confession in pantomime and an unconscious one!"

"Did you do anything to check the sleepwalking?"

"Did I? I went to see Feng first. You know the old definition of a gentleman — 'a person who never asks questions'?"

"Certainly rules out detectives," murmured Basil.

"Well, it describes Feng. I felt safe with him. But you can imagine how I felt when I ran into you there! Later that day I got Feng alone in his office at Southerland Hall. I told him I'd been sleepwalking — I didn't tell him where or when or how and he didn't ask, as I knew he wouldn't. I begged him to give me something to stop it at once but he said there wasn't anything. It might be controlled after a long period of treatment but it couldn't be stopped overnight. I wanted it stopped at once because I didn't know what I might reveal in the sleepwalking state.

"That's one reason I was so upset Sunday night at supper. After I got upstairs I remembered some sleeping medicine I always carry — phenobarbital, the big capsules that are supposed to ward off night attacks of epilepsy, not the little capsules used for ordinary insomnia. I thought I might conquer sleepwalking if I could induce a deep sleep. So I locked my bedroom door and took a double dose."

"Worst thing you could have done," interpolated Basil. "Phenobarbital may discourage an ordinary epileptic attack but not sleepwalking. You're more likely to walk in a deep sleep than in a light one."

"I didn't know that. I fell asleep in my bed and I woke up outdoors — halfway between Southerland Hall and the Dean's house. The front door was locked but a living room window was open. I must have left the house that way. At least, that was how I returned."

"The Dean and I heard you leave the house," said Basil. "We were in his study and we both heard something. But by the time I had opened a window there was no one in sight."

"It wasn't very late when I got back — only one o'clock. But I didn't dare go to sleep again. The room I had is used by Dr Lysaght's son when he's in New York. I rummaged around for something sharp and I found a pair of spurs. I took off my pyjama jacket and sat up in bed reading with a spur on either side of me so that whenever I dozed off and slumped down I was sure to fall on one of the spurs and of course the rowel would gash me and I'd be wide awake again. It wasn't pleasant but the only way I could keep from sleepwalking was to keep from sleeping."

Halsey did not seem to mind questions that gave him an opportunity to talk about himself. Apparently he had forgotten Bartlett taking his blood pressure every few moments and Duff recording every word he uttered in shorthand. His eyes never left Basil and he talked as easily as if they had been lunching together.

"Monday morning I played tennis because I had an idea that physical fatigue might do more to make me sleep normally than drugs. And then you came and found Amy Salt's body. I didn't know when she'd been killed. But I knew that her body had been found outdoors and that I'd been outdoors sleepwalking the night before. Again I had no memory of anything that happened before I woke and found myself halfway between Southerland Hall and the Dean's house. I might have killed her, and the uncertainty was worse than a certain knowledge of guilt. My one idea was to get away from the Dean's house before I walked in my sleep again. But you wouldn't let me leave. I thought you suspected me of both murders. I couldn't find my phial of sleeping medicine and I thought I might've dropped it somewhere near Amy's body if I'd killed her. It's always with me at night — under my pillow or in the pocket of my pyjama jacket.

"After that I was afraid to sleep at all. Last night I tried to sit up in a chair all night reading. I put the spurs on top of the back of the chair so I couldn't rest my head there. I drew down the shades to keep out the moonlight and turned on all the lights and I locked the bedroom door. But it didn't do any good. I must have dozed off about midnight and unlocked the door in a sleepwalking state."

Basil sighed. "You'd have saved us a great deal of unnecessary work if you hadn't been so determined to hide your epileptic condition."

"It's not the sort of thing one cares to tell people."

"I can understand that. But of course there are some people you must tell."

"*Must!*" Halsey wasn't used to the word and he didn't like it. "Whom *must* I tell?"

"Well." Basil's eyes met Halsey's and held them. "Anyone you were planning to marry."

Halsey was suddenly quiet. His agate-grey eyes seemed cloudy and sightless. He spoke hardly moving his lips. "Do you suppose my father wants the Halsey fortune to go to my cousins who aren't even named Halsey? I have as much right to marry as he did! He never stayed sober for 24 hours in his life."

The words were so low that Duff had to lean forward to catch them. Halsey was no longer conscious of Bartlett or Duff — but only of Basil. "They say I've got to lead a normal life and money can make up for a lot of things. It isn't as if I were…well, mad, you know. Epilepsy is no worse than a bad neurosis. And everybody's a little neurotic. It's nothing to be ashamed of…nothing!"

"Then why not tell her?" At that moment Basil himself had almost forgotten Duff and Bartlett.

"I can't. I might lose her." Neither of them mentioned a name — it wasn't necessary. "I'll tell her what I please when I please, and you have no right to interfere. I believe you're only doing it because you want her for yourself!" Halsey's voice rose to the shrill, inhuman note it had reached when he discovered Konradi's body. "You shan't have her! She's mine! I don't care what anybody says — I don't care! I—"

He fell forward in his chair, jerking the blood-pressure apparatus out of Bartlett's hands. His head was on the table and he was crying.

BY THREE O'CLOCK that afternoon it was so dark that Basil had to turn on the light in Prickett's laboratory. His luncheon tray stood untouched on a corner of the big table. The ashtray was choked with cigarette stubs. He was surrounded by a mass of papers — blood-pressure records now plotted in graph form and an analysis of the two association tests expressed in mathematical terms.

He was alone when Inspector Foyle entered and there was no sound except the jerky scratching of his fountain pen as he scribbled a row of figures. What he saw made him frown. His pen idly traced a cross surrounded by a circle and then a woman's profile.

"She looks like Gisela von Hohenems," observed the Inspector with interest.

A drop of ink gathered on the tip of the pen and made a blot. "Confound these things!" Basil threw down the pen and mopped his fingers with a loose piece of blotter. "Why is it anything mechanical always gets out of order as soon as I buy it?"

"What about this junk?" Foyle jerked a thumb toward the analyses of the lie-detector tests. "Did you learn anything?"

Basil looked at the "junk" which represented four hour's work. A sudden light danced in his eyes. "How'd you like some really expert opinions?"

"Huh?"

Basil strode to the door and looked out into the corridor.

"Prickett and Feng are both in their offices. Even if they wouldn't take the test, they ought not to grudge us a little professional advice on the analysis."

"If you think it's okay to let them in on this…"

But Basil had left the room already.

EXCOGITATION

F eng was reading what appeared to be a student's theme — an appearance confirmed by the alacrity with which he put it down.

"You wish me to check the results of the test I refused to take myself? That is heaping coals of fire on my head! But I'll be glad to help…if I can."

Prickett was on his knees filling packing cases with books.

"Just…er…tidying things up." He smiled gingerly as if his muscles were unused to the exercise.

"Can you spare a moment from your packing? I'd like your opinion on the lie-detector tests."

Back in the psychological laboratory, Basil spread his mass of papers on the table before Prickett and Feng while Foyle stood watching. "These are stenographic records of questions and answers. These are stenographic records of association tests. These graphs represent blood-pressure readings taken during both proceedings. And this is my analysis of the results."

Prickett gasped as he saw Halsey's name. "Feng!"

"Yes?"

"Did you know that Ian was taking this test?"

"No."

For some minutes the room was still except for the rustling of paper. Foyle yawned and relaxed in a chair. Basil stood at the east window watching the mist.

"Good God!" It was Prickett's voice.

Basil turned his back to the window in time to catch Prickett's stare at Feng. "Did you know about Ian?"

Feng nodded.

"How?" cried Prickett.

"Everything suggested it. His father was a drunkard and he was an only child — presumably his mother's first child and therefore more liable to injury at birth. He's always been irritable, wayward, self-centred with that poverty of imagination and lack of sympathy that Jung calls 'emotional stupidity.' The moralistic stuff about the absolute truth is just as characteristic."

"Why didn't you tell me? If I'd known, I would never have chosen him for the sham criminal, and I would never have included wine in the sham crime!"

"You forget I didn't know the identity of the sham criminal."

Foyle peered at the record of Halsey's test over Prickett's shoulder. "What's wrong with it? Looks okay to me."

Feng sat back in his chair and looked at Basil. "I suppose this is confidential?"

"Unless it has something to do with the crimes," amended Basil.

"How could it?" Feng hesitated. His glance shifted to Foyle. "Prickett has just discovered Halsey is an epileptic. His association test shows all the symptoms. An exceptionally slow mean reaction time. A tendency for the slow rates to mount like a ladder. A tendency to react several times to different stimuli words with the same reaction word, usually a vague, general term such as *condition* or *article.* A tendency to react to one stimulus word twice in succession as in *car — wheel, house — steer,* both *wheel* and *steer* being reactions to *car.* A tendency to react with another form of the stimulus word as in *sweet — sweetness.* And finally a tendency to amplify his response with synonyms as when he reacted to *warm* with *warm — too hot — sultry.* As for the nonsense word *fensid — * that is a danger signal. When anyone responds to a stimulus word with his own concoction it shows a drift toward dementia and epilepsy can develop into dementia."

Prickett was growing worried. "Then that was why—"

Swiftly, Feng cut him short. "That was why Halsey refused to take the lie-detector test."

"Isn't homicide the commonest of all crimes among epileptics?" persisted Prickett. "Especially violent homicide without motive?"

"Your cigarette has gone out." Feng tossed a packet of matches across the table.

But Prickett would not be distracted. "It never occurred to me that Ian—"

"Of course it didn't." Feng interrupted again. "Doctors of medicine often fail to diagnose an epileptic by his behaviour alone. A professor of psychology might easily make the same mistake."

"I didn't mean that. I meant I've never seriously considered the possibility that Ian might be the...the murderer." Prickett seemed to balk at the word in connection with Halsey. "If I'd known he was an epileptic I'd never..." At last he saw the pitfall from which Feng had tried to divert him. "I mean...I...I...would've behaved rather differently," he finished lamely.

Foyle interrupted. "In plain English, Dr Prickett, you'd

never have protected Halsey by joining him in a refusal to take the lie-detector test, if you'd known that he was certainly an epileptic and therefore quite possibly a murderer. Right?"

Prickett's lips moved, but no sound came.

"We can guess the inducement Southerland offered you," said Basil. "We've been making some inquiries about stockholders in the Argus Advertising Agency."

A faint pinkness tinged Prickett's high cheekbones.

"But I'm still at a loss to explain Feng's refusal to take the test." Basil turned slowly toward the Chinese man. "You seem less vulnerable than Prickett. You've no wife or children to support and poverty has no real terrors for you since you've deliberately chosen a life of privation in order to send money to the Chinese cause. Everyone says you were Konradi's only intimate friend here — you admit it yourself. What inducement made you obstruct our efforts to find the murderer? Did Southerland or the Mercantile Bank promise financial help for the Chinese cause? A bond issue perhaps?"

Feng's face was stoical. "I was not offered money or financial help — either for myself or the Chinese cause."

"Then what were you offered?" cried Foyle.

But Feng came of a people whose discretion has survived centuries of judicial torture. Tranquilly he took out his amethyst fingering piece and turned it over in his hand. "No one has offered me anything or required anything of me. When I refused to take the lie-detector test I was acting on my own initiative. Suppose we say that I was entirely disinterested — that I had no motive except my desire to protect a most unfortunate boy whom I believed innocent?"

"In that case," said Basil, "you should be willing to take the test — now that we know about Halsey."

Feng's smile appeared charmingly spontaneous. "I've never forgotten Francis Galton's comment on the association test: *It exhibits a man's mental anatomy with more vividness and truth than he would probably care to publish to the world.* I have no secret like poor Halsey's but I prefer to keep my mental anatomy decently veiled." Feng pushed away the mass of papers before him and settled back in his chair. "Why have you shown us this analysis, Willing? Everything is in order. You don't need our help."

"But I want to know if your conclusions are the same as mine."

Feng's glance sought Prickett's.

It was Prickett who answered. "Precisely the same. The blood-pressure records show clearly that Gisela von Hohenems lied throughout the latter part of her test, while Halsey told the truth. In the association test, his reaction time in responding to words connected with the crime, such as *blood* and *shot,* was perfectly normal — neither too slow nor too quick as compared with his mean reaction time in his response words. The association of such words as *blood* — *stone* and *blank* — *paper* is obviously innocent. It's too bad Gisela didn't take the association test, too."

"Then," said Basil, "you would both support me if I told Inspector Foyle that the murderer is Gisela von Hohenems or one of the five people who refused to take the test — yourself, your wife, Feng, Salt or Southerland?"

Feng smiled appreciatively. "You've put us in a bizarre situation, Willing. Now I see why you wanted us to check your analysis of the test. You're actually asking us to confirm the possibility of our own guilt! No one could suspect Mrs Prickett of committing murder. It's equally impossible to believe that Salt would kill the wife he loved so devotedly or that Southerland would murder the biochemist whose cancer research he had just endowed. Therefore, the net result of the lie-detector test seems to be that Miss von

Hohenems, Prickett or myself murdered Konradi and Mrs Salt."

Prickett moistened dry lips with a pale tongue. But Feng seemed to be enjoying the situation. Through the haze of Prickett's cigarette smoke, he was a smiling Buddhist image bathed in clouds of incense.

Basil answered, "There is one other possibility. Is it very far-fetched to believe a criminal might discover some way to cheat the lie-detector? Just as other criminals have already learned to forge fingerprints?"

Feng's face was suddenly blank. But Prickett's astonishment was open to inspection.

"What on earth do you mean?" he gasped.

"Suppose this murderer devised a way to cheat the lie-detector. Suppose he planned from the first to commit his murder and then 'prove' his 'innocence' afterward by passing a lie-detector test with flying colours. Of course, he must make sure beforehand that the police would use the lie-detector — by planning his real crime to coincide with the sham crime in a lie-detector experiment. Then the police would be certain to try the lie-detector on any suspect who consented to take it — as Southerland pointed out the first time I saw him."

"But it's impossible to cheat a lie-detector!" Now that Prickett no longer feared he would have to take the test, he leaped to its defence with his old fanaticism. "There just isn't any way you can keep your reaction time from becoming slower than normal when you respond to a word that rouses feelings of guilt. And when your reaction time is measured so finely in thousandths of a second you can't substitute one reaction word for another without causing an even longer delay."

Basil found a chair and leaned back in it, contemplating Prickett impersonally. "Suppose you delayed *all* your responses? Then there would be no variations. Your mean reaction time to both guilty and innocent stimulus words would be the same. All your reactions would be so slow that you'd have time to substitute one reaction word for another whenever you wished."

"Preposterous! Any competent examiner would notice that old trick the moment he saw that all the responses were abnormally slow!"

"Ordinarily, yes." Basil was watching his audience closely. "But—" he smiled at Prickett "—what if these particular responses were supposed to come from an epileptic? Then any competent examiner would expect all the responses to be abnormally slow."

Feng's mind seized the idea while Prickett was still fumbling for it. "'Supposed to be an epileptic'? Then you're suggesting that Halsey is a normal boy pretending to be an epileptic to cheat the lie-detector?"

"It's one possibility, isn't it? The difference between his real reaction time and the slow reaction time of his assumed epilepsy would give him a margin in which he could select any reaction words he pleased — such as *paper* for *blank* instead of the more compromising *shot,* and *stone* for *blood* instead of *stain* or *spot.* Any reactions slower than his real reaction time would be concealed by the uniform slowness of all. In most circumstances no one would use this method to cheat a lie-detector because no normal person cares to be branded an epileptic. But to escape a murder charge — it might be done."

Feng nodded agreement. "Halsey's been studying abnormal psychology under me, so he knows the symptoms. They aren't difficult to fake and his are exaggerated enough to be spurious. I first noticed it in midwinter. I suppose you're inferring he began to plan Konradi's murder as long ago as that?"

"It's a theory — an unproved possibility rather than an

inference," protested Basil. "But he has been free to do pretty much as he pleased this winter with his parents in Egypt."

"They would know the truth!" cried Prickett. "Southerland must know. And the family doctor."

"But that won't help us. Even if his claim to epilepsy were false, his parents wouldn't give him away if he told them it was his only chance to escape conviction for murder. Neither would Southerland or the family doctor or the nurse he had when he was a baby. There's nothing new about a perjured insanity defence in a murder case. The only new thing is that it may have been planned before the murder for the purpose of disarming suspicion by cheating a lie-detector."

"What about his blood-pressure readings?" demanded Prickett. "He couldn't fake those!"

"Are you sure?" returned Basil. "Anyone with a knowledge of abnormal psychology might keep blood pressure down regardless of excitement by taking a heart depressant just before the test."

Foyle had been silent for a long time, but now he had an inspiration. "What about Halsey's sleepwalking stunt? You needn't tell me a boy is normal when he can space corrections on a blank page so they coincide with errors on a typewritten page he can't see!"

"I don't believe Willing is suggesting Halsey is normal," answered Feng. "It's an axiom of abnormal psychology that no sane person ever pretends to be insane. There's no such thing as malingering in mental disease for no truly normal man will assume the stigma of insanity voluntarily — a fact apparently unknown to scholars who wrangle over Hamlet's sanity. Halsey may or may not be an epileptic. But if not, the fact that he has been faking epilepsy would prove him abnormal in some other way — perhaps a worse way."

"I thought you liked the boy!" exclaimed Prickett.

"I do But I don't like murder."

"Don't you?" said Basil gently.

The word hung in the air between them for a moment. Then Feng pocketed his bit of amethyst quartz and rose. "If you'll excuse me, I'll get on with the dreary business of reading undergraduate themes."

It was an orderly retreat. But at the threshold he spoiled it. His eyes veered toward the side door.

"I wonder if I might take a look around Konradi's laboratory. I've never had a chance to observe the actual scene of a murder, and I must confess to a little curiosity. Morbid, I suppose, but there it is."

Foyle was startled. "We're not letting anybody in there just yet," he said rather curtly.

"Oh, I beg your pardon. I have no wish to interfere with your arrangements. Some other time will do."

PRICKETT HAD GONE. The police had gone. It didn't seem worthwhile for a patrolman to guard Southerland Hall three days after the murder.

The library clock struck three deep, vibrant notes. Basil had been working steadily since nine and had had no luncheon. But he felt reluctant to leave the building. Basil had an overpowering impression that Konradi's laboratory was the focal point of all three murders.

He entered it and switched on the lights. All empty rooms are haunted but especially an empty room filled with the intimate belongings of someone dead. Konradi's rubber gloves lay on the edge of the sink where he must have laid them Saturday afternoon when he hurried out to look for the missing laboratory notes. One of his old overalls hung in the half-open locker. There were cultures in test tubes Konradi had prepared.

Basil looked at the test tubes more closely and saw that the cultures were dry and dead. Had he neglected them as he had neglected the charts? Or had no one bothered to keep the cultures alive since his death? Already there were signs of disuse. The cages of mice were gone, and a powdery film of dust was over everything.

What had Feng really wanted in Konradi's laboratory? A "person who never asks questions" does not succumb to curiosity without a reason. Yet what could Feng hope to find that had been missed by Homicide Squad detectives trained to search for the smallest clues? By a municipal toxicologist far more familiar with the technical side of Konradi's work than Feng?

A Chinese psychologist's patriotism — an American banker's sentimental interest in cancer research because his mother had died of the disease — an Austrian biochemist's experiments with irritant chemical compounds as sources of cancer — his arrest by the Nazis, his alleged escape from Dachau and his solitary life in America — the murder of a German exchange student — were all these part of one pattern? Had Amy Salt been close to the truth when she said that Southerland, Feng and Konradi were all "in something" together? Had she died because she said that once too often?

An idea glimmered faintly in Basil's mind. Slowly he turned and looked at the electro-chemical machinery Lambert had envied. Basil knew little about such things, but anyone could see that such a mechanism must be expensive and use a great deal of current. Of course, a foundation endowed by Souther-land could afford such toys for its research laboratories.

The old typewriter was the only shabby machine in the

magnificent array of shining glass, brass, copper, steel and platinum which Southerland had provided so lavishly. After the police failed to find any fingerprints on it except Konradi's, no one had paid much attention to an object that seemed commonplace against the glitter. Its nickel plating was dull, its black paint was peeling, but it was in good order — an Underwood machine, desk size, several years old, exactly like thousands of others in New York offices and workshops.

Basil stood looking down at it — and suddenly he knew that he had found a leading clue to the murderer. But the motive?

He rose and went over to the work bench. The things Lambert had been examining were still there. A glass jar filled with brilliant crimson crystals labelled with the chemical formula for chromic acid. A rough lump of unfinished metal — a stony grey speckled with something that gleamed like mica. It was labelled "ferro-chromium" — of course, Lambert had said that Konradi was interested in the fact that the metallic form of chromium was not poisonous like the oxides and chromates.

It was very still in the empty building. The mist seemed to shut off the University from the rest of the city. But now, quite close at hand, he heard a creak. It might have been the unoiled hinge of a door. Wasn't the building empty after all? His hand closed over the lump of metal. It would make a handy weapon. A man without great strength or even a woman might strike a hard blow with that clasped in one hand. He looked down at it — had it been used as a weapon already? Surely Lambert would have found some microscopic traces of blood or skin unless it had been rinsed in some strong solvent. There were plenty here in the laboratory.

There was a second sound — a quick, light, feminine footfall. Basil slid the lump of metal in his overcoat pocket and stepped into the corridor.

Gisela was coming toward him. Beyond her the front door stood open. White mist surged against the doorway.

"Did you meet anyone just now — as you came here?"

"No." The question surprised her. "I couldn't see very far in this fog. I want to talk to you."

She was carrying a newspaper folded under one arm. She was bare-headed, and the mist had precipitated a few rain-drops that shone against her dark hair. Fatigue made her eyes larger and darker, her face paler than ever. The brave scarlet of her lipstick only underlined the sadness of her mouth.

She sat down on the work bench and looked around the laboratory as Basil had done a moment ago. Her glance came to rest on Basil. "It was I who took the notes. Not for myself — for someone else."

He stood looking down at her. "Dietrich?"

"How did you know?"

"A lie always gives away more than it conceals. When you denied talking to Dietrich Saturday night that was just one way of telling us there was something incriminating about your talk with Dietrich. Where are the notes now?"

"Weren't they found among his things?"

"No."

"But they should have been." She was puzzled. "How did it happen?"

"I saw someone with a flashlight in Konradi's laboratory Friday night when I was walking near the chapel. I knew Konradi wasn't there, so I went in and found Dietrich going through Konradi's papers. The laboratory was locked, but he seemed to know all about locks; he had skeleton keys. He had asked me about Konradi's work several times. I always got out of answering by saying I didn't know anything about chem-

istry. But Friday night Dietrich said that no matter how ignorant I was I must know at least which notes dealt with cancer
of the lungs. I couldn't open the safe — I didn't know whether
Konradi had taken the notes home with him. But he would
have them in the laboratory the next day. Dietrich forced me
to promise I would meet him on the campus Saturday night
and bring him the notes dealing with cancer of the lungs and
all the notes that came after them chronologically."

"Forced you?"

She clasped her hands on the newspaper in her lap and
looked down at them. "My father was in Prague. When I left, I
thought he would be safe on Czech soil. Now it is German
soil."

"And Dietrich threatened to denounce your father to the
police as an anti-Nazi?"

She nodded without looking up. "An anonymous letter
would be enough. They wouldn't bother about proof."

"Was Dietrich himself a Nazi?"

"I was never sure. He wouldn't tell me anything. I have no
idea why he wanted Konradi's notes on cancer of the lungs.
One day he drew on a piece of paper a cross surrounded by a
circle. He told me that if anyone ever showed me that sign, I
would know it was a messenger from him. But no one ever
did."

"Why didn't you tell Konradi this?"

"There were some things about Konradi that I didn't
understand. He had animals brought to the laboratory every
day — but for the last two months he never went near them. I
couldn't tell just what he was doing — but even I could see he
was only pretending to work on cancer while he was actually
doing something else."

"So you did doubt Konradi?"

Her shoulders moved — something between a shiver and a

shrug. "When I realised he wasn't working on cancer, I couldn't help wondering about him. I didn't dare confide in him. I dare say he wondered about me sometimes. He never confided in me. You Americans can have no idea how suspicion breeds suspicion. I remember when the Russian refugees first came to Vienna. Each one would solemnly assure you that all the others were Bolshevist agents. Then the Italian refugees began coming and each one thought all the others were Fascist agents. We were very scornful of them. We used to say such things could only happen among decadent Italians and barbarous Slavs. German-speaking people had political and scientific education. Such things could never happen to us, we said; just as you say now that such things could never happen to you."

"Did Konradi suspect you of taking the notes?"

"He must have. But he didn't say so. Saturday afternoon he discovered they were gone. I came into the laboratory and he said he had mislaid some notes. He asked me if I had seen them or if I had let anyone in when he wasn't there. I said no to both questions. I had taken home some unimportant notes I was copying and he said he would come to my apartment that evening about 7:30 to see if the missing notes had got among those by mistake. He was standing by an open window and he said suddenly, 'There's some paper drifting on the wind… perhaps the wind took them.'

"That was possible because the notes were in a loose-leaf book and he often unfastened the rings and took them out when he was working. He hurried outside and didn't come back. I didn't see him again until that evening."

"Did you tell anyone he would be there?"

"No. I changed into a house dress so he wouldn't suspect I was going out as soon as he had gone. He looked through the notes I had been copying — but the missing notes were not there. I think the real reason he came was to give me a chance to confess I had taken them. It was dreadful because I wanted to confess and I couldn't. Perhaps he would have accused me if it hadn't been for that phone message that called him away. It happened just as I told you, except for one thing: Konradi said, 'That was someone who knows what has become of the missing notes. I'm going to meet him at Southerland Hall.' He wouldn't tell me who it was. He said he had promised not to tell. He was particular about promises. The murderer — if it was the murderer who phoned — must have counted on that.

"I was puzzled by that telephone message because no one could have seen me take the notes. I was alone in the laboratory at the time with the doors locked and the shades down. I thought it must be someone who knew Dietrich was after the notes. But I had to deliver them to him just the same. As soon as Konradi had gone, I threw on a coat and hurried out without stopping to change my dress. He had stayed so long I was afraid I'd be late for the appointment with Dietrich.

"You must have seen me when I was giving him the notes. I've never seen anyone so frightened as he was then. I asked him if he was afraid of the police. He said he could always deal with police...this was something more dangerous. I understood him to mean someone else was after the notes — someone he feared.

"It was just after he left me that I met you on the pathway. When you asked me the way to Southerland Hall and said you had an appointment there, I thought you must be the man who had phoned Konradi — who knew that Dietrich was after the notes. That was why I tried to discourage your going to Southerland Hall. If Konradi were told Dietrich had the notes, he would take steps to recover them. That meant my father would be arrested. Dietrich had told me that would happen if he failed to get the notes.

"Even after I knew Konradi had been murdered I didn't dare tell about Dietrich for fear something would happen to my father. Even after I knew Dietrich was dead I couldn't tell because he had hinted he was not working alone. If I had told the American police about Dietrich's activities, the men working with him could have delivered my father to the German police."

Basil studied her face. "If Dietrich was working against Konradi, why should they both be killed in the same way — obviously by the same person?"

"I don't know." She lifted her eyes at last. They were brilliant with unshed tears.

"You did love Konradi, didn't you?"

She looked down at her hands again. "That was what made it hard. And I could see that he would never love me. He cared for nothing but his work."

"Why is it you aren't afraid to tell this now?"

"You haven't seen the afternoon papers?"

"No. I've been here all day."

She opened the newspaper she carried and spread it on Konradi's work bench. There was a small paragraph on the second page:

Prague, May 6th, by Occidental News Service — Count Alois von Hohenems, resident of this city and former supporter of ex-Chancellor von Schuschnigg of Austria, has disappeared during the last few days. Nazi officials deny that he has been taken into protective custody and sent to the Bavarian prison camp at Dachau, or that he is seriously ill there.

17

EXPOSURE

I t was nearly four o'clock when Basil passed under the archway that led to the School of Mines.

The elevator man admitted rather cautiously that the Department of Metallurgy was on the third floor. Yes, some of the professors were still in their offices. He had taken up Dr Farquharson a few minutes ago and he was still there unless he'd come down by the stairs. His room was 302. Basil walked down a bare corridor and knocked on a door of ground glass.

"Come in!"

Dr Farquharson was small and sandy and incredibly Scottish. Basil introduced himself and took the lump of metal from his pocket.

"Can you identify this? It's labelled 'ferro-chromium,' but there may be some mistake about that."

Dr Farquharson adjusted his glasses and examined the ugly, shapeless chunk of metal minutely.

"Whaur did ye get this?"

"Suppose we leave that in abeyance for the moment."

Dr Farquharson had a sympathy for taciturnity. He nodded

gravely. "It will be ferro-chromium…" he rolled his R's like the ruffle of a drum "…but if you would be wanting absolute scientific sairtainty I'll take it into the metallurgical laboratory for a while." He looked less sure when he came back. "Would ye be leaving the wee bit metal with me for a day or so?"

"Then it isn't ferro-chromium?"

"I'll not be saying it is and I'll not be saying it isn't." A faint gleam came into his pale, blue eyes. "We'll be leaving that in abeyance for the moment."

"At least you can tell me what's making you doubt your first opinion?"

"The melting point. A bit too high for ferro-chromium. And that's uncanny because there will not be many metals with a melting point higher than ferro-chromium."

"Just what is ferro-chromium?"

"An intairmediate compound of the mineral chromite in the manufacture of chromium steel. Not the cheap chromium plating used for plumbing fixtures and modernistic chairs, but the expensive chromium alloy steel that will stand continuous sairvice at a temperature of 2,300 Fahrenheit."

Outside in the corridor Basil noticed some brass letters over a double doorway: *Metallurgical Reading Room.* The librarian was a faded woman with a fluttering manner. He asked her for the latest yearbook of the US Bureau of Mines and Minerals.

"We have a great call for that book," she said when he returned it. "All the students of mining and engineering here have secret hopes of getting a job with Mr Southerland after they are graduated. They always look in that book to see what is produced by his African Mining Company, and when they find it's manganese they always want to major in metallurgy."

"But it isn't manganese," protested Basil. "It's chromite."

"Oh?" She smiled vaguely. "They're pretty much the same — I mean they're both used for alloy steel."

The Mercantile Bank and Trust Company dominates a corner where Wall Street meets another old lane that was named "New Street" when anything North of Bowling Green was "new." Inside, the great marble hall four stories high was dimly lighted and artificially cooled. Basil had to interview five different people before he reached Malcolm Southerland's private secretary. Mr Southerland could see no one — he was on the floor, but the secretary didn't know just where. Basil took out a visiting card and scribbled one word: *ferrochromium.*

The secretary was more deferential when he returned. An express elevator took them to the top floor. As they left the balcony that overlooked the public rooms of the bank, the hum of voices receded. At the end of the corridor, the secretary led the way through two small offices to an oak door.

Basil stepped into a lofty room more like a drawing room than an office. Southerland was not "on the floor" — he was sitting at a carved rosewood desk. It wasn't a worker's desk at all. It was bare as a parade ground except for a silver-mounted, rose-coloured blotter that had never been used to blot anything and a silver pen and crystal inkwell that had never been sullied by contact with ink. There was also a bowl of cut crystal filled with water and long-stemmed Hermosa roses.

Another man sat, almost reclining, in a deep armchair covered with dark red leather. Basil recognised Yorkville's Visiting Professor of Abnormal Psychology — Albert Feng Lo.

"This is an unexpected pleasure, Dr Willing," said Southerland aridly. "Marcus, move that other armchair up to the desk, please."

"Will there be anything else, Mr Southerland?"

"No." He didn't speak again until the secretary had gone. He was holding Basil's card delicately between thumb and forefinger. "The message on this card is rather...cryptic."

"If it had been cryptic you wouldn't have seen me," retorted Basil. "I'm tired of fencing, Mr Southerland. You can't manage murder like a stock exchange ramp with the truth hidden from everyone except an inner circle. Don't you think it's about time you told the police all you know about Konradi's discovery?"

"I've told the police everything I know about Konradi's cancer research."

"I'm not talking about Konradi's cancer research. I'm talking about the thing he stumbled on in the course of his cancer research — a synthetic chromium substitute for the metal now derived from natural chromite."

Basil's glance travelled to a framed photograph on the wall. It looked rather like the ruin of a Roman amphitheatre, but it was an open-cut mine, roughly circular, in tiers and terraces.

Southerland turned Basil's card over and over in his fingers and suddenly Basil saw him as an old man. When he lifted his eyes all the disillusion of age was visible in his face. "Does anyone else know of this yet?"

"No."

"How did you find out?"

"I knew Konradi had been working with chromic acid because of a characteristic lesion between his nostrils. Therefore I knew you lied when you said he was working on alum — and I wondered why. As the mice in his laboratory showed no signs of chromium poisoning it looked as if he had interrupted his biochemical experiments to work on a purely chemical problem. What remained of his notes suggested he had been trying to isolate the irritant factor present in chromic acid and absent from metallic chromium. That might lead to the discovery of a substitute for natural forms of chromium such as chromite.

"Such a discovery would explain the theft of the laboratory notes and your attempt to conceal that Konradi had been working on chromium. He had the equipment for such work — including an electric furnace that would produce high temperatures. Had he refused any laboratory assistants because he didn't want to trust anyone with this secret? Had he avoided his former students and other biochemists on the faculty because he didn't want anyone to become involved in what he was doing? Did he refrain from keeping textbooks in his laboratory because he didn't want anyone to know what books he was consulting? Did he instruct the keeper of the animal room to bring mice bred for cancer of the lungs to his laboratory every day so that anyone who discovered he was being supplied with chromic acid would assume he was still working on cancer of the lungs? Did he employ a secretary ignorant of chemistry so she could not understand anything she saw in his laboratory or among his papers? Did he avoid other German-speaking refugees because a Nazi agent might pass as a refugee and the Nazis wanted his discovery for their own use?

"This afternoon Dr Feng showed an interest in Konradi's laboratory that was not characteristic of his usual circumspection. Later I found a lump of unfinished metal in the laboratory labelled 'ferro-chromium.' Dr Lambert, the city chemist, had taken the label at its face value, but when a metallurgist told me it hadn't the same melting point as ordinary ferro-chromium made with chromite, I thought I was on the right track. I was sure of it when I verified my recollection that you and the Mercantile Bank had heavy investments in African chromite mines."

Southerland seemed to brush all this aside as unimportant. "Was Dietrich a Nazi agent?" he demanded.

"Don't you know?"

"I never suspected it until you told me about his suicide Sunday evening."

"There must have been a Nazi agent," said Basil. "Dietrich is the most likely candidate. A Nazi symbol was found along his trail and all secret political agents use some symbol by which they can recognise each other. The swastika is the logical symbol for a Nazi — unfortunately it's been too well advertised. But the primitive swastika — the cross surrounded by a circle — is known only to a few. It was just the thing and Dietrich was just the man because his abnormal thymus gland made him look immature enough to pass as a German exchange student."

Southerland crushed the card in his fist. "Did Dietrich get word of the process to Germany before his death?"

"I think not."

"Why?"

"Count von Hohenems was arrested by the Gestapo in Prague after the news of Dietrich's death must have reached the German news agencies. That was reprisal."

"Thank God!" The crushed card fell on the blotter as Southerland's hand relaxed. "Germany is one of our best customers for natural chromite in peace time. But what had Hohenems to do with it?"

"Dietrich tried to get the laboratory notes from the daughter by threatening the father. When he failed, the threat was carried out."

"And Dietrich killed himself because he failed?"

"No. Dietrich was killed by the same person who killed Konradi."

"But that can't be!"

"Why not?"

"Why should anyone kill *both* Konradi and Dietrich? One a refugee from the Nazis, the other a Nazi agent?"

Basil answered with another question. "Am I right in assuming that Konradi wanted his chromium process used in America?"

"Perfectly right."

"And Dietrich wanted it used in Germany. So you see they did have one thing in common: both wanted to use the chromium process. Both were killed by someone who wanted to prevent *use* of the chromium process — probably for financial reasons."

The scent of roses was heavy in the room. For an instant there was no sound. Then the harsh, thin chimes of Old Trinity pealed the quarter hour.

Feng sat perfectly still. Southerland moved uneasily in his chair. "I suppose you think I murdered both?"

"You had a motive."

Feng spoke for the first time. "So had I."

Basil turned to look at him. "As a professor of abnormal psychology, which would you consider the stronger motive for murder — patriotism or greed?"

Before Feng could answer, Southerland took command. "Willing, I am relying on you not to repeat anything we say here this afternoon. The bank is in no position to lose its investments in the African Mining Company — to say nothing of its investments in the railroad and shipping lines that transport chromite to Europe and America. The failure of the Mercantile Bank might involve the whole world."

"Aren't you exaggerating?"

"Am I? The failure of one bank — the *Creditanstalt* of Vienna — was the whisper that loosed an avalanche in 1929. The world is an economic whole today — the conflict between our economic internationalism and our emotional nationalism is destroying us. I'm putting all my cards on the table. But first I want to make one thing clear: I did not kill Konradi and I don't know who did."

"Then why did you hide so many facts from the police?"

"Let me put the whole situation before you. Then you can decide whether I murdered Konradi."

As Basil listened, he reminded himself that Southerland was not really a banker but a successful press agent — a man who had reduced persuasion to an exact science. He was speaking now in the easy voice of a man who feels that he has reason on his side.

"...The SS men who wrecked Konradi's laboratory in Vienna in 1938 were young toughs with little education and as far as he could see no knowledge of chemistry. It never occurred to them that he might have made a discovery invaluable to the Third Reich. They knew he was not an industrial chemist, but a biological chemist working on cancer. They didn't realise that no one can draw a hard and fast line between industrial and biological chemistry.

"Before burning Konradi's laboratory, they sent all his papers including his notes, to a higher officer whose duty was to see if there were anything that would further incriminate them or their friends. Apparently this officer had some knowledge of chemistry, for he understood Konradi's notes well enough to realise that the most important part was missing. Konradi's study of chromium was only one phase of his study of cancer of the lungs, but in the course of it he stumbled upon a substance much cheaper and more accessible than chromite.

"Can you imagine the feelings of that Nazi officer when he first caught a glimpse of synthetic chromium from the hints scattered through Konradi's notes? Chromium alloy steel with its high tensile strength and resistance to heat and rust is essential to the armour plate, bearings and valve steels used in modern war. To make it now you must have a large supply of natural chromite. This makes chromite one of the so-called 'strategic materials' which may make the difference between the victory or defeat of a nation at war.

"Germany's courtship of Russians, Turks and Africans of German descent is prompted by chromite hunger — Russia, Turkey and Africa are the chief chromite-producing nations. Of 28 essential minerals Germany has only 13 within her territory. All research laboratories in Germany today are geared for the discovery of substitutes for the strategic materials she lacks — rubber, gasoline, tin, copper, manganese, mercury, molybdenum, tungsten and...chromite.

"Konradi must have watched the SS men in his laboratory with sardonic appreciation. When they wrecked and burned it, they were too stupid to suspect that they might be destroying something Germany needs. Intelligence is also a strategic material — one for which there is no substitute even in totalitarian states. Of course, Nazi chemists went over the ruins of Konradi's laboratory, but all the metals were so fused and transformed it was impossible to find any clue to the process of manufacture. The heat of the fire had been intense because inflammable chemicals were stored in the laboratory."

Daylight had begun to fade. Southerland's hand trembled slightly as he switched on his desk lamp.

"Do you mean to tell me the Nazis could find no way of getting the process from Konradi himself at Dachau?" cried Basil incredulously.

Southerland hesitated. "They did try," he said at last.

"There wasn't a scar on Konradi's body!"

"Konradi's scars were mental rather than physical. He had the whip hand — in a way. If they tried their usual methods of persuasion, he might have gone insane or died before revealing the process. There were no hostages they could threaten. His parents were dead, he had no wife or children, and both his laboratory assistants died shortly after arrest. For once the Gestapo was forced to try subtlety. They borrowed an idea called the 'torture of hope.' Police call it the 'cat-and-mouse method.'

"You subject your prisoner to the worst possible conditions — solitary confinement, darkness, filth and a starvation diet. Then one night the jailer 'forgets' to lock the door as he goes out. For the first time in weeks the prisoner feels the dreadful emotion of hope — he thinks he has a chance to escape. Of course, he's carefully watched all the time. But he's allowed to go quite far — in some cases he's allowed to escape and enjoy the illusion of liberty before the police decide to pounce and take him back. This is repeated several times. No matter how often the prisoner has been fooled, each time he sees the door ajar he can't help hoping just a little. The alternation of hope and despair is said to break the most stubborn will in the long run. When hope is finally dead, he'll do or say anything required of him."

"But Konradi's will didn't break?"

"A jail is only as strong as its weakest jailer. Some of Konradi's German students were in the Nazi ranks. Whether they were converts or working for some underground anti-Nazi movement, he never knew. But they got word to him that something would go wrong in the powerhouse the night of his escape. For a few moments there would be no electric current in the barbed wire and no floodlights for the machine gunners. With a man of his resolution, that was enough to turn a staged escape into a real one."

"Are you quite sure it wasn't staged after all?" murmured Basil.

"What do you mean?"

"A Nazi agent with a knowledge of chemistry could have used Konradi's name and reputation to gain access to this country. Did you have real proof of his identity?"

"Indisputable proof." Southerland smiled. "His process for making synthetic chromium. No one else with a knowledge of chemistry could work out the details of an original process as brilliantly as Konradi."

"Then you have the process now?"

"I've destroyed all my notes on it."

"How could you?"

Southerland's smile vanished. "Do you suppose farmers who plough under cotton really want to do such a wanton thing? They've got to if they're to get a decent price for their cotton! They're prisoners of circumstances. So was I."

"And so was I." It was almost a whisper from Feng.

Southerland was not proud of his own part in Konradi's story. It was several moments before he continued. His eyes were on the roses, avoiding Basil and Feng.

"Like the SS men, I forgot that there's no hard and fast line between biological and industrial chemistry. Even when Konradi said something to me about working here on an industrial process he had discovered in Vienna during his cancer researches, I never associated cancer with chromium steel. Even when I saw the itemised bill for his equipment, I went on thinking of him as primarily a biological chemist. If there'd been any chance for me to make money out of his discovery, I might have been more alert. But I knew the patent would go automatically to the University. It always does when a member of the faculty makes a discovery during his work there."

"Why hadn't Konradi patented the process in his own name before going to Yorkville?" asked Basil.

"He couldn't be sure of the details until he was able to repeat his experiments in a laboratory," explained Southerland. "He had to do the whole thing over again without the help of the preliminary notes the Nazis had confiscated in Vienna and he wasn't sure he could pull it off. That was why he didn't tell me more about it. He chose a university rather than an industrial laboratory because he was a biological chemist and he wanted to go on with his cancer work afterward."

"So you actually financed your own ruin?" said Basil.

"Exactly." Southerland achieved a wry smile. "Konradi knew I was a vice-president of the Mercantile Bank, but he didn't know that I and the bank were deeply involved in chromite mines. Neither he nor I had any idea he was using money derived from the sale of natural chromite to perfect a process of manufacturing synthetic chromium which would make natural chromite unsalable. You know what happened to the Chilean nitrate industry when European chemists learned to extract commercial nitrates from air. The bank couldn't obtain the patent on Konradi's discovery. Legally it was the property of the University and Konradi insisted that he was obliged to inform the trustees of any discovery he made. I knew they would insist on the University's right to the patent. The bank would be left holding the bag while the University sold the process directly to the steel companies on a royalty basis. Konradi had an absurdly exaggerated idea of his obligations to the University and when I suggested that he suppress his discovery he even accused me of disloyalty to my own government."

"Why?"

"America lacks seven of the minerals essential to modern war and chromite is one of them. Synthetic chromium would lessen our dependence on chromite-producing nations.

241

Synthetic chromium would secure our supply of a military essential, chromium steel, within our own borders. Konradi thought this fact should influence me more than financial considerations. Outside his own rather narrow field of chemistry, he was a little naïve.

"Only when I pointed out that every miner in the chromite mines, every worker in the African Coastal Railway and every sailor on the Afro-American Freighters would be thrown out of work by his discovery, to say nothing of the people who would be ruined if the bank got into difficulties — only then did he begin to understand. He wasn't converted to my point of view. But he finally agreed to wait two weeks before speaking to the other trustees about his discovery."

"What good was the delay?"

"I hoped it would give me a chance to get rid of some of my stock in the various companies that would be affected — selling a little here and a little there so no one would smell a rat and investing the proceeds in something absolutely safe. Then if the bank did crash, I could save something from the wreck."

"Nice for the bank," murmured Basil. "And all those workers in the mines and the railway and shipping company."

Southerland flushed. "It wouldn't help the bank or the miners if I were ruined, too, would it? If I'd warned the other directors, they'd have started selling and there would have been a panic before any of us were safe! There's no sentiment in business!"

"There certainly isn't!" agreed Basil. "But wasn't the delay dangerous after the process was on paper? Why didn't you get police protection for Konradi? Or private detectives?"

"Konradi wouldn't have them. He believed that detectives can be bribed or intimidated — that triple locks, burglar alarms and special guards simply advertise the presence of something immensely valuable. He thought the safest way to protect a secret is to let no one know that it exists. Just as he thought Gisela von Hohenem's ignorance of chemistry would protect her. It seems he was wrong, but — she upset his calculations in more ways than one."

"Meaning he fell in love with her?"

"What do you think?" Southerland smiled again. "He was an exile and she was home — she was the Ringstrasse on a May morning and all the waltzes from Strauss. But he couldn't tell her so. He knew he was always in danger and he never forgot those moments at Dachau when he was glad there was no one in his life who could be held as a hostage...no parent... no woman...no child. You can imagine how angry he was when Mrs Prickett began to gossip about them. Even in this country he was always on guard against the Nazis, but so far as I know he never suspected the German exchange students seriously —least of all Dietrich, who looked about sixteen."

"And then?"

"There's not much more to tell," answered Southerland. "Only last Friday I heard of Konradi's discovery from Konradi himself in his laboratory. Saturday — the day he was murdered — I went to see him again, still hoping to convert him to my point of view."

"And when you went into his laboratory that afternoon you discovered that his notes were missing?"

Southerland's eyes narrowed. "How did you know that?"

"You told me you looked at some books and that they were too technical for you. But the only book in Konradi's laboratory was the telephone book. You must have been doing something you didn't want to admit. You're not a chemist, so Konradi's papers were the only things likely to interest you."

Southerland was almost embarrassed. "Ordinarily I wouldn't think of looking at another man's papers. But when

Gisela went to look for Konradi I realised suddenly that if only I could destroy his notes, it would take him some time to reconstruct the series of experiments from memory and that would delay publication of his discovery still longer.

"It was a great shock when I found the notes were missing and an even worse shock when I learned Konradi had been murdered. I felt sure the murderer had stolen the laboratory notes on the process, but I didn't know why. If someone like Feng or myself had stolen the process in order to suppress it, I ought to hang onto my African Mining stock. But if a Nazi agent or a common thief had stolen the process in order to make use of it, I ought to dump my African Mining stock as soon as I could. Finally I decided to hold the bulk of my chromite stock while selling some of it — and using the proceeds to buy an annuity as a lifeboat in case of sudden shipwreck.

"I didn't know what evidence of his work Konradi had left in his laboratory and I was naturally afraid the secret of his chromium process would come to light during a murder investigation. That would destroy the value of my mining stock and show the police I had a motive for killing Konradi. So I did everything I could to make you think his death was a simple suicide not worth investigating. I got a research worker on my press relations staff to look up suicides among German refugees and he found that stuff about blank-shot suicides that I passed on to you.

"With so much to conceal, I couldn't risk a lie-detector test. But if only I were to refuse the police would suspect me. Therefore I induced several others to refuse at the same time, to weaken suspicion by distributing it. Feng and Halsey had their own reasons for refusing. Prickett was easily handled. For years he's been pestering me to get him a job in some advertising agency. He used to dedicate books to me and all that, but when I didn't prove responsive, I really believe he nursed a sort of grudge against me. I thought it particularly fortunate to have the two professors of psychology refuse the lie-detector test. That should discredit its psychological value in the eyes of the police. If you think my procedure was rather high-handed, I can only remind you that I was desperate. With so much at stake, I would stop at nothing."

"Nothing?"

There was an uncomfortable hush.

"Almost nothing, I should have said."

"And you, Feng?" Basil turned to the man who had remained impassive throughout Southerland's story. "What was your stake? Do you own stock in the African Mining Company? Or has the Mercantile Bank promised a loan to the Chinese government?"

Feng shook his head. "I told you I had not received money in any form — for myself or the Chinese cause."

"Then…?"

"The future independence of China depends largely on the behaviour of other nations." Feng selected his words slowly. "As long as America, England and France have commercial stakes in the East, we can still hope. But should all three of these nations withdraw from Asia, we will be dominated either by Japan or Russia. When Britain and France are at war in Europe, America is our chief hope. Her stake in the East is not only her trade with China, but their lines of transport in Asiatic waters. She must keep these lines open if she is to obtain necessary raw materials from British and Dutch colonies in Africa and Asia — strategic materials essential to national defence. That is why America keeps most of her navy in the Pacific and leaves patrolling the Atlantic largely to the British.

"In other words, America is bound to Asia and Africa by a

rope woven of several strands — tin, tungsten, rubber, silk, selenium, quinine, manganese and…chromite. If only one of these strands is broken, the rope is that much weaker. When Konradi discovered a process for making chromium steel without natural chromite he was breaking one of the strands. The silk strand may be broken by nylon. The rubber strand may be broken by synthetic rubber. I didn't want a third strand broken — the chromite strand. For if ever America should learn to synthesise all these strands the rope would break — she would withdraw from the Far East altogether. Britain and France would probably have to withdraw as well — Britain could hardly patrol both Atlantic and Pacific alone — and China would be dominated by Japan.

"I learned of Konradi's discovery Friday afternoon when Southerland came to my office to enlist my aid. He knew how I felt about the future of China and he knew I had been friendly with Konradi all winter. He thought my political arguments for suppressing the discovery would carry more weight with Konradi than his own financial arguments. I saw Konradi in his laboratory Saturday afternoon, but I could not persuade him to suppress the process. He argued that it was impossible to save democracy in China now, but that it could still be saved in America. But…" Feng lifted his eyes and looked Basil full in the face "…I am not American. I am Chinese."

A rose petal drifted down upon the desk.

Feng sighed. "Konradi was my friend. To suppress evidence related to his chromium process I have had to protect his murderer by suppressing evidence related to his murder. Perhaps my conscience urged me to help you subconsciously. I like to think that is why I lost Konradi's drawing of the primitive swastika in your car last Sunday and perhaps that is why I talked so much about chromium when I took you to the squash court Monday morning."

Basil looked at Southerland. "So at least three people had a motive for killing Konradi?"

"You mean Dietrich, Feng, or I might have killed him to suppress his discovery?"

"No. Dietrich's murder clears him. But the failure of the Mercantile Bank would have been as bad for Ian Halsey as for you."

"Ian knew nothing of Konradi's discovery!" cried Southerland.

Basil explained the flaw in the air-conditioning system. "Anyone who happened to be in the squash court under Konradi's laboratory on Friday when you talked to Konradi or on Saturday when Feng talked to him could have known all about Konradi's discovery. Anyone in the squash court Friday night when Dietrich talked to Gisela in Konradi's laboratory would have learned that Dietrich was after the process. The missing notes weren't found by the police among Dietrich's papers. But it was he who had them last — Gisela gave them to him Saturday night. The murderer must have taken them when he killed Dietrich."

"Then...he must have them now!" Southerland was appalled. "He may patent the thing and sell it to the steel companies! And we don't know who he is! We don't know anything about him!"

"We know one thing — he plays squash. We know he was in the squash court Saturday afternoon because he phoned Konradi at Gisela's apartment Saturday evening. The only way the murderer could have known Konradi would be there was by overhearing him make the appointment with her, through the air-conditioning system. Konradi told no one he was going, and she told no one she expected him." Basil rose, conscious of Southerland's probing eyes.

"Where are you going?" demanded Southerland.

"Back to Konradi's laboratory. Now I know what to look for, I may find more clues to the process."

Southerland had risen. He pressed the switch of the ceiling light to illumine Basil's way to the door. He paused, his hand still on the switch. "How many people know about the chromium process?"

"I'm the only one besides yourself and Feng and whoever has the laboratory notes." Basil felt as if Southerland's shrewd glance were appraising his whole personality — estimating its price. He smiled slightly. "No use, Southerland. I don't want to become psychiatric adviser to an advertising firm and I don't own any stock in the African Mining Company and I'm not Chinese."

Southerland's hand dropped. "So you're the only one who knows." His voice was hard. "It's a dangerous secret. It has already cost three lives in three days."

Basil's smile broadened. "Is that a warning — or a threat?"

18

EXEUNT

Yorkville University streetlamps were lighted along the gravel paths, their rays drowned in mist. At Southerland Hall there were lights in Prickett's laboratory and Salt's office. Basil's step in the corridor brought Prickett to the threshold. Through the half-open door Basil saw Ian Halsey.

"Are you making any progress?" demanded Prickett.

"We believe so."

"You mean there'll be an arrest? Soon?"

"Perhaps tomorrow. I expect to find my last piece of evidence in Konradi's laboratory tonight."

"You think that wise?"

"Why not?"

Prickett's eyes grew speculative. "You'll be alone in the building. Nothing will induce Ezra to sleep here again and the police guard has gone."

Basil smiled. "My job takes me among queer people all the time. I can take care of myself."

"Anything I can do to help?"

"No…unless you can tell me if Southerland knows how to use a typewriter?"

"I don't know—" began Prickett.

Halsey intervened. "Yes, he uses an old Remington portable he bought in his newspaper days about 1919. He says it brings him luck and he won't even have it repaired though the E is worn smooth and the dollar sign looks like an ordinary S."

"Touch system or hunt and peck?"

"Touch. Do you think Southerland—"

"Ian, Dr Willing has work to do," said Prickett. "You and I had better clear out."

Alone, Basil unlocked Konradi's laboratory and switched on the lights. Apparently nothing had been disturbed. He left the door ajar and dropped his coat and hat on the work bench. Night had come swiftly — a black, moonless night that turned the great panes of glass into mirrors reflecting the lighted room and the shining array of apparatus. He shaded his eyes with his hands trying to see into the darkness. But the mist hid every sight and deadened every sound except the moaning of foghorns in the harbour. He glanced at Konradi's shelves without much hope of finding another lump of synthetic ferro-chromium.

Steps came along the corridor. Basil turned quickly and came face to face with Julian Salt.

This was no longer the man who had seemed stricken at word of his wife's death. There was a flush under the sun-browned skin, the hazel eyes were brilliant.

"Cigarette?" Salt smiled and the white teeth in the brown face were oddly suggestive of the feral animal baring its teeth before giving battle.

"No, thanks."

Salt lit his cigarette and lounged against the bench. "I heard what you said to Prickett just now."

"That's why I said it. I knew you'd listen."

Salt went on imperturbably. "Most murderers are caught because they are stupid and uneducated. This murderer is neither. You may be able to guess his identity. But you'll never be able to prove his guilt beyond a reasonable doubt. Rather tantalising — isn't it?"

Basil returned the smile. "Must you stick to the third person?"

"Not necessarily. I know I didn't overlook any clues that would be admitted as evidence in a court of law. That leaves me free to say whatever I please when there are no witnesses. I can always deny it afterward."

The moment Salt admitted his guilt, Basil knew that he was not intended to leave the room alive. To do so he would have to match Salt's coolness and audacity.

"You share the weakness of all murderers — vanity."

Salt was amused. "I can afford the luxury of vanity because you can't prove me guilty."

"Quite sure?"

"Quite." Salt's relaxation was assumed. His eyes never lost their vigilance. "But I'm curious. How did you happen to pick on me?"

So that was it. Salt wasn't quite sure, and he had to find out.

"You made the most fatuous mistake a murderer can make — you told unnecessary lies. A lie always reflects the image of the truth; it inverts like a mirror."

"Very clever. But not legal evidence." The hint of temper in Salt's voice encouraged Basil. A man who loses his temper can always be outwitted.

"Just after Konradi's murder, when you walked into Southerland Hall you asked Prickett, '*Did you break that window?*' A moment later you said to Foyle, '*By eight, I must*

251

*have been somewhere on the path between the chapel and Souther-
land Hall, walking toward the library. I reached the library a little
after eight. I've been there ever since. I came out of the library and
saw lights in my office across the quad, so I decided to come over
here and investigate.'*

"If you try to visualise those assertions spatially, you'll see
that they contradict each other. We all know the library is east,
the chapel is south, and Southerland Hall is west. The library
and Southerland Hall face each other across the quadrangle.
And the janitor's window faces the campus — north. If you
went east to the library just before eight by way of the southwest path between the chapel and Southerland Hall and then
recrossed the quadrangle from the library to Southerland Hall
— from east to west — how could you possibly know that a
window on the north side of Southerland Hall had been
broken just after eight o'clock? You couldn't have seen the
broken window from inside the building when you entered it
after the murder, because you didn't go down the corridor
beyond your own office, the first to the right of the entrance.

"As soon as I worked that out, I suspected you were the
man in the moonlight. It took youth, agility, nerve and presence of mind — the attributes of a man of action — to
remember the one breakable window on the ground floor
when you found yourself locked in the building — to crash
through it and escape by outrunning any pursuit. Prickett,
Southerland and Feng are middle-aged men leading sedentary
lives. Halsey is mentally unstable and always loses his nerve at
the first hint of danger. The other suspects were women. You
were the one man of action who must have faced all sorts of
emergencies among Indians in the hinterland of Mexico.
Southerland once described you as athletic. When I realised
the significance of the squash court, I was almost certain of
your guilt."

"Neat enough." Salt's hand was steady as he lit a second cigarette. "But flimsy. It isn't a crime to be a field worker in anthropology. In court I could say I got my topography mixed when I talked to Prickett and Foyle the night of the murder. I'm still waiting for evidence that would convict me beyond a reasonable doubt."

"The most revealing lies are the inventive lies that draw on the imagination of the liar," went on Basil. "We had three of those on the night of Konradi's murder — three detailed descriptions of the man in the moonlight, each one different. We knew all three were false because none of the three witnesses could have seen him so clearly by moonlight at that distance. It didn't matter whether those false statements were lies or mis-observations. Inventive lies and mis-observations are both stories that a witness builds with his own imagination. Therefore both reveal the emotions and memories that haunt his imagination, as a dream reveals them. That's what makes inventive lying dangerous to the liar — it's partly an unconscious process he can't control.

"Those three witnesses were so eager to describe the man in the moonlight because each wanted to divert suspicion from himself by identifying someone else as the murderer. If you are trying to pin a murder on someone consciously you choose someone you don't like. Exactly the same thing happens when you try to pin a murder on someone unconsciously through mis-observation — you choose someone you don't like without realising it. When Woodman tried to divert suspicion from himself by describing another man as the murderer, his imagination seized upon Prickett because he was angry at Prickett for fooling him over the sham crime. Prickett's own imagination seized upon Southerland. For years Prickett has resented Southerland's refusal to help him get a job with an advertising agency. Both these mis-observations were wholly unconscious. Woodman denied that he had described Prickett, and Prickett denied he had described Southerland.

"You described that fugitive in the moonlight as a woman with high heels, long, trailing, dark coat and long pale dress. When I heard that your wife had worn high heels, long sapphire blue coat and long pale blue dress that night, I began to wonder if it could be she your imagination had thrust into the dangerous role of murderer when Foyle forced you to find a substitute for a figure that was actually your own. If so, I believed you must hate her — consciously or unconsciously — more than Foyle had realised when he overheard scraps of your quarrel with her at dinner on the night of Konradi's murder. When you drew that portrait of your wife you forgot that *portray* and *betray* have the same root and a portrait may betray artist as well as subject."

Salt's face had changed at mention of Amy. "I hated her consciously! I—"

Basil interrupted, pursuing his advantage. "As long as you stuck to fact, you concealed your hate. But whenever you lied, you told the truth, for the creative imagination must always suggest the true emotional state of the creator. The morning we notified you of your wife's death, you had to pretend you didn't know she was missing. You claimed you had been alone working on your plans for the Southerland Expedition to Mexico since early that morning, so you didn't even know she had left the house. Would you have been so busy with your work the first morning your wife was at home after months of separation, if you had loved her as you pretended? Of course not. But in concocting that yarn, your creative imagination automatically assumed that truth — that you did not love your wife — in which case your story was perfectly logical.

"Your principal emotional response to the news of her

death was rage at the police for failing to protect her, instead of grief at her loss. But grief would have been more natural if you had loved her. Was your rage assumed simply because rage is more easily counterfeited than grief? And was this false rage of yours directed at the police so that you wouldn't have to help us by taking the lie-detector test? You would have been obliged to take it after your wife's death if you had remained on good terms with us. We unearthed reasons why Halsey, Southerland, Feng and the Pricketts refused to take the test. But we never found any real explanation for your refusal to take it.

"Another lie that betrayed you was your ingenious theory that the man known as Konradi might have been a Nazi agent. You timed that tale to divert attention from yourself at a crucial moment — the discovery of your wife's murder. The story was planned to confuse us by alienating our sympathy from Konradi and suggesting that we must look among anti-Nazis for his murderer. But it did more than that. It told us that you had an ingeniously criminal imagination — and we knew that an ingeniously criminal imagination had planned the blank-shot suicide of Konradi.

"As you elaborated your false theory, you were carried away by the creative enthusiasm of a truly artistic liar, eager to fit everything that needed explanation into the pattern of his lie. You asked why Konradi should be killed 'at the same time and by the same hand' as Dietrich — unless both were Nazis? But how did you know Dietrich was killed 'by the same hand'? The only evidence of that was that Dietrich and Konradi were both killed by the same method. The newspapers announced Dietrich's death as suicide. How did you know it was murder — unless you were the murderer? That was one thing you couldn't have overheard through the flaw in the air-conditioning system, because Feng said he was alone in the squash court when he overheard it and there was no reason to believe you and Feng were working in collusion."

Salt tossed his last cigarette on the floor and rose.

"Do you think a jury would swallow all this bunk about the truth in lies? You'd be laughed out of court and you know it! It happens to be true — in this case anyway. But you can't prove it, so — what are you going to do about it?"

"There's one more point — the suicide note you signed with Konradi's name and left beside his body. A misleading clue is like a lie — a leading clue to the mind that conceived it and the hand that executed it."

"You're bluffing!" Salt almost shouted. "There were no clues in that note! I used Konradi's own typewriter and notepaper from his desk. I wore gloves so I would leave no fingerprints and I handled the paper carefully so Konradi's fingerprints wouldn't be blurred. I even typed the signature so I wouldn't have to risk imitating his handwriting."

"And yet you left a clue in that note."

It took a great effort of will for Basil to turn his back to Salt. But he must appear completely sure of himself and he believed that Salt would not try to kill him until he had told Salt what the clue was — especially now the suicide note was in the hands of the police.

Basil uncovered Konradi's typewriter, slipped a sheet of paper into the roller and began to type:

Sorry to selfishly involve Yorkville in this miserable affair...

"You're crazy!" Salt pushed him aside. "I didn't say 'miserable affair' — I said 'rotten business'! And I never split an infinitive in my life! This is what I wrote — I remember perfectly!"

Looking over Salt's shoulder, Basil watched the words as Salt tapped them out letter by letter:

Sorry to involve the University in this rotten business, But life is hopeless if one loses friends ho;e country , , , everything , , , F, Konrqdi

"You see—" Something in Basil's eyes stopped Salt.

"I see that Konradi is spelled with a Q, that the word *home* contains a semicolon in place of the letter M, and that there are commas in eight places where there should be periods. Exactly those same errors occur in the original copy of the suicide note you left beside Konradi's body, and each error corresponds to a difference between the keyboard of a French typewriter and the keyboard of an American typewriter."

"I don't understand."

"You wrote the fake suicide note on this typewriter of Konradi's — an American Underwood just like thousands of others in New York offices. But your own typewriter is one of the Remington portables made for the French trade — I saw it when I first went to your house. You were brought up in France where your father served as consul and you probably never used an American typewriter before, or you would have anticipated the risk you took in changing from the French keyboard to the American. To a superficial glance, the two keyboards appear the same, but there are a few differences. The positions of A and Q, Z and W, as they occur on the American keyboard, are reversed on the French keyboard. The punctuation marks are re-shuffled on the French machine to make room for the accents. The French semicolon takes the place of the American small M, the French period replaces the American comma and so forth.

"People never realise these differences until they switch

from one keyboard to the other and find that they are eternally putting Q for A and a comma for a period. Manual reflexes don't adapt themselves quickly to changed circumstances and a good typist, like a good pianist, relies on hands instead of eyes. He never notices his mistakes until he reads over what he has written. As you typed Konradi's suicide note in the dark, you couldn't read over what you had written.

"But darkness couldn't account for your errors. To type in the dark, you must have used the touch system and even the blind can type by the touch system without making mistakes. If you typed well enough by touch to spell a long word like *university* correctly without seeing it, there was no reason you should make a mistake in a short word like *home.* Neither could chance account for one error repeated eight times — the eight commas that should be periods. For all your careful, conscious planning of the crime, you betrayed yourself unconsciously through the arbitrary pattern of motor impulses which habit had stamped indelibly into your nervous system."

"Anybody might have a French typewriter!" Salt was shouting now. "Perhaps Southerland—"

"Of the four people who had motives for murdering Konradi and Dietrich, only you are in the habit of using a French typewriter. Halsey has a Corona portable. Foyle fixed the fact that it was American by remarking that it was just like his own — I knew Foyle would never buy a French typewriter. Feng uses a Royal. When I went to his rooms, I noticed that most of his possessions were American, including his typewriter. Southerland keeps an old Remington portable for personal use. When Halsey said that the dollar sign was worn out, I knew it must be an American machine, for the French keyboard has no dollar sign."

In blind rage, Salt sprang at the man who had outwitted

him, but Basil was on guard. The blow that caught Salt on the point of the jaw and jarred his brain into unconsciousness was surgically neat and quick.

"WHY WERE there no misspelled words in the fake suicide note that Salt signed with Dietrich's name?"

The sun was shining in the Dean's garden when he asked his question a few days later. Basil and Foyle were with him.

"Wasn't it written on an American typewriter?" went on the Dean. "Dietrich's own Smith portable?"

"Yes, but the text of the note didn't happen to include the letters A, Q, Z, W, or M," explained Basil. "There were some significant errors in punctuation. Such a phrase as 'To whom it may concern' is usually followed by a colon or comma. In that note some such phrase was followed by a period. Again, after the word *undersigned* a colon or comma would seem appropriate, but in that note it was punctuated with another period. That gave us two more errors corresponding to differences between the French and American keyboards making a total of twelve in the two fake suicide notes. Of course, Salt didn't type Dietrich's note in the dark, but those errors in punctuation were so slight that he didn't notice them in his state of excitement immediately after Dietrich's murder when he must have typed the note."

The Dean asked one last question. "Why? Why should Julian Salt, a scientist and scholar, want to suppress Konradi's discovery of synthetic chromium?"

Foyle watched a gull coasting above the river as Basil answered the Dean's question.

"Do you still think of a scholar as someone living remote from political and industrial forces? That may have been scholarship in the Middle Ages or even in the nineteenth century, but not today. Every university and every research foundation depends on endowment from industry or the state. That means that every scientist and every scholar has a vital interest in industry or politics. There is no refuge from these issues today. Even in the infinitely remote world of the molecule Konradi ran afoul of Nazi policy. Salt, the anthropologist, had just as personal an interest in preserving the market for natural chromite as Southerland, the capitalist. A job is just as much a vested interest as invested capital.

"Salt lost his assistant professorship at Yorkville when the trustees decided to economise. But by rare good fortune he secured an even better job with the Southerland Foundation's expedition to Mexico. Feng told me that all Southerland's gifts to the University and the Foundation were in the form of preferred stock in the African chromite mines. Synthetic chromium would make these stock certificates worthless. Then there would have been no Southerland Foundation, no expedition to Mexico and no job for Salt. He had no means but his earnings. The little luxuries he loved because they distinguished him from professors like Prickett — the remodelled house, the Herat rug in his office, even the gold cigarette case — were made possible by his wife. And she was about to divorce him.

"Like all specialists he was the prisoner of his specialised training. It was too late for him to adapt himself successfully to work in any field other than anthropology. He understood this because he was always haunted by the shabby, defeated figure of his friend Trevor, the specialised man out of a job — living from hand to mouth while his special talents and training go to waste. Unlike most men whose jobs are threatened by a technological invention, Salt knew the circumstances beforehand and had the opportunity to save his job by destroying the invention and murdering the inventor. Like the

Luddites of England who smashed the machines that made their hand labour unnecessary, Salt's aggression was fear turned inside out. He was murderous and bold because he was frightened. As Konradi himself said, 'Courage is simply the active form of fear.'

"If Southerland had killed Konradi his motive would have been love of wealth. But Salt's motive has driven men and even nations to far more desperate acts — fear of poverty — the one motive that doesn't have to be explained to a jury. Southerland had only to trade a block of chromite shares for an annuity before the crash came and he would be safe. Southerland only *thought* he was desperate. Salt was *really* desperate."

"I can understand why Salt killed Konradi and Dietrich," put in Foyle. "But I don't see yet why he killed his wife."

"When he first learned of Konradi's discovery Salt tried to induce Amy to come back to him. Then he wouldn't have been so utterly dependent on his job with the Southerland Foundation. But she refused. The bitterness you saw in Salt's face at the restaurant Saturday evening was not frustrated love but humiliated egoism. Amy was Salt's last chance and he had lost her. It may have been while you were watching him that he took his final decision to kill Konradi and Dietrich.

"How he must have writhed when Amy did come back to him — after the murders of Konradi and Dietrich, when his job was safe and he no longer needed her money! She was foolish enough to say, '*I'm almost glad Konradi was murdered because it has brought us together again!*' No wonder he cried, '*Don't say that!*' with real emotion. It's only human to externalise remorse. Doubtless he was thinking, '*It's her fault! If she hadn't left me, it wouldn't have happened.*' But he had to pretend he was glad to see her or the police might ask awkward questions about his change of heart.

"And he began to be afraid she would discover his guilt. No one had a better opportunity, and she was observant. She had noticed already that Southerland, Feng and Konradi were all 'in something together.' Perhaps she found a clue in something he did or said. Or perhaps he simply couldn't stand the strain of anticipating such a possibility any longer.

"I think Salt had hated Amy for a long time. That was the real reason she left him last autumn. He had grown weary of his burden of gratitude to her and he couldn't hide it any longer. In primitive patriarchies the husband buys the wife, and Salt was one of those men who can never adjust themselves to the more civilised custom of the wife buying the husband. Yet he had wanted the comfort Amy could bring him enough to marry her in the first place. The very fact that he had to go without some of that comfort when she left him this winter must have exacerbated his feeling of antagonism for her."

As the last rays of the sun gilded the Long Island shore the Dean walked to the campus gates with them.

"Remember our first interview, Inspector? I hope we shall have the pleasure of welcoming your son to our freshman class before long."

"Thanks, but I haven't quite decided. Maybe I'll just put him in the Police Force after all."

"I thought you wanted to get him away from the police atmosphere of crime and criminals?"

"Yeah." The Inspector's gaze dwelt on Southerland Hall for the last time. "I do."

That evening for the first time Basil went to the apartment on 79th Street where Gisela lived. He found her at her piano improvising a formless melody in minor key. Perhaps her little sitting room with its rented furniture was dingy and commonplace. But he was conscious only of the picture she made in the lamplight — dark head bent over flying hands, the veil of hair that hid her face almost black above the pale pink of her housecoat.

"What would you like?" she asked. "Schubert? Or something modern?"

"I'd like to talk to you."

Her hands were still but she didn't look up. "Is it about Ian? You needn't bother. He told me the truth about himself this morning. He said I had you to thank for that — poor Ian!"

"Pity is hardly a healthy foundation for marriage," ventured Basil.

Her fingers brushed the keys lightly. "I'm not going to marry Ian — or anyone else." He recognised the opening bars of the nostalgic *Wiener Wald.* Was she thinking of Konradi? Or her father?

He laid a hand over hers and the harmony dissolved in a blurred dissonance. "Life can't go on without a great deal of forgetting. You can decide about marrying later. But you've got to dine with me tonight. That's not an invitation — it's an order!"

THE DEADLY TRUTH

HELEN MCCLOY

CHAPTER ONE

A butterfly in a beehive could not have looked more out of place than Claudia Bethune in the vestibule of the Southerland Foundation. The piratical rake of her black straw hat and the sly cut of her black crêpe dress came from the world of fashion and frivolity. The brilliants that winked from the rim of her onyx watch would have kept one of the Foundation's research chemists in comfort for a year. The staccato click of her three-inch heels wakened echoes unfamiliar in a hall where ears were tuned to the rubber-shod tread of laboratory assistants, and the delicate spice of Angèle's *Nuit de Mai* bemused nostrils that had savoured nothing more subtle than carbolic for years.

But more than all else it was her eyes that made her look alien to this world of work and thought. Pale turquoise, almond-shaped, lidless and tilted wide apart under a sloping brow, they were flat, bright and uneasy as the eyes of a wolfhound with too much wolf blood.

Claudia allowed a blue ribbon of amber-scented smoke to trail from the cigarette in her ungloved hand as she passed the

"No Smoking" sign. She extinguished the ember by dropping it in a vase of carnations on the receptionist's desk.

"Mrs. Bethune to see Dr Slater."

The receptionist pursed thin lips innocent of lipstick. Such superb insolence was as foreign to the Foundation as Parisian perfumes and Egyptian cigarettes.

"Dr Slater is engaged in most important research work." Miss Squibbs made her voice as starchy as her white apron. "If you would care to see his secretary and make an appointment with her—"

"I'll see him — now," interrupted Claudia, blandly. "Just tell him I'm here, will you?"

Miss Squibbs was becoming aware how richly the turquoise eyes contrasted with the golden bronze hair and creamy skin. From a purse Claudia took a small box gay with Limoges enamel in sapphire and emerald. Two hundred years ago it must have carried snuff. Today it was fragrantly dusty with Angèle's tea-rose powder. Claudia consulted a mirror in the lid and plied a lipstick of lobster pink. Miss Squibbs looked with disgust at the damp cigarette butt polluting the water around the stems of her carnations. But to her own surprise she made no further protest. She wasn't quite certain whether it was the woman's assurance or her beauty or her diamonds, but something about her made Miss Squibbs reach meekly for the house telephone and dial extension 806.

"Yes?" Dr Slater's tone made one word sound like six: *What the hell do you want*? Of all bio-chemists in the Foundation laboratories he was the most impatient of interruptions.

"Mrs Bethune to see you." Miss Squibbs kept her own voice impersonal.

For once Dr Slater seemed at a loss. Then he said curtly. "Send her up."

"To the visitors' room?"

"No, to my lab."

This was unprecedented but it was none of Miss Squibbs' business. "Certainly, Dr Slater." She turned back to Claudia. "He'll see you in his laboratory. That's on the eighth floor — Room 806. You take the first elevator on the right."

Claudia sauntered towards the elevator as if Dr Slater's time were of no more value to humanity than a popcorn peddler's. Miss Squibbs stared after her, wondering what such a woman could want with such a man. Miss Squibbs saw Dr Slater every day and she was not impressed by his growing reputation as a scientist. She thought him a very ordinary, very disagreeable young man. He was short and thick-set, with a sulky face so swarthy that it never looked quite clean. He had no money but the frail salary of a staff research chemist. In Miss Squibbs' opinion he was a person of no importance. What had he to offer the "fabulous Mrs Bethune"?

The phrase came to Miss Squibbs' mind unbidden. She had seen it a few days ago in one of the newspaper gossip columns. Gradually the whole paragraph came back to her.

Mr Hitler's latest gift to New York is the fabulous Mrs Bethune, who was as much a part of Paris in the old days as petits suisses *or* petits bleus. *Some of her experiments in the art of party-giving were original to say the least. The recipient of a card to one of her more intimate evenings was fortunate indeed if he awoke the next morning with nothing more serious than an ordinary hangover. Claudia Bethune's sense of humour verged upon the eccentric but everyone always enjoyed the joke — except the victim. It remains to be seen if she will find New York as tolerant as Paris, where eccentricity was always permitted — at a price.*

Roger Slater did not rise from his work-bench when Claudia entered the laboratory. He spoke to her with the not unfriendly rudeness of a brother to a sister. "I thought I told you I was pretty busy just now."

"Did you?" Claudia drifted towards the work-bench and looked down at his quick, rubber-gloved hands without apparent interest or even curiosity. "I'm awfully busy too. Philippe is designing a new coiffure for me at two, I have a fitting at three, and I promised Mike to get back to Blessingbourne in time for dinner. I just dropped in to ask if you could come along. I need an extra man."

"I shouldn't imagine you'd ever run short."

Claudia opened her pale, bright eyes very wide like the baby in the song who had never seen Christmas yet. "Why, Roger! Is that a compliment or an insult?"

"What do you think?" Roger's hands were still busy. "Who else is going to be there?"

"Nobody particular. Charles Rodney, Peggy Titus and, of course, Phyllis."

"Of course. No party of yours would be complete without Phyllis, would it?"

"I think it's terribly noble and broad-minded of me to have Phyllis!" Claudia's pout was wasted, for Roger did not look up.

"What does Phyllis think?"

"She must like to come or she wouldn't accept, would she? She's still terribly fond of Mike and she lives in such a poky little apartment it's marvellous for her to have a few days at a big place like Blessingbourne now and then."

"And Mike? Is he terribly noble and broadminded, too?"

"Mike doesn't care a hoot what Phyllis does now."

"How nice for Phyllis."

"Don't be stuffy, Roger. Are you coming? Or do I get somebody else?"

"You get somebody else. I don't like these ex-wife and ex-husband parties."

"But it isn't a party really. Charles is only coming to talk business with me. Phyllis and the Titus girl will just loaf and invite their souls."

"Who has the Hut this year?"

"A Dr Willing."

"Why not ask him? A tenant can hardly refuse his landlady."

"This one can. I've asked him a dozen times but he won't come — he doesn't approve of me... What on earth is that?" One long, coral-pink nail touched a little mound of greyish powder in a porcelain dish Roger was holding.

"I haven't named it yet. How would you like to have it named after you?" At last Roger looked up at her. His dark eyes were hard and challenging.

"You mean the way gardeners name a new rose after you? Like Dorothy Perkins and Mrs John Lang?"

"More the way physiologists name a newly discovered part of the body after you. Like the Islands of Langerhans, I decided long ago that if ever I discovered a new curlicue in the small intestine I'd call it 'Mrs Michael Bethune.'"

"I suppose that's your idea of humour." Claudia's glance went back to the greyish powder. "What is it? Something you've just discovered?"

"In a way, yes." Roger eyed the powder with a certain proprietary pride. "It's a derivative of scopolamin that I've just succeeded in isolating. Here it is in tablet form."

From a cupboard he took a handful of aluminium tubes and opened one. It contained a row of flat, square, greyish tablets. "Five grains each with a little gum arabic as a binder. Easier to take that way."

"Oh, it's some kind of medicine?"

"Not exactly." Roger's grin was tight-lipped. "At least, not physical medicine. You might call it moral medicine."

"Moral medicine! Do you mean poison? Saki's idea that most people would be enormously improved by dying?"

"No, it's not poisonous. That's the whole point. It's scopolamin with the dangerous properties eliminated."

"Is this that truth serum you said something about last spring?"

For a moment Roger hesitated — but only for a moment. A peacock unfurling his tail before a peahen or a small boy walking along the top of a picket fence to impress his best girl would have understood the suddenly expansive impulse that made Roger tell Claudia a secret which was not his property but that of the Foundation.

"Scopolamin isn't a 'serum' at all. 'Truth serum' is just the popular name. Actually, it's an anaesthetic which dulls pain without obliterating consciousness. It was called 'twilight sleep' when used in childbirth because it creates a twilit state between sleeping and waking. There is no realisation of pain or fear and the inhibitions created by fear of painful punishment are relaxed. A man doped with scopolamin speaks stark truth regardless of consequences to himself or others. Same principle as *in vino veritas.* Repression is stupefied, but the older, deeper desire for expression stays wide awake. In several cases police have used scopolamin to force truth from a suspected criminal."

"Sounds unconstitutional!"

"What's the Constitution between policemen? They would use scopolamin as often as they dared, but for one thing — it causes confusion, almost delirium. A suspect doped with it wouldn't lie to them purposely, but he might mislead them inadvertently just because he was in a fuzzy mental state. That's why a group of police officers asked the director of the

Foundation some time ago if we could develop a new form of scopolamin with all the advantages of the original drug and none of the disadvantages."

"And this is it? Roger, how clever of you! Did you do it all by yourself?"

"Well, I had two assistants who helped work out some of my ideas." Roger's tone suggested that the two assistants had done little more than sweep out the laboratory and wash up the flasks and retorts. "I've spent nearly six months tinkering with the scopolamin molecule and this is the result. 'Novopo-lamin' I suppose it might be called. It's scopolamin with the delirium factor eliminated just as novocaine is cocaine with the habit-forming factor eliminated. A five-grain dose of novopolamin does not impair accuracy in perception, speech or reasoning. But it does kill a man's desire to dissemble anything he knows or feels — even if it's to his interest to do so. A man doped with it appears to be in a perfectly normal state except for one thing — he tells the truth."

Claudia didn't laugh. "For just how long?" There was a world of cynicism in her tone.

"It takes effect in fifteen minutes and lasts for about three hours. Then you fall asleep for about five hours and on waking revert to the normal state of mendacity."

The wide, pale eyes opened still wider. "You mean you've actually tried this diabolical stuff and it really works?"

"Oh, yes." Roger couldn't keep the note of triumph out of his voice. "I've tried it on several fellows here in the lab. I've even tried it on myself."

Pale eyes narrowed and lengthened. "It must've been refreshing to hear you speak the truth! I wish I'd been there."

"Perhaps it's just as well you weren't." Roger shut the tube in his hand. "It would be diabolical indeed in the wrong hands."

"I'm sure that's what the Wright brothers said." A smile played around the corners of Claudia's mouth.

"The authorities plan to control the manufacture and distribution of this very strictly," retorted Roger. "It will be sold only to police officers and psychiatrists and people like that."

Claudia's smile broadened. "They control the manufacture and distribution of morphine very strictly and yet — it does get into the wrong hands. Before you know it you'll have bootleggers selling — what is it called?"

"Novopolamin."

"Nonsense! You said you were going to name it after me. Now I know what it's for, I shall hold you to that. Call it 'bethune.' No — people might think it was named after Mike. Call it 'claudine'."

"Sounds more like the name of a French farce than a new drug."

"Well then, 'claudaine' or 'nux claudia' or 'claudinite'. I insist on your keeping your promise and naming it after me." Limoges enamel glittered in her hands again as she plied her lipstick. "Roger, I must dash — it's nearly two. You are coming down to Blessingbourne this evening, aren't you?"

"No." Roger dropped the tube on the work-bench and went to the window as if the sea of slum streets that seethed around the Foundation building had suddenly become a matter of absorbing interest to him.

After a moment Claudia touched his arm lightly. "You'd better!" The touch lingered and became a caress.

"Claudia!" He turned swiftly, his heart in his eyes, only to meet mockery in hers.

"No. I'm not coming to Blessingbourne." His voice was sullen. "I don't want to be just another scalp dangling from your belt."

"No?" Claudia dropped her powder box into her handbag. She seemed to be enjoying herself. She shut the bag with a snap and tucked it under her arm.

"I can imagine nothing more dull and conventional than the party you describe." Roger had recovered his fraternal rudeness but he wore it less easily now Claudia could no longer be deceived by it. "An old fogey like Charles, a clothes horse like Phyllis and that gawky kid — what's her name?"

"Titus." Claudia's smile lingered as her touch had lingered — insinuatingly. Then her rare laughter rang out—clear as a bell on a frosty morning. "You may be right about some things, Roger, but you're wrong there. I give you my word, it won't be a conventional party."

She went to the door, taking quick, stilted steps on her tall heels. At the threshold, she paused and looked back, her eyes ambushed under the shadow of her hat brim. "If you should change your mind at the last moment, don't hesitate to come…"

"Fat chance!"

The door closed. Roger went back to the bench. Automatically, he counted the aluminium tubes before replacing them in the cupboard. Then he frowned and counted them again. And again. He had taken twelve from the cupboard. Now there were only eleven.

Furiously he snatched the telephone. "Miss Squibbs! Has Mrs Bethune left the building?"

"Yes." The receptionist's voice was as impersonal as ever. "She just passed my desk."

"See if you can catch her. It's important."

A moment later Miss Squibbs was saying: "Sorry, Dr Slater, but Mrs Bethune has just driven away in her car. I called and waved to her from the steps outside, but she didn't seem to hear me."

"No, she wouldn't." Roger stared at the telephone. "She was right. It won't be a conventional party… for what could be more unconventional than truth?"

"What's that, Dr Slater? I can't quite hear you."

"Nothing." Roger slammed the telephone back in its cradle, tore off his white overall and reached for his grey flannel jacket. "Johnny!" he shouted to the laboratory boy in the corridor. "I'm leaving for the day. If anything important comes up, I'll be at Mrs Michael Bethune's. You can find the number in the Suffolk County telephone book."

WANT TO DISCOVER MORE UNCROWNED QUEENS OF CRIME?

SIGN UP TO OUR CRIME CLASSICS NEWSLETTER TO DISCOVER NEW GOLDEN AGE CRIME, RECEIVE EXCLUSIVE CONTENT, AND NEVER-BEFORE PUBLISHED SHORT STORIES, ALL FOR FREE.

FROM THE BELOVED GREATS OF THE GOLDEN AGE TO THE FORGOTTEN GEMS, BEST-KEPT-SECRETS, AND BRAND NEW DISCOVERIES, WE'RE DEVOTED TO CLASSIC CRIME.

IF YOU SIGN UP TODAY, YOU'LL GET:

1. A FREE NOVEL FROM OUR CLASSIC CRIME COLLECTION;

2. EXCLUSIVE INSIGHTS INTO CLASSIC NOVELS AND THEIR AUTHORS; AND,

3. THE CHANCE TO GET COPIES IN ADVANCE OF PUBLICATION.

INTERESTED?

IT TAKES LESS THAN A MINUTE TO SIGN UP, JUST HEAD TO

WWW.CRIMECLASSICS.CO.UK

AND YOUR EBOOK WILL BE SENT TO YOU.

facebook.com/crimeclassics
twitter.com/crimeclassics

Printed in Great Britain
by Amazon